I0692936

Divine Scream

A Novel

By
Benjamin Kane Ethridge

JournalStone
San Francisco

JOURNALSTONE
YOUR LINK TO ARTISTIC TALENT

JournalStone books may be ordered through booksellers or by contacting:

JournalStone
www.journalstone.com

ISBN: 978-1-942712-19-0   (sc)
ISBN: 978-1-942712-20-6   (ebook)

Library of Congress Control Number: 2015933040

Printed in the United States of America
JournalStone rev. date: April 24, 2015

Cover Design: Rob Grom
Cover Photograph © Shutterstock.com

Edited by: Aaron J. French

Divine Scream

Chapter 1
Jared

The doctor was afraid. Jared didn't need to be a mind reader to understand that much. The receptionist had stressed Jared make the appointment as soon as possible, and that had been prompted by the doctor's review of his labs and the chest X-ray. He knew it had to be bad news. You don't get a call if your labs are normal, typically. So why was the doctor shocked now? Shouldn't he have been prepared, a week later, to lay it on Jared? Maybe he still wasn't sure what the results meant, or maybe, being only a few years older than Jared, he had second-guessed himself. Either way, the doctor with the GI Joe-cropped blonde hair and shrapnel acne scars down his cheeks had a look of paralyzing disbelief on his face, and he hadn't spoken a word for the past five minutes.

When he finally did, Jared could hardly believe it.

"I'm uh… would you excuse me for a moment? Since you're new with me, I just want to verify something with Dr. Saxon."

"Verify?" asked Jared.

"Just one of these results. I'm having—I mean, it's probably me. Just, uh, yeah. I'll be back in a jiff. Is there anything you want?"

"Sorry?"

"Something to drink or something?"

Jared shrugged. "I guess not."

"Hang tight, sir."

What else could Jared do but push back against the butcher paper on the exam bed? The crinkling sound embarrassed him, brought attention to the vulnerable state of being a broken human. Nervous as he was, he would sit and wait and do as he was told. At least they hadn't made him get undressed and put on one of those big gowns made of napkin paper.

Doctor GI Joe took one more look down at the papers in his folder, as though a second glance might strike him differently. It didn't; he pressed his lips together in a well-meaning smile, probably for Jared's benefit, and got the hell out of the exam room.

I'm dying, thought Jared. Right away he felt disgusted with himself. *You don't know anything yet. Take a deep breath and wait to hear what the results are.*

But then there was that opposing voice, the little storm cloud to piss rain over any sunshine, which replied, *With all those irregular heartbeats and that weird cough you've had—all that trouble breathing when you sleep—and now Doc Junior looks at the results like a chimp with a calculus problem. Signs point to very bad things, Jared. Sooner you accept it, sooner you can deal.*

"I'm not accepting it," Jared whispered to the empty room. He scrubbed at the burning disquiet in his eyes. "And I won't feel sorry for myself."

Lost your mom, lost your dad, and now you. Bam, bam, bam. Genetics is telling you something. Your family aren't survivors.

Jared squeezed his lips together between his fingers. They felt corpse dry.

He searched around the room for distraction. Next to a bio-hazard waste disposal box mounted on the wall, a long poster detailed a cartoon man sliced in half with all his organs exposed. His gaze looked so serene... there was even a hint of a smile. What kind of a sick joke was that? It was mockery, put there just to disservice him. Hey there guy, here's an example of brightly colored, untarnished organs, *whereas all those fleshy things inside you, Jared, are probably black, brown, or polka-dotted with corruption.*

Jared inched forward on the butcher paper, trying to get a better look at the heart's location in relation to where he'd felt the odd palpitations.

The door opened quickly with a rapid knock-knock. Though unnecessary, it wasn't much of a warning and Jared started. A triple heartbeat pulsed through his chest and a painful warmth spread down his left arm. The GI Joe lookalike stuck his head in. "Hey bud, just want you to know that Dr. Saxon will be coming over as well to discuss these results."

"I also have my dad's old friend, Dr. Revel. For a second opinion. He reviews all my medical results as well."

GI Joe seemed uninterested. He peered back into the hallway and smiled a greeting at someone. Casting a furtive glance back at Jared, he said, "Well that's a good thing if it makes you feel more secure, of course. Sure you don't need anything to drink? Saxon said it'd only be ten minutes. I don't recommend coffee, but we have water and juice."

"I'm fine."

With a nod, he gently closed the door and Jared let out a sigh that ran with shivers.

What the hell is this about? Why are they torturing me?

He took out his cell phone to call Kaitlin, but then remembered she had an audition. She'd probably tell him to chill the hell out anyway.

Several minutes passed with Jared just listening to the murmuring sounds of receptionists behind the thin walls. He considered looking at Facebook or playing one of his phone games, but the bitterness in his mind made those options bleak and exceedingly depressing. A reddish shadow glided over the room and vanished near the window. Must have been a reflection from a passing car outside—except the blinds were shut, so that couldn't be possible.

Something clicked against the window. Jared knitted his brow. He was just jittery. That was certain.

Several seconds later, the sound repeated.

Most likely birds dropping things, or squirrels in the rain gutters. But then, there weren't really any ideal squirrel trees around this part of the city, so yeah, probably birds...

The sound came again, *louder.*

Jared hopped off the exam table and drew the accordion blinds up with one tug. Several pebbles struck the window. He glanced down and beyond the rusted fire escape to a woman standing in the alley. He was awestruck. Even at a distance, it was clear she was damn beautiful, with a piercing intelligence behind eyes like Caribbean water. Her gaze locked onto his and she made a gesture to open the window. When he stood there, staring like a dumbass for a few moments, she moved several strands of hair off her shoulder, showing impatience, and made the gesture again. Her dark brown hair had waves of purple, blue, and magenta through it, but in the midday sun the streaks almost had a metallic quality to them. Jared had never seen such an effect from hair dye. Must have been a new punk rock thing. Probably so, since she wore some strange skin-tight gray jumpsuit, which had a military look, save for the V-cut neckline.

Jared turned his eyes back to the door, expecting the doctor to burst in again. *Knock-knock!*

"What the hell," he muttered.

The window latch was difficult to turn over, as though it hadn't been opened in years, but the window itself came up so quickly it hit the framing above.

"Were you calling to me?" he asked.

"Hi up there," she answered. "Can you help me out? My car—"

How weird to ask someone up in a building for car help rather than find a nearby auto shop. Her beauty could capture all manner of greasy mechanics. "Sorry, don't know anything about cars." Jared reached to pull the window back down.

"It's only that I dropped my keys and kicked them under my car. I just need a longer arm to reach them. It won't take a minute."

Her voice had a sweet-as-cherries, musical quality to it. That and the deep plunge of her neckline had Jared staring. When he realized his inappropriateness, he moved his eyes away. *Classy. Way to stay a gentleman...*

Noting his silence she swayed a little, looking flighty. "You're kind of my only hope right now."

Jared frowned. "I'm sure you can find someone down there."

"Look, it'll only be a few minutes. Come on, there's a fire ladder right outside. Or is the view too good up there?" She offered a luminous grin.

Face flushing, Jared concentrated his attention on the brick wall behind her. "Wish I could help. I'm in the middle of something important. I'm really sorry."

"What can I do for a little assistance here? It'll be quick. I swear."

"I shouldn't be climbing ladders."

"Nonsense."

"Really, I should go—"

She tilted her head. "You're not scared of me are you? What will it take to convince you I'm friendly?"

He looked back incredulously and before he could avert his eyes, she drew down her top and flashed her breasts.

Jared nearly fell through the window. "Wh-wh-what, why—did you?"

She put herself away and folded her arms, no hint of embarrassment on her face. "I like seeing you blush, and besides, you're now obligated to help me. I gave you a freebie. It's only fair. Hey, you were looking anyway—thought it might help you do the right thing."

"The *right* thing?"

"Help this distressed woman who graciously, although briefly, shared her bosoms with you."

This had to be a fever dream. Jared shook his head, and yes, indeed, he was pretty damned lightheaded. "But I didn't ask... I mean, I'm sorry, thank you for that, but I can't help. I'll get someone in the office here—"

"*Jared*," she said firmly. "Don't be a baby. Get your ass down here. This is serious shit."

Her words slapped him into silence. He stood there at the window, blinking. "H-how did you know my name, are you—"

The woman pointed to the ground. "Get down here. *Now*." Her brown purple eyebrow arched. "Before I do something fancy and make you come down. Nobody can help you up there. Only *I* can. Move it. You are in grave danger."

A sharp point of truth stabbed through Jared's inconsistent thoughts. He didn't want to hear what those two doctors had to say, and this mystery woman knew him somehow. She knew his name and where to find him. Something about her tone of voice too. It reminded him of his childhood, *no, his entire life*, like she'd personally read aloud to him every memory that ever involved him. The sound was uncontaminated emotion, unmistakable. Riveting and terrifying. She almost sounded like... the voice of his conscience.

For that and for all the fears he might escape here in the exam room, Jared poked through the window and grabbed hold of the fire escape. It was sturdier than expected and reminded him of climbing the one outside his parents' apartment in LA as a kid. His heart beat strangely in its new rhythm as he carefully took the ladder off the side. Each of his steps on every rung were calculated with full prudence. He must have been going too slowly because the woman started gently slapping her hip and fidgeting.

When his feet thankfully touched the ground, he said, "Okay, I need to get back. Where's your—"

Jared couldn't get the rest of his words out. He was forced against the building.

"What are—"

"Quiet!" She pushed her body closer. Her hands wrapped around his and pressed his fingers down. Hot whispers tickled his ear: "Clench your fists."

"Huh?"

"Clench your fists. Clench them. Stop the questions. Do it."

A myriad of considerations passed through Jared's mind. She was going to rob him. She was going to hurt him. She's a female serial killer. He had fallen into her trap to be murdered—over boobs.

"Good," she said in his ear. "Keep them shut. Don't open your hands until I say so. Keep your voice low."

"Look, I'm far from being a rich man and…"

Her body pressed harder into his and Jared's heart made another strange throbbing lunge. This stress couldn't be good for his condition, whatever that condition was. Then something else happened. He felt his body react to her closeness and he stiffened against her, despite all his confusion. The woman leaned back and her beautiful ocean eyes fixed on his. "Like me, huh?"

"Come on, what is this—"

"Shhh!" Her head whipped around and her eyes thinned on the far end of the alley. A figure ambled out with all the shrugging grace of a marionette. It must have been the distance, but the person appeared to be naked and badly burned from head to toe. *A homeless person?* The once Caucasian flesh had a bumpy, bubbled texture that clotted the skin up to the head, which was an even more disturbing sight: a skull exposing a glistening red brain that grew into an obscene nose with nostrils large enough for fists. In one of the clumpy hands, the person carried a small crossbow.

Jared cried out and a hand immediately slammed over his mouth. It smelled faintly of ash and lavender. "Let's scream on the inside," said the woman, sparing no playfulness. "The scouts may be blind, but they aren't deaf."

The creature stopped and watched the alley, its big nostrils dilating.

Jared shivered. *I've lost my mind.*

"Keep your fists closed," she warned. "Otherwise the scout will smell your lifeline."

The scout moved back and forth for a moment, its brain erupting with blood that drenched the nose and its twisted shoulders. Up went the crossbow, quick and ready, and the scout took two measured steps forward and aimed straight for them. For a heartbeat. Then it aimed at a nearby dumpster. Taking a step backward, it angled the crossbow to the rooftops. The nostrils quivered into a loud snort that sounded like a prehistoric warthog. After a few silent moments, the scout withdrew and walked out of the alley, vanishing around the corner.

The woman pulled at Jared's wrist. "Let's be on our way now, but keep your hands closed in the meantime. Tight. No opening them until I say."

Numbly, he let her take him a few paces away from the wall. In this moment of chaos, this upending of the natural flow of his life, Jared needed to focus on something tangible or he feared he'd panic. His head dropped and he noticed the woman had no shoes on. Surprisingly her feet looked clean and her toenails flawless. In a way, the perfection of them was almost stranger than the deformed scout.

"I really need to get back to the doctor. There's something really wrong with me," he pointed out.

"I agree," the woman said, leading him on.

"So you didn't lose your car keys?"

To this she chuckled and gave him a sly, backward look.

Jared halted now. The woman wasn't getting it. He was in trouble. His heart was failing. Maybe he wasn't getting enough oxygen to his brain. Something was horribly wrong. He must have wandered out of the doctor's office somehow. Who knows which events really happened? And in what order. But he was sick. Maybe most, or all of this, had been hallucinations.

"I gotta go back," he pleaded.

"Jared, now is not the time to lose your shit." She got closer and carefully studied him. A fond expression entered her already sweet face. "It's nice knowing you can see me now. Never imagined I'd have this chance."

"What do you mean?"

"That doesn't matter right now. Your soul is in danger. I'll explain more once we've reached relative safety—"

"But how do you know me? What are you doing here? Where did you come from?"

The woman was silent for a few seconds, seeming to consider whether she should say more. She checked the alley and bit her lip before relenting. "I've watched you my whole life. I'm an *Utumm-Resona*, or a banshee, if you like."

Jared's brows knit. "A banshee? Are you joking?"

"No, and in case you're wondering," she added, "we're not ghosts and we're not from Scotland."

"Wait a minute." Jared grinned and wagged his finger at her. "This smacks of Kaitlin. Making fun of me for watching *Lord of the Rings*. She probably sent you and that guy in the burn victim suit, huh? Probably got the doctor in on this too, to freak me out?"

"Rather elaborate for a prank, don't you think? Especially for the likes of you, honey. No, no. Your pal Kaitlin's got nothing to do with this. She's at an audition in Burbank right now. Not doing that well either, I might add."

"So you *do* know her?"

"I've watched everybody in your life and in many other lives. That's my job, my duty, my curse, what have you. Understood? So let's beat cheeks here." She tugged at him again. "We can play catch-up once I transport us to the beach."

"Beach?"

"You'll see. That's your only chance to be spared."

It all sounded so frank coming from her. Disturbingly frank. Jared felt the world unraveling around him. This had to be mental failure. There was no way. "No no no. Can't be a part of this lunacy." He stopped walking and waved his hands in a *that's enough* gesture. "You're very pretty, but either you or I have to be crazy. Or both maybe."

The banshee snatched his right hand and shook her head. Her gaze traveled from his palm back up to his eyes. "Nice work. You opened your fist. The scout has smelled you now, dummy."

"I don't—"

With incredible strength, she locked her hand around Jared's. "I'm going to need to do the scream here and hope for the best. *Don't let go of me.* Whatever you do. Understand?"

He nodded and she turned her head in sideways appraisal. "You sure? Because so far you suck at following directions."

"I understa—"

She broke into a sprint, nearly pulling Jared's arm out of joint.

Sniffing sounds followed them. Jared turned back and watched in horror as the scout loped toward them, its legs rising and falling rapidly like a deer's. Rich, corded black veins pulsed all through the brain-head. The scout waved its crossbow. It had been too far to see before, but as the creature closed in on them, Jared got a much better view. A long net wiggled from the end of the bolt.

"Remember," said the banshee through deep breaths. "Don't. Let. Go."

Her blue eyes had become so real, so intense and commanding, Jared almost didn't believe this was a psychotic dream anymore. He gripped her hand tighter. A thin vibration hummed in the air, indistinguishable at first, and then it *thickened* with other layers of the same sound, a series of universe-moving machines revived from eons of silence. A pulse went through the banshee and through Jared's hand to shock his elbow. The source of the strange sound came from an angelic braid of silver and gold that lighted under the skin of the banshee's neck—it looked like a peculiar musical instrument, a sophisticated, harp-shaped set of vocal cords. Her mouth parted and miniature sunbursts and eclipses spread through the air on every note.

The scout let out a growl of frustration and shot its net gun. Jared followed the tangle of black webbing as it sailed overhead... and then... the air pulled back, away, the net hewed into minute, dim fragments. Everything surrounding Jared and the woman suddenly did the same. Buildings stretched out on strings of pebbles that raced into the sky, where they threaded in an immense tapestry of grays, greens, and browns. Lacing. Bending. Joining. And slowly, that tapestry pulled down east and west of them in long luxurious trails that could have been earthen taffy. Dark steam lifted from the sidewalks and streets and buildings alike. Plumes roiled around Jared and the banshee before little stars blinked in the space around them. It was as though he and the banshee had become galactic giants thrashing their way through space; they were juggernauts that moved around a micro-sized universe that had been shrunken exclusively for them. Comets the size of houseflies zipped past, asteroid fields scattered like suspended pools of pebbles and dust, and planets slipped around their bodies, frozen eggs moving briefly before returning to orbital position.

Jared looked over his shoulder. The scout struggled out in the darkness. It clawed and shifted violently but could not gain control. Its nostrils collapsed and the exposed brain hemorrhaged in torrents. After one more flail of its body, the scout drifted away, useless and frozen in the nothingness.

Jared's ears buzzed as the banshee's bizarre scream ended. The tunnel of open space that forged through the city buckled and shook, almost angrily.

"Oh, damn it!" yelled the banshee. "Shit!"

"What?" He could hardly hear himself.

"A *Disturbance Paradigm*. Keep holding on to me, Jared!"

Gravity pulled from several directions. His grip on the banshee's hand started to give. She swung around and grabbed his wrist with her other hand. They were floating now. Pebbles, rocks, bricks, and stones rained down, some bundling together before falling apart and then rebuilding again. The banshee pivoted, turned him away from the dangerous debris. A cluster of something that looked like a halved portion of a dentist's office twisted down from nowhere. The banshee threw her arms around Jared and rocked him away, just dodging the office as it fell past.

The sensation of being sucked through a straw overwhelmed him then and bile rose in his throat with a horrible wave of claustrophobia. A force pushed him and his protector forward into shards of hot white light and in the next moment—

Jared sat on the curb of Eighth Street, just across from his favorite *pho* restaurant, which had to be at least five miles from the doctor's office. He glanced back and saw the dentist's office, unaffected, people waiting in chairs by a fake plant. Hadn't that whole building just blown past them, as though weighing nothing? And yet it was here again. Nothing was fragmented or weightless. Everything was grounded and whole again. All of the madness of moving through space had ended like a dream.

The banshee sighed and held her forehead. "Not what I counted on... damn it. We were supposed to make it to the beach. That Disturbance Paradigm really screwed things up. Oh... this so sucks. So sucks. So sucks."

Jared gaped at her a moment. Her agitation faded and she drew back and clapped him on the shoulder, successfully scaring the shit out of him. "Well, enough bitching I guess. We'll get to the beach still. But that was a good job, Jared. I'm proud! You didn't let go of my hand."

She helped him up and he searched his surroundings, dizzily. "What else would have happened had I let go?"

She shrugged one shoulder, her metallic purple and brown tresses swaying with the motion. "Reality probably would have bent into a pretzel that ate it itself and then vomited... Best way I can describe it. Anyhow, we have much to discuss and little time to do it."

"By all means." Jared brushed off his pants. "Start where I'm connected in all this."

"Great," she replied. "So you're ready to talk about your death?"

Jared absently nodded.

And then fainted on the sidewalk.

Chapter 2
The Banshee

The banshee studied Jared as he sat there, searching the sidewalk in a daze. How many times had she watched him this way? Lost. Out to sea. Scared of what the future might hold for him. He'd spent most of his life that way, and she'd been there for it all. Still, she could never be inside his head, so there would always be more to learn.

An old lady driving a brand new Cadillac slowed down and peered suspiciously over her sleeping husband in the passenger seat. The window slid down. The banshee smiled and the woman smiled back, a little embarrassed. "Is he okay?"

"Tequila shooters for breakfast," said the banshee.

The woman shot them both a disapproving glare and pulled the car away. Neither of the older people in the Cadillac were her assignments, but she could still read their lives. They'd both be gone from this world by this time next year. The woman would break her hip next Saturday and die during surgery a month later. The man would give up on life, drink scotch and eat nothing but Del Taco for the year thereafter. In the end, relatives would say he died of a broken heart. And this would technically be the case, due to organ failure.

Jared blinked up into the sun. Dark blonde hair, hazel eyes, just a slight shade of stubble on his jaw. He was incredibly handsome. She'd always thought so, even as a little boy. His shyness and lack of confidence, however, ultimately masked his good looks. Women who got to know him interpreted his reluctance as weakness, rather than taking it as a good sign and accepting it as a challenge. The banshee didn't understand females in this world. They mostly chose strength and protection in men when modern society had rendered such qualities superfluous. With so many good hearts out there going to waste, women should have been cultivating these flowers and watching them bloom to fullness. Instead, they chose the man with more confidence than he deserved and spent most of their lives chipping away at that confidence to reshape them into someone closer to Jared. That was working in reverse. Jared was a hunk of stone that hadn't been worked into a statue yet. She loved all the possibilities lying within him.

"I've never fainted before," he said.

"I won't hold it against you," she replied. "I thought you had a stronger stomach. My apologies, Jared. We won't talk death right now."

He pinched between his eyes. "Who are you? Do you have a name?"

"No. None of us do. Our own lives don't matter. We aren't people."

"You look like a person to me."

"We are mechanisms. We perform a required job. I'm like a spiritual air traffic controller. When I give the go-ahead, someone takes flight into the great unknown, and never before."

"I thought we weren't talking about that right now." Jared closed his eyes and took a quivering breath through his nose.

"Oops. Yeah. Sorry about that."

His eyes flew open, vitally renewed. "I need to understand what's happening. I mean, what was that back there? What the hell— what *in the hell* was all of *that*? And that thing you did, that sound that came out of your throat—"

"That was a Cosmos Scream," the banshee explained. "It severs all realities at once to form a short-cut of sorts through time and space. It usually works more smoothly than that, and we could have covered a lot more miles, reached our ultimate destination, but unfortunately one reality rejected our presence and the conflict formed a *Disturbance Paradigm*."

"Come again?"

She offered her hand and Jared carefully took it. She pulled him to his feet and grasped his shoulders for a moment to make sure he had balance. For a few seconds she massaged his muscles and stared deep into his eyes. This made him squirmy and she drew her hands away.

"As I said before, it's like a reality pretzel, but that paradigm back there was teeny-tiny. I've seen far greater DPs than that, so count us lucky. Anyway, let's get moving, huh? We can talk as we walk."

Jared flinched. "You're not going to do that cosmic thingy again, are you?"

"Cosmos Scream? Not likely."

"What does that mean? 'Not likely?' That you *are* going to do it again? I—I can't go through that another time."

"Oh, poor baby. Want me to hold you?" She put her arm around his waist as she guided him down the street. "I could sing you a soothing song. I know many."

"You're making fun of me?"

"Hell yes I am. Look, breathe in and breathe out. I won't be doing another Cosmos Scream. No more bending reality. From here on in, reality stays rooted. I'll use every other scream I have to help you. Everything within my limits, anyway."

"What are you actually helping me with, though?"

"You ready to talk about that? Maybe sit down first," she said, regarding him with a maternal concern.

"I'm not there yet."

"Didn't think so."

He sighed and blinked rapidly, trying to form another thought. "You have other screams then?"

"Of course I do, dummy." The banshee spotted a small eating establishment near a Korean bank. Her heart leapt. "Hey is that a pretzel place? Oh man, what a coincidence! I was just talking about those. Oh buy me one, Jared. I've never had food here before. And a soda. I want one of those, too. There's no line. It won't take us long, will it?"

"I guess— not." Jared stumbled forward at her insistence.

Mr. Softy's Pretzels had only one patron, a tattooed woman with a pompadour, who had finished her food and was busy thumbing the screen of her phone. As they made their way over to the counter, the banshee studied the woman. This human wasn't her assignment either but the mark of death was clear: three years from now, head-on collision while texting and driving, coming home from a Tool concert. She will leave behind a six year old daughter and a boyfriend who is "the one."

The banshee shook the thoughts from her head and drew closer to the counter. A middle-aged man with a salt and pepper mustache smiled warmly at them. "I like your hair," he said to the banshee. "Interesting colors."

"Thank you," said the banshee. "I like your mustache. Very manly. Jared, you need to grow one."

"Yeah, Jared," the man chuckled. "Grow one. It would suit you."

Jared blushed. After a moment of silence he said to the banshee, "Aren't you going to order?"

"I want a pretzel with that cheese sauce, and one of those soda things."

"Which kind?" asked the man.

"The best kind."

"Sorry?"

"Give her your favorite," Jared clarified.

The mustached man half-smiled. "Don't drink soda really."

"Give her a 7-Up then."

"Got it. Anything for you?"

Jared shook his head. They waited there while the man got everything. She took a drink of the soda first. This world had such focus on the senses—not like in her reality, where the senses were fabricated; no, in this world they were on display, like delicacies to be sampled but not feasted upon, delightfully pronounced and adorable compared to what they really could be. She brushed the waxy cup's surface with her thumb. The perspiration up and down its sides. The carbonation fizzling within like microscopic fireworks. The plastic straw inside her mouth. The soda *glurping* as it traveled up. Ice rattling below. The beverage burning her nose, sweetly. It was a very interesting experience when considered simultaneously. Life was good in this moment. Yes, this made her content.

The man rang them up, and with all the grace of a robot, Jared took out his wallet and paid.

"Thanks you two," the man said.

The banshee shared another smile with him. In twenty-two years pancreatic cancer would claim his life. The heartening thing, however, was he'd be more than ready to go by that time. That's a luxury not many human beings enjoyed.

She turned her thoughts back to the matter at hand. If she was going to do anything else interesting on this trip, she'd have to get him close to the beach before anyone in the Deeper Unseen found out what she'd done. Especially if *they* found out.

Which way was south?

She didn't have a firm grasp on direction yet; things moved differently now that she had a foothold in this place. She could faintly smell the stench of sea salt on the air. The ocean wasn't far, luckily for them both. It was both reassuring and devastating. If they succeeded, for Jared it would mean his soul escaping eternal pain, and for the banshee, it would mean... being rid of her accursed job for good.

Jared didn't need to know how that would ultimately happen, and she had no plans on letting him know. He already looked thoroughly disturbed as he watched her munch on the pretzel, another refined sensory experience to be sure.

"Hey, remember what I said earlier?" she asked, and playfully gnawed the end of the pretzel. "Watch, Jared, I'm eating reality. Mmmm! It's salty!"

He smoothed his hands over his face and shook his head. She shrugged and dunked the remaining part of the pretzel into the tangy cheese sauce. Good while it lasted.

"Where are we going, banshee?" he asked. "I should—I should go back to the doctor's. Really. He had to tell me something important."

"It wouldn't help. The doctor's still confused by what I did to him anyway."

Jared stopped. "What you *did* to him?"

The banshee pushed him along. "Keep walking. I used a Bewildering Scream—made all his memories of your results like smeared Aramaic writing inside his mind. It'll be days before he can recall what he needed to tell you."

"Why—"

"I had to get him out of the exam room. I figured he'd go for help and that'd give me my chance."

"Did you see the results?"

She hesitated, and then said, "Yep. Sure did."

"And?"

"Ready to talk about this, are we?"

Jared steeled himself and nodded. "Yeah, please. What's on the report?"

"Can't tell you that. It's forbidden to disclose how you actually die."

"So I am?"

"What?"

"Going to die?"

"Oh, what a completely unforeseen shock, all you humans die."

"It's the *when* I'm worried about," he said and swallowed.

"It's not for me to divulge precise details. Technically, I can't say exactly *when* either. I can only be vague. If I allowed everything to slip, I could no longer be your banshee and then I'd be of no assistance to you."

"So what are you actually assisting me in? Cheating death?"

The banshee laughed. "Oh no. That's above my pay grade."

"Then—"

"How about cheating eternal agony? Sound better?"

"Honestly? They both sound shitty."

"You creatures think all death is bad, even when you despise living. Funny, that. But there are good deaths and bad deaths, believe me."

Jared's face went green and he broke away from her hold of his waist. "So the doctor's concern was real?"

"All I can say is that you're scheduled to die this summer. Nothing is fixed though. It could happen a lot sooner if you don't follow my every direction."

This did nothing to improve Jared's color.

"Nobody ever wants to hear about their mortality... but there are worse things than dying. After that Cosmos Scream going wrong, there is a good chance that *The Assembly* approaches. Every hundred years, a new gift is made of a person about to die. You are that gift, Jared. After patiently waiting, the Assembly intends to collect you."

"They take me before or after... it, I mean, death... happens?"

"Under normal circumstances, the Assembly kidnaps you at the moment of death, before your spirit can release. *Spiritual interruptus.* That's funny, right?"

"Hysterical."

"As a gift, nothing will be the same again. You'll be taken to my reality, the Deeper Unseen, and you'll be made immortal and become their toy, their property."

"What do they do with gifts?"

"I really shouldn't scare you..."

"What does it mean?" he asked.

"Remember the scout?"

Jared nodded.

"That thing was one of their gifts. At one time, it too used to be human, and it wasn't even as gruesome as some gifts I've seen. At least that one could still walk and had flesh... well, kind of. Being the Assembly's eternal plaything is worse than death. *Far* worse. Anyhow, since that scout showed up it's obvious the Assembly has been given permission to claim you early. They have discovered my plan to protect you. They know I broke my pact with them and that's why we cannot slow down until we reach our destination."

Jared checked himself, touched his chest and face. His breathing quickened. "I'm dreaming. This is a really, really crazy dream. Am I already dying? Lying on the floor of the doctor's office?"

"Get a grip."

"I can't."

"Put this in your pocket." She handed him the wax paper the pretzel came with.

He took it without question. They walked quietly for a few moments before Jared spotted a trash can with a green grate around it. He tossed it in.

The banshee couldn't believe her eyes. "You didn't just throw that away?"

"It was trash."

"Damn it all. I wish you'd listen!" She stepped up to the trash can and peered in the small hole at the top that was encircled by cigarette sand and butts. Sticking her arm down inside, she searched for a few moments, shaking her head. Her fingers touched nothing. The trashcan must have been recently emptied and the inner can was surrounded by heavy concrete. It would seem that someone who worked for the city could open the padlock on its side, but there was no chance in overturning it to get the piece of wax paper back out.

"Shit," she muttered.

"What did I do?"

She pulled her arm out of the trash can. "Forget it. Just... Jared, you really have to stop screwing up so much. Really. This isn't going to be an easy trip. You have to listen to *everything* I tell you to do. I know you're scared, but trust me, there are worse things in store for you."

"I'm sorry."

"Don't be sorry, just be better."

He bowed his head as they started off again. She watched as Jared's eyes darted up the street to the horizon. "Are you going to run on me? You look pretty flighty right now."

"What do you mean by that?"

"I mean that without me, the Assembly will find you. No question, they'll find you. And they'll be so jolly they might celebrate by force-feeding you buckets of glass on your first day in their fortress."

Jared swallowed. "Why would I run?"

"Because, despite my twisting reality right before your eyes, you still don't frigging believe me, you're trying to explain this away!"

"No I'm not—"

The banshee got hold of her frustration and let a breath escape through her teeth. "Here, the story might go like this: you give me the slip, nearly get killed, and then have an epiphany which convinces you I'm telling the truth. I swoop in, just in time, and save you. No more setbacks after that. We're then on the same page.

"Problem is, that cliché doesn't ever get to happen. If you leave my side—even for a moment—your slim chance becomes no chance at all. Once you leave and I can't find you, there won't be an opportunity to say 'oh wow, she's sexy *and* telling the truth,' because the Assembly will be dragging you under. So don't run off, okay?"

"You obviously don't know me that well."

The banshee laughed. "You totally find me sexy. Don't even start with that."

"That's not what I meant—"

"You'll also find that I'm goddamn brilliant most of the time, but don't let that threaten you. Just accept it. And I'm well aware of who you are. I know you *very* well." Jared scowled. She pinched his cheek and gave it a light smack. "I was assigned to be the one who hails your death. I've watched you for a very long time, dearest. Believe me, *I know you.*"

"Watched me... where?"

"From the time you get up in the morning until you go to sleep, on some days."

"You've watched me? *Everywhere?*"

She tittered at his vexed expression. "Bathrooms are sacred, of course. But only because I'm classy."

"You've seen me undress?" He lifted a skeptical eyebrow and folded his arms.

She reached around and pinched his ass. Jared jumped as though electrified. "I sure have, sweet cheeks. You have three very cute moles on the left side, reminds me of a constellation. What else... let's see. Oh, you're circumcised. Average length. All in all, a very handsome joystick. That's more of an opinion though."

Jared's jaw fell open.

"Not impressed yet? Let talk about your habits. When you aren't eating your neighbor's cooking, you eat shredded beef tacos from *Los Amigos* like you're expecting a global tortilla shortage. You smooth out ketchup and hot sauce packets while you wait for your food, and then you stack them in neat little piles. You lose your keys at least five times a week. Old Spice body spray is your go-to cologne when you actually do have dates. Let's see, hmmmm... Your favorite lotion is Jorgen's Cherry Vanilla, but you only use it for—"

"That's enough. I believe you." He hung his head down, blushing.

A bitter, razor-blade taste flooded the banshee's mouth. *Not good.* The fates of many individuals had suddenly changed. Like a series of bells, one after another... death schedules had changed. Only *they* could be responsible for such a thing. It meant they were given permission by the Silent Kings. They were using their three grants.

She tugged on Jared sleeve. "We ought to quicken our pace."

"The Assembly? Are they close?" He glanced around breathlessly. "I thought they still hadn't found out. You said—"

"Don't flip out on me. Keep calm, for crying out loud."

"I can tell in your eyes—you're worried."

"Don't overreact," she said.

"You think they'll find us, don't you?"

"Just walk faster. I've got to plan something."

"We can take a bus, you know? I have a pass and it doesn't cost much. Where are we going, anyway?"

"I cannot ride in vehicles," she said. "We have to run."

"Really? How far? Where is this destination you keep talking about?"

"The nearest beach."

Jared spluttered. "Wow. That would be Seal Beach and that's one hell of a run."

"Darling," she said, "with the Assembly tracking us, you can bank on that."

Chapter 3
The Assembly

Things change over thousands of years, but there is always a constant in that love guides our Assembly and always will. It is, however, important not to become too muddy-minded with adoration when approaching our task. On this planet, in this reality, our presence is tenuous and we must keep our feet as near to the soil as possible. This is an unfortunate circumstance, but we will recover our gift, nevertheless. We can only establish where our scout first disappeared: an alleyway behind a modest two-story office building.

It was a mistake being too aggressive with sending the scout, and we possibly deserve having the creature now embedded in a reality transom—but the confounding anguish of losing our property and our lack of patience were the compelling factors. We could not help being possessive, but we could try to be less impulsive. And smarter. We left our work in mid-cycle and that's why that Disturbance Paradigm unfolded. The main fault rested with that lying, betraying *Utumm-Resona*. We salivated for the moment when our serrated saws ravaged that beautiful voice box from her neck. It must be said, she did inspire wonder in us. Yet, how? It was wonder, not admiration, for that we knew. It had us perplexed though. How did that deceitful scourge accomplish all that she had?

Our ten formed a semi-circle around the fire escape. The proteinous scent of a gift was faint on the rusted iron fixture. The breeze through the alley had disintegrated its exact signature, but we had a suspicion our gift climbed down here shortly before the scout discovered him. Alas, we could not track him with this limited information.

Simultaneously all ten of us craned our heads up to the window at the top of the fire escape. In that room up there, we could get a full nose of him. What an unexplainable marvel! How did the *Utumm-Resona* get our gift to descend? Most of her more invasive screams we would have detected at once and she was smarter than to send such a signal. She couldn't have climbed the fire escape, because she's bound to the dirt and rock just as much as we are in this reality. So what happened here?

"Physical connection with another body will keep our residence in this reality," we said. Some of this morning's spoils of torture had settled down the left side of his face, making an eye-patch of hardened gore. "We can make a ladder of bodies. Need at least twelve—no—twenty to stack high enough to reach that window. We can climb up then."

"Alive?" we asked ourselves, all ten of our mouths saying the words in unison.

"Dead would be easier," we replied.

Then laughed together.

"That would change the death schedule. It would mean asking the Silent Kings for one of our grants," we went on. "Do we wish to use one so soon on this mission?"

"The banshee and our Gift draw farther away as we debate."

"It will still be painful for the climber," we added. "It will not be a firm enough connection."

"There is no time for pain." We sucked the foreign air past our blood speckled lips and closed our eyes. "For our first grant, we wish to change the death schedule, oh Silent Kings. It will serve our purpose."

A moment later a pulse of affirmation went through our bones.

We smiled.

Looking at the coin-op laundry mat across the way, we then found our resolve.

Two of our number, the Second and the Fifth, circled the building to post at the front door, and one posted in the alley. One at a time, the remaining seven pulled machetes from corridor shadows near our scarlet soaked feet. The Ninth took hold of the backdoor handle in his fist and ripped it clean out of the wood. The sorry piece of metal clattered in the silent alley. He reached into the hole and pulled the door open. Single file, we entered the laundry mat to gather the materials for our ladder.

It was a busy laundry day, luckily for us.

* * *

We rolled the bodies out the back door at a furious pace, but in the process, we still tried to study the deceased. Those who had kept their faces, we honored with a brief look of awe. This was a special day, and even though, inevitably, when the blood begins to fly all sense of the individual is lost, the least we could do was appreciate some of these spectacles of life uprooted from their mundane tasks.

A young blonde man with a white shirt speckled red with the words BABY CAKES across the chest in Old English font. His wallet was still in his hand. His driver's license indicated his name as Jason Stolarik. *Pleasant travels, Jason. Thank you for being one of our rungs.*

Unlike this one, the others remained nameless to us.

A bearded man in his forties, short cropped hair, black Harley Davidson t-shirt. He'd been smiling at a woman when one of our machetes bifurcated his forehead.

The lady he spoke to was a sixty-three year old woman with dyed auburn hair, overweight, and in a loose-fitting yellow blouse. Her eyes thinned when she laughed at the Harley man's joke, so she didn't see the first blow coming for her neck.

A younger brunette woman in flower patterned bell-bottomed jeans had run for the exit. The blade went through her gut fluidly and spread crimson immediately over her white tank top. She started coughing and grunting until we lengthened the wound to her breastplate.

Others went down more quickly: an elderly African man with yellow-tinted sun glasses and wearing a golf hat had his neck snapped without ceremony; with precise chops to the spine, an obese middle-aged couple dropped like enormous flour sacks; a well-built man in Army fatigues that should have lasted longer than two seconds ate the end of a machete when he screamed out; and the others became a delicious blur to us, as always: screaming faces, bloody teeth, bulging eyes, a kaleidoscope of pain and delight. We hoped they enjoyed it as we did, for the short while it lasted.

Even though we stood in a different reality, we could feel the vibrations of *Utumm-Resona* screams sending these people on their way. We pondered if those banshees were anything at all like the traitorous scum who spirited our gift away. Possibly so. They might all be treacherous in nature. And that would be our defense to the Silent Kings for needing to come here! The blame would squarely fall on that miserable thing's shoulders. After all, it was she who knocked over the domino stones. This massacre is an echo of her vile actions, and grant or no grant, if changing the death schedule became a point of contention, we would certainly let the Silent Kings know where the guilt rested.

Yes... we would never trust any of those golden-voiced women again. They were all sinning thieves lying in wait, ready to take our cherished prize. We would forever give them sidelong looks. We would never forgive or forget this. We were gullible to allow them access to the fortress archives. Had we been shrewder, the gift decree would have never been discovered. But it wasn't our oversight—we hadn't thought this an issue before. The *Utumm-Resonas* did their jobs and kept in line. Deceit, we had thought, wasn't in their nature, and for that, we were completely blindsided.

Never again, we whispered, three hundred and twenty teeth clenched at once.

Never again will we be foolish enough to trust them.

Yet this wasn't the time to lose focus. The variety of the eighteen corpses' shapes had made for an awkward ladder. The bloody slime between the individuals made them slippery and the pile unstable. We leaned into the body ladder, giving the support needed. The Eighth and the Fifth climbed up, one after the other, while we dug our heels in and crushed our backs against the quivering mass. Grunts of pain turned into barks of agony as the Eighth and the Fifth felt the disconnection from the ground catching up with them. Without the bodies providing some buffer they would have likely burst into flames by now and their ashes scattered in the wind. We were getting our gift back though, and this pain could be endured a while longer.

The Fifth climbed onto the Eighth's shoulders, bringing him eye-level with the window. He leaned over the fire escape and took in a ragged breath. The next moment, the glass shattered as his fist went through it. This was a doctor's office. But no doctor, nor patient, was present. The Fifth snorted and laughed. He licked his lips, tasting, enjoying, loving the smell. Through him, we all tasted it. A second later he descended from the Eighth's shoulders and the pair of them made haste to return to the ground.

Once they were safe, we pushed away from the dead people. More than ten bodies slipped off, twirled, and crashed to the ground. A few skulls did not take the landing very well and broke open.

The scent in our noses was powerful and developed into something quite tangible. Immediately we discovered a remnant odor of our Gift drifting on the wind. Our nostrils flared. Our fists clenched to the point of knuckles splitting. We broke into a sprint down the alley and took a left at the street. Our feet flew underneath us. Faster. And faster. Buildings blurring at our sides, we ran for miles, cutting in and out of traffic, ignoring the stares of onlookers. At one point we believed we might have lost the scent, as it was fleeting.

But then we stopped at a trashcan and found treasure.

The wrapper inside had large, stinking salt crystals in it, but otherwise smelled of two individuals. Our Gift, definitely, but the smell was hers mostly. That damnable *Utumm-Resona*.

Nonetheless, all that mattered was our Gift was detectable on the wadded paper. That meant they were still together, at least at this point. A new breeze kicked up and we smelled him again. He was near enough to taste now. Oh, it was entirely too enchanting.

We're coming for you, Jared, and we'll love you more than she does.

Chapter 4
Jared

When Jared was five years old...

He would walk to the park on Grand Avenue with his father. They'd bring a Ziploc bag with two heels of their weekly Wonder Bread. Jared was actually the only one in his family who liked sandwiches with the heels but he sacrificed them to feed Fatso, the seagull. Seemed other people at the park had the same giving nature, hence him being the most rotund and shiniest gull in the entire park—he was probably the size of two and a half seagulls by Jared's estimate.

They had been feeding Fatso for months before the lake closed for restoration of its pumps. When the lake reopened, Jared went back for a schoolmate's birthday party and he and some other kids discovered Fatso had become thin and sickly. If Jared hadn't spotted the little bald spot under the bird's chin, he wouldn't have been recognizable. The seagull had taken to living under a crevasse in the sidewalk. The entire turn of events disturbed Jared and on the way home his dad explained that since Fatso didn't have any handouts during the restoration he had starved. This further disturbed Jared that Fatso could die so easily without help, so he decided on the next trip he'd bring three slices of bread to get his friend healthy again.

Then one afternoon, his dad went down to the park for a company softball game by the lake. Jared's mother was working late, so he had to stay at the sitter's. That night his parents had an awful fight and his dad came in to say goodnight before leaving. Before he could even say a word, Jared asked about Fatso. His dad looked at him, blinking, as though he didn't understand the question. He said he hadn't looked for Fatso that day, but it sure seemed like his dad knew more, like there was something he wouldn't tell Jared. That's how adults were. They never thought kids could handle knowing everything.

Especially when it came to their relationship. Even though they didn't say so, Jared knew his parents were having big troubles. For this, he found himself more and more at the sitter's house. Bella Boyd. The woman had to be on meth or crack or something speedy, but nobody could say she didn't always put that hyperactive heart to good use. She was affordable and took Jared at the drop of a hat, never cared if he got sick, would never make him stay home. And he *liked* Bella. She was funny and had more energy than his two parents combined.

Problem was... she was pretty liberal when it came to safety. Bella had no problem letting Jared stroll up to stray dogs and pet them—had no issue with him climbing the tallest trees in the neighborhood wearing shorts and sandals—or letting him explore the entire neighborhood while she drank Miller High Life in a lounge chair on the driveway, reading kissy books. Jared was nearly six years old, after all. All of Bella's sons had done the same thing. One was in jail for grand theft auto and the other was a bouncer at a strip club in Vegas, but as she liked to mention, "they both made it quite safely to adulthood on my watch."

So the day Jared decided to go to the park and see for himself what had happened to Fatso, his sitter thought he was collecting tadpoles at the run-off channel up the street. Jared made up the tadpoles—he'd seen them on Sesame Street once, the letter "T" episode. He didn't even know if tadpoles existed in California, but obviously Bella had no trouble buying into his plan. Her show, The View, was on, and that meant she got to pace the living room with a mug of coffee and cuss out the stupid things someone was bound to say.

Jared knew the walk to the lake well, his parent's apartment being only one block away. He missed having his dad with him today. Since his parents stopped loving each other, he had seen less and less of the man. His dad must have been angry at Jared, too, for some reason. Maybe it was because of whatever happened to Fatso? That seemed to be the moment his dad went away to live at his friend Carl's place. His eyes had told something meaningful and sad the night he said goodbye and rather than ask what his mother had done to make him in so much pain, Jared had chickened out and asked about Fatso. Oh those eyes of his, they could have said many things, but Jared read them only as, *how can you ask me about that bird right now?*

Which only made Jared want to know even more. What had become of his big, fat feathered friend? It would be the answer to so many of his questions. Armed with a single heel of Wonder Bread, he headed down the hill, past the sundried run-off channel where his imaginary tadpoles lived.

He looked both ways like he was supposed to and hurried across the street. His eyes shot over to the crushed body of a crow. It didn't look real. Looked like a billowy black puppet that never could have been alive. Jared thought of Fatso and his father's silence and started running. The next three streets were empty and he got across without any problem.

Then came the major intersection at Grand Avenue. That's when everything got tough. He saw the crossing sign was the green man—that meant "go." Jared knew this. So he walked out into the crosswalk and hadn't gotten even halfway when a blinking red hand lit up. Red meant stop. And the red hand meant you shouldn't be in the street anymore and that a car would hit you. *Didn't it?*

Jared ran back to the curb, heart hammering in his throat. He thought about going back to Bella Boyd's house. She was probably still chewing out Barbara Walters and had no clue he'd gone. But even thinking of going back there right now made him shake his head. He would still want to know about Fatso. The park wasn't much farther. Just across this street and around the market, and he was there.

A tall pick-up truck with giant tires screeched to halt, almost coming to a stop in the intersection. Cowboy music blared over its revving engine.

The green man lit up again.

Jared had to circle the truck. It was so tall he doubted the driver could even see him. He decided to sprint for the other side of the street. It was different without his father holding his hand, making him keep up with the grown-up pace.

A horn blared and Jared yelled out in surprise, dropping his slice of bread in the street. The truck honked at someone making a right-hand turn. Jared turned back to pick up the bread—without it, there would be no point.

A man from the pick-up shouted, "Yeah, kiss my ass!"

Jared bent down and saw the red-hand light up again. The truck revved again, back tires kicking out white smoke. Another car's horn blasted and someone punched their middle finger up into the sky. Jared had stopped cold in the street. He couldn't go back the way he came. He'd have to run to the other side. This was dumb! He was going to get hit!

Gripping hard onto the bread, he flew for the opposite side of the street. A dark sedan slammed on its brakes and a green jeep turning right broadsided it. Jared jumped up on the sidewalk and grabbed the street light.

He cried for a long time in a daze. It wasn't even clear what was happening when a stricken, red-eyed Bella Boyd jumped from her Corolla and swept him into her arms. She looked to have been crying just as long as he had.

The accident, Jared later learned, had happened because the woman in the jeep freaked out and stomped the gas pedal rather than the brake. The black sedan probably wouldn't have hit Jared, but it was too close to call. A lady busted her nose on the steering wheel and her boyfriend, an older man, was taken away by the paramedics for heart troubles. The young woman in the jeep was able to drive away.

As much as he'd been missing his father, Jared hadn't looked forward to seeing him that night. While his mother sobbed in her bedroom, he sat down Jared on the couch and lectured and shouted and lectured some more. "You can't just make stupid choices like that. You have to think about everything you do! You have to be safe, Jared! You aren't able to make choices like these. You'll get hurt. This world will eat you up. Don't you understand?"

Jared only nodded and cried.

"You did that for the bird? Is that why? What were you thinking?"

He didn't have words for his father. As an adult, Jared still couldn't explain why he needed to be sure about Fatso. It made no sense then or now.

The blame ultimately came to fall on Bella Boyd. After that, Jared wasn't allowed to stay with her anymore, and shortly after she lost her rental and moved away. Jared always felt bad for her. She'd seemed so happy where she was and he'd wrecked it. He never felt safe or behaved well for any other daycare providers, and so after a string of failed attempts, Jared had to join his mother at her office job, which entailed staying quiet in the corner with *Dragonlance* books and hand-held videogames. His dad moved back in, but the relationship never improved. His parents did take him back to the lake regularly every weekend, before it was filled in and made into basketball courts.

Jared never saw Fatso again, but long imagined other gulls guiding him back to the ocean where he'd heal and be loved.

* * *

As they continued down the all-too familiar city streets of his Southern Californian childhood, Jared watched the banshee, his feelings still on a tilt-o-whirl. Long hair drinking in the sunlight across threads of purple and magenta steel awash in a chestnut storm, she was outrageously attractive to him. So human looking and yet... alien. He was both enamored and terrified with the very concept of her. Even so, there was a strange trust between them, like a parent and child, but unique unto itself. He would follow her anywhere and that scared him more than anything else.

"How did you know the Assembly were near?" he asked.

"People died today who were not scheduled. That was *their* doing. It isn't permitted to rearrange the schedule, but they are owed you."

"People died," muttered Jared. "Because of me?"

She ignored this question, lost in thought. "Still, I can't believe the Assembly was given permission to abuse the death schedule for so many, not even for a grant from the Silent Kings." The banshee glanced down. Then her face darkened. "They mean to blame me... if I survive, I'll be made to answer for these unplanned deaths."

"What do you mean, *if* you survive? You aren't a person. You can't die, can you?"

She looked at him as though she'd let something slip. "Everything can die, Jared, even those life forms that cannot age have a means to expire. Even banshees can die. It's difficult, but there are ways."

"But who hails your death then?"

The banshee pressed her lips together, thinking a moment. Somehow it made her more beautiful to him.

"I've met my own banshee three times now, but she rarely visits the Deeper Unseen," she replied. "She has red hair, is slender, with rather fierce looking features—but kind eyes. Just as with me, she has no name. She has watched me all my life, just as I've watched you."

"That's weird that banshees have banshees."

"Everything with a soul needs to be given passage. All that energy goes to the same place, in the end. I'm lucky none of my assignments are other banshees—those assignments are long term, if not eternal, and require tracking just like any other. I can't imagine the patience it would require." The banshee winced at something and stepped off the sidewalk.

"What's wrong?"

"Even walking on this concrete makes my soles sting a little because it's not as solid a connection to this world. That's why I had to get you to come down from the second floor of that doctor's office. I couldn't go up there myself. The farther away I get from the ground, the more I lose connection."

"Why is that, banshee?"

"This isn't my reality, Jared. I belong to the Deeper Unseen. That's my home. And without using the Cosmos Scream, I have to remain anchored when I have physical presence in this dimension. That goes the same for the Assembly, for that matter."

"But, banshee—"

"What, human?" She eyed him. "That's getting annoying, you calling me *banshee*. I must say."

"You have no name though."

"Well use your imagination and give me one."

Jared thought about it, but he'd never considered assigning a name to someone before. Pets yes, people no. He shrugged. "I don't know... some of my friends in school used to shorten my name to Jare. How about we shorten banshee to Banch?"

"I hate it."

"Okay," Jared said, clearing his throat. "Let's stick with Bs though. Beatrice, Bella, Beth. Oh! At the data entry place I work, they just hired a woman named Betty. How about that? It's catchy, right? Yeah, Betty the Banshee."

"No way."

"How about Cs? Carol? Chantal? God, I can't think of anything else."

"Dig deep."

"Heather! Helga!"

She rolled her eyes and groaned. "Just call me Banch, I suppose."

They walked down the street past a few empty shops. She stopped short, spying something at the base wooden trim of a Wells Fargo Bank.

"What is it?"

"We might need to buy some more time. We need to remove the scent of the Gift—they'll find us quicker if they've somehow acquired it."

"I don't follow. There's nothing—"

Then Jared spotted a flickering auburn shadow just above the layer of bark shavings in the planter. The shadow rested against the bottom of the wall, the size of secret hidden within a child's fist.

"I've seen these shadows before, back at the doctor's office," said Jared.

"Yes," Banch replied, "I was searching for you and since I had some residence here, you could see the *corridor shadows* open, just as you see this one now."

"What are they?"

"Holes between dimensions? Well, sort of, think of the wedges of an orange as you pry them apart."

"Got it."

"Like that. Pry those wedges apart and create an opening to a specific location in the Deeper Unseen. I happen to know that this shadow opens to nothing more than a field of bare earth and small rocks and pebbles. Perfect for what we need."

"Earth and pebbles?"

"We are going to rub the dirt all over that handsome mug of yours and your arms and legs for good measure. It'll complicate the scent of the prize and make it more difficult for the Assembly to track you."

"Whatever we have to do, I guess."

"Reaching through the shadow can be painful if not done with precision. We need to widen the opening so we can get a decent amount of dirt. Go ahead and put your fingers through."

Jared stiffened. "Why me? Didn't you say this could hurt?"

"A little."

"Why can't you do it?"

"It'll be good for you. Stop being prissy."

"*Prissy*? I'm not a—I just don't see why I have to do it."

Banch leveled her gaze and folded her arms. "Because I'm not doing everything on this trip for you. *That* is why. It's important. You have to get your feet wet. This is going to be a long day, trust me."

Jared scowled and reluctantly dropped to his knees. The bark bit sharply into his jeans.

"Wow. You mind pretty well." Banch laughed.

"Hey!"

"Okay, okay. So put your fingers through and delink the strands of antimatter."

"Pardon me?"

"You'll know them when you find them—"

A buzz went through Jared's arm, making his teeth clatter and the hair on his neck stand on end.

"—and when you don't," Banch finished.

"Uh, ouch!" Jared smacked his lips in disgust. "It tastes like I ate an aluminum can."

"Good, that means you went the wrong way."

"*Good*?"

"It's important to know the wrong way to go, just as much as the correct way. So find the other side now."

Jared wiggled his fingers until they encountered something like a knot of dry twine. He probed it a moment and then plunged his fingertips through. Immediately the shadow widened on the wall.

"That is great work, Jared, really."

"Yeah?" He smiled despite the cold sweat forming on his shoulders.

"Now one more. That should give us enough aperture to pull a sufficient amount of dirt through and fix you up. It'll be a little more challenging."

He searched around for two seconds before electrified tiger's fangs slammed down on his wrist. Jared leapt to his feet, screaming, holding his arm. A middle aged couple walking their brown pit-bull stopped across the street.

"He's good. Mental health issues! *Prissy-itis!*" Banch shouted. The couple shared a few whispered words and continued on more briskly.

"What *the hell*?" Jared continued to dance around in circles. Smoke flaked off his arm in lavender wisps. "My damn arm is frying!"

"You're golden. You're fine," said Banch. "Just try again, babe."

"No."

"Yes."

"No."

Banch stepped closer to him, their lips nearly touching. "Yes."

"It was larger and more complex to move around. I got, I don't even know how many shocks before a big one came and I'd hardly searched around. I am NOT doing that again."

With a snort, Banch said, "Do you need Mommy to hold you?"

"Stop making fun of me." Jared turned away, rubbing the singed spot on his sleeve.

Sputtering, Banch dropped down and stuck her arm inside the shadow.

"Easy for you to do," said Jared. "You know all about this interdimensional flim-flam."

The banshee focused as she searched. "I know—" Her body went rigid with an apparent shock. "As much—" She moaned through the pain. "As you do..." Another shock came and she clenched her eyes shut for a moment. "...about this particular shadow."

With a look of defiance, she tugged free a fistful of lime green dirt. "Here," she swallowed, "rub this on your face and arms."

Jared accepted the dirt, which felt and smelled like soil of a normal sort, nothing strange at all except the color. He applied it to his arms and noticed it left a slight discoloration on his skin for a moment before fading. Banch retrieved two more fistfuls and set them on the sidewalk. "For your legs," she said, and then wearily stood. "From your knees down should be enough, but get your feet too."

Jared caught sight of her arm. A couple burns streaked there and one had ruptured and seeped a vibrant red trail of blood down to her elbow.

"Banch, I'm sorry—"

"Forget it. Let's get the dirt applied so we can get moving again. There's more to masking the scent than just this."

Jared did as he was told. He took off his shoes and lifted his jeans up to his knees. When he was finished, he still felt horrible. He'd given up too quickly and had disappointed her.

"Banch... I was scared it would get worse. That's all."

She turned to him and placed a cool hand on his cheek. "I know, Jared. I know. No worries right now, okay?"

She pulled her hand away and he was sad to feel her touch go. She started off and he followed, the dirt making him tingle all over.

"We need a couple items from your apartment."

"What about the Assembly?" he asked.

"This involves keeping them at a distance. No dawdling. Move it."

Jared hurried to her side. "Banch?"

"Yes?"

"Who is going to hail my death if you die?"

She hesitated, then said, "There are plenty of other banshees to take your assignment. You'll be seen to."

He nodded, then said, "I'd rather have you though."

They continued down the street a few paces before Banch glanced over at him, a sad smile in her eyes.

Chapter 5
The Banshee

"It's good that cosmos thingy you did spit us out so close to home. That would have been a bit of a walk from the doc's office. Pretty lucky."

"And lucky you live on the first floor," said Banch.

"There's that too." Jared fumbled with his keys. He looked nervous with Banch standing so close behind him.

"Yeah, it was all lucky. Nothing but." She blew on the back of his neck and he jumped.

Jared grabbed his neck in reflex. "You mean, it was planned—you made it bring us here? Why didn't you just take us straight to the beach?"

"That would be because of the inception of a disturbance paradigm. This was the best I could do. We're good that we pulled through where we did." Banch gave an *ahem* and rolled her hand for him to continue opening the door.

"That sounds like a risk you shouldn't have taken then."

"Had I not used the Cosmic Scream, you would be in the Assembly's possession and I would likely be facing punishment in the lowest dungeon in their fortress."

"What about—"

"Jared!" Banch seethed. "Open the frigging door!"

He hummed discordantly, but obeyed. As he pulled open the door a rush went through Banch; she'd lingered on the fringes of Jared's personal space since his birth, but the rooms he dwelled within, observed from her own dimensional axis, were only shadows within shadows. Such a familiar territory brought her a smile, despite not having had an actual presence in this place. A familiar warmth spread through her, a homecoming, even if she'd frequented many homes in this world. Still, there wasn't time to get nostalgic. There wasn't time for much of anything now that the Assembly had arrived. She would have to find a way to keep them from heading them off at the beach. A slight detour might be necessary.

"Do you think Eun Sun can spare a box of detergent?" she asked Jared. "We'll need an entire box."

Jared turned to her, brow softly furrowed. It was apparently still difficult for him to grasp how she knew everything about his life, including his neighbors, the Kangjun family, who fed him and did his laundry.

"Uh... we can ask her," he finally said. "I think she's home."

"No," Banch said, rethinking the idea. "On second thought, let's not involve anybody else. We can buy some detergent on the way to the beach."

"So why are we here then?"

"To finish what we started with that dirt. Now we need to get you into some blue clothes."

"Blue?"

"Do I have a speech impediment?"

"I... don't... think so?"

She rolled her eyes. "Can you find it inside yourself to just let some things go unquestioned? We really need to move quicker than we have."

"Sure. Blue clothes. All of them?"

"Underwear, shirt—uh, those jeans aren't blue enough—pants then, and socks. Oh, and wear your old Nikes under your bed, they're mostly blue."

"This is so crazy... that you know so much." Shaking his head, he went through the living room, past the kitchenette and into the hall. "Why do I need to wear blue?"

Banch groaned. "Oh great shit, fine, I'll explain while you search."

The bedroom was plastered in movie posters from the 80s and 90s, with some abstract art prints he'd taken a liking to when he'd briefly attended art school. Over the single window was a stop sign he and Kaitlin had stolen from that very same time period.

He rounded the unmade bed and opened the top dresser drawer. "Okay... Blue."

"Some of these things aren't easily explained, Jared. In my world the senses are unified and transferred interchangeably at times. The color blue will further distort your scent with the green color of the soil perking beneath your skin. It adds another layer over the scent of the Gift and will make it more difficult for them to sniff you out."

"Makes sense."

"Does it now?"

"Not even remotely. But very little does make sense today." Jared tossed some blue boxers on the top of the dresser.

"The ones without the stripes," Banch noted.

He glanced over his shoulder.

She snapped her fingers. "Today, guy, today."

He went back through the drawers and found the blue boxers, some navy dress socks, and a sky blue t-shirt. It would have been better if every article was a similar tone of blue, but it would work almost as well.

"I have some blue sweatpants next door in the laundry, but that's it for my pants options. I guess we can go buy something."

Banch shook her head. Too many detours. They really needed to get out in front of the Assembly; the farther, the better. "We have to get you clothed quickly or the blue won't grasp the green as well."

Jared snorted. "Well that sucks."

"Oh hush."

"I can run over there to the Kangjuns," he said, shutting the drawer and standing up from the dresser. "You can wait here. I'll be fast."

"I can't leave your side."

"Not even for five minutes?"

She took his hand and pulled him close. His eyes didn't leave hers. His whole life, all in those eyes, and now in his death… She didn't want to think of it. Even without the Assembly involved, the news of her favorite project's early demise had twisted her heart. Death wasn't fair. She knew that better than most, but why him? Why so early? Why couldn't he have more time to grow into himself? Many special people had been taken and she was weary of it. So unbelievably weary. With the right guidance, Jared could evolve into greatness; the universe needed more like him. He just needed a chance. And now, he would never have one. All she could try to do was prevent the agony that the Assembly promised for him. It was the one way to show him how much he meant to her.

As they lingered, she drew even closer to him, thinking these thoughts, feeling the warmth of this apartment and of him. His lips approached hers. "This really is real," he said. "Isn't it?"

"Do you want it to be a dream instead?" she asked with a grin. "Would it be mine, or yours?"

He swallowed loudly. "Mine, of course."

"Don't be so sure."

Suddenly she got hold of herself, took in a deep breath, and pulled away. Awkwardly, she patted his shoulder and squeezed it.

He nodded. "Right, yeah, we should..."

"Go," she added. "Yes."

With a shy signal to the hall, he led her out of his bedroom. "Since we're seeing Eun Sun, we can ask if she has that detergent we need. As strange of a request as that is, I have left that part of this unquestioned. Proud of me?"

"Always, honey. Always."

Jared blushed and looked away.

Banch really needed to focus on why she was here. This wasn't wish fulfillment. This was saving Jared from an afterlife of endless pain and spiritual torment. *Then* doing what she needed to do for herself. The one selfish part in all of this, but it would be her reward if they made it to the beach.

* * *

Banch could feel the Assembly's unease. They were regrouping and she'd have to be ready for their next move. As Eun Sun answered the door, Banch went through some of those moves in her head and tried not to flinch when the woman's eyes moved from Jared's to hers. It was strange to realize people in this place couldn't taste your thoughts. After that bracing realization came over her, Banch's heart brightened. Meeting Eun Sun in person was an honor she'd not expected. The woman and her husband Bae had been so gracious for Jared helping them with their English. They'd treated him like a son for years. Since Jared couldn't cook—or was afraid to try—Eun Sun prepared his breakfast and his dinner. Before the Kangjuns had moved in, he'd always eaten out, three meals a day. He was saving money now, losing weight, and no longer had his friend Kaitlin coming over to help with the coin-op laundry down the street, a chore which she'd been giving him a hard time about for years.

"This is?" asked Eun Sun, extending her hand for Banch.

Banch returned her soft, sincere handshake. "It's not Betty, that's for sure."

"Eun Sun, this is my new friend, Banch. We were just, well, I needed to find my sweatpants in the laundry."

"Not washed yet." Eun Sun's eyebrows lifted with grim concern. Laundry was a source of dignity to the woman. She'd often make Jared strip off wrinkled shirts at the table and flee the table to iron them rather than finish her own breakfast.

"It's good that it's dirty," said Banch. "More of your scent."

"That's fine, Eun Sun," Jared insisted. "Really."

"Please, come." The older woman beckoned them inside.

"Oh, do you have another box of detergent? I'll buy you a new one. We need one right now."

Eun Sun looked positively startled. "You want... clothes washed... someone else?"

"No no, this is for my friend Banch. We are... uh, testing out her new washing machine."

After a moment's thought, Eun Sun nodded. "I see, you, and you, want to eat? Too early? For dinner—no, lunch?"

"Oh thanks, but we're in a hurry. We have to go soon."

A quick nod and Eun Sun shuffled down the hall.

"She's come a long way. You've tutored them so well," said Banch.

"They've taught me a lot too."

"You're a good teacher. I've always wondered why you didn't teach kids. Isn't there good money in that?"

Jared shrugged one shoulder. "Not really. And besides, I'm not much of a kid person."

"Got to make peace with kids."

"What?"

"It's like reconciling the past," Banch told him. "I was never a child so it's a foreign idea to me, but I think it's useful to make peace with children. It's coming to understand life in its rawest form."

"If you say so. Snotty, loud, and destructive, as far as I care to know."

Banch laughed. "So they are..." Her eyes lit on a fish bowl and suddenly her mind raced with an idea. She picked up the bowl. Two circling purple fish seemed to be stirring the mixture for her. She sniffed the water. *Beyond perfect.*

"What are you doing with that?" asked Jared.

That would do nicely. She dipped the bowl on its side and spilled half the water on the carpet near the door. The fish swam around madly as their world lessened.

"Banch! What's gotten into you?"

"They aren't fresh water variety," she explained.

"They're going to be the no-water variety if you keep holding it that way!"

"My apologies." She set the bowl back down. Jared looked at the puddle on the floor, awestruck. "Do I need to go fill it up with more water?" she suggested.

"No! Just don't touch anything else and we'll be good."

With slow grace, Banch ran a finger down the side of his smooth arm. "Gonna sue me now?"

Eun Sun emerged with a basket of Jared's clothes. "Sorry no more—extra? Box of soap, the, the, the…"

"We got it, that's okay. Thanks for looking."

Jared bent over and rummaged through his clothes.

Eun Sun looked at him and then Banch, searching for the right word. She smiled. "He… good person. People? Good man."

A faint smile came to Jared's lips, but he didn't look up from his work.

"Geuneun ibnida," said Banch. "Naneun olae jeon-e geuwa salang-e ppajyeossda."

He is. I fell in love with him a long time ago.

Eun Sun blushed and sniffed out a little laugh. Jared drew up his sweat pants from inside the basket and regarded them both. "You two up to no good?"

Banch put a hand on her hip. "That's the best way to be up."

"Thank you," Jared said to Eun Sun, and put his sweat pants over his arm. "Say hello to Bae for us."

"Dinner… tonight?" she asked.

"Not tonight."

Eun Sun nodded with a sly smile and saw them to the door. She noticed the puddle on the carpet and studied it in confusion.

"Jared neun mulgogi geuleus eul heul lyeoss-eo," said Banch. Joesonghabnida, geuneun seotuleun."

Jared spilled your fish bowl. Sorry, he's such an oaf.

Banch and Eun Sun burst out laughing and Jared watched them both, sensing the joke revolved around him. They left into the hall, and Banch already missed this home. She would have loved to play cards with Jared and Bae at their dinner table and try a large bowl of Eun Sun's beef soup.

Banch put Eun Sun's and Bae's deaths out of her mind, even though she knew the events well. Thinking in the moment always did her heart so much better.

Chapter 6
The Assembly

We wouldn't lose our prize. The Silent Kings' promise will be fulfilled to our number. We've kept the light and dark from converging and we've suffered for it. So it was our due to release the last century from our trembling, scabbed hands onto another. It was our reprieve. It was our right. Sometimes, it was the only reason we believed for our existence, even more than sorting shadows and sunbursts for the glory and health of all the dimensions. After the day was done and we laid on the cold stone floor of the fortress at the elemental hinge, covered in our blood and filth, we dreamed about the next Gift who will release the woe of our lot.

We hated this banshee for taking that away, especially since it is something she would never understand, for whatever reason, out of selfishness or cruelty. She was decidedly both, and craftier than we cared to deal with at the moment. Somehow she had played a move ahead of us again. The scent of the Gift was gone or so faint, it remained undetected now. This was undoubtedly her doing. For all the trouble we went through to acquire the scent, and wasting one of our three grants to claim those lives, she'd suddenly made all that meaningless. How we'd have loved to pull that golden voice box from her neck and share bites while she stared at us, aspirating, hemorrhaging. Relying on fantasy didn't get us any closer to the Gift however.

"Bring out the scroll," we growled.

The Seventh reached into a pocket in his gore-covered slacks and lifted out the dripping sanguine document. He unrolled it with a jerk, spattering blood over the faces of the Second and the Eighth. The blood remained there on their faces in fresh streamers, a history in red. We lived through blood: the scarlet, the pink, the brown, and the blackest of rot.

"Where does Jared die?" we asked.

The Seventh read for a moment and grunted. The new information spread through all of our minds. The Gift would expire at his place of work, an office building a mile or so from here. To the north, with a short turn on Styx Street.

We broke off, a pack of muscular frenzy and need. Some humans in running clothes watched us from across the street. From their dull eyes and gaping mouths it was clear they'd never seen or even thought about anything like us. But that was not such a surprise. A mite cannot lift its ugly head to the sky and understand the approach of a world-ending meteor. It is not fair to ask something like that of nothinglings.

Our pace became a trot, which became a sprint. The air dried some of the blood on our bare backs and in our tangled, ratty hair. New blood would replace it soon. A relished certainty.

Several of our number quit the sidewalk for the street, the connection with this world becoming stronger and less biting to the bones. It was a sensation that our entire number sensed, so all ten followed suit. Yes. The connection was better. We felt stronger and more aware of this place, and the pain of not having complete residence was but a slight tingle in our soles.

We arrived at the office building that was luckily only a single story structure, making this stop much easier. WESTCOAST DATA EXCELLENCE. The double doors slid open without manual operation. We filed into the lobby and stood before a reception desk. A small Japanese fountain bubbled near the wall with a lonesome bamboo shaft poking through the pebbles. Beyond the lobby area, a sea of cubicles stretched to the outer reaches of the building, a blue-gray morass.

"Oh *God*! What?" A curly haired woman in a blue pantsuit rounded the desk, a cell phone clutched in her hand. She stood away from them, terrified and watching the blood pitter-patter on the floor. "Leave here at once. I'm calling the police."

"Give us Jared Kare's address," we demanded. "Then we will leave your building."

Her eyes widened, stricken by our communal voice.

She retreated further into the hall and glanced at her phone. The Sixth moved to her and caught her wrist.

"The police," she said with a yelp.

"We don't care about your blue-coated strongmen and their metal. We bear the fabric of time and its billion fibers tearing across our exposed hearts, flayed open to welcome the falling acid from the universe's teeth. Now..." we told her. The Sixth tightened his grip and the phone tumbled from her hand and clattered on the beige tile floor. "Give us the address."

The woman gulped and sealed her eyes shut.

"Rose!" called a bald man, standing stock still at the side of the desk.

"Bill..." she whispered, opening her eyes partway.

"Jared Kare, his address," we insisted. "Or we will fill her womb with enough darkness to bring a litter of devil dogs."

The Sixth forced Rose to the wall, ran his hand down his bare stomach until it reached the buckle in his right suspender. He unfastened it and his pants slid sideways, revealing the side of one of his bloodstained buttocks.

"No," cried Bill. "I can get his personnel file. Just don't hurt her."

"Hurry," we whispered. The Sixth nudged his seeping scarlet lips against Rose's cheek as he said this with us and the movement left a violent flower of color on her.

Bill almost slipped as he tore away to a file cabinet down the hall. He crashed into the water cooler and it gurgled loudly.

The Sixth grabbed Rose under her knee and hefted up her leg. He brought his hips closer to her and softly nipped at her pale neck. We watched with fascination, enjoying the shared excitement and need surging at the two bodies.

"Here! Jared's stuff." Bill waved a paper overhead and charged back to us, his loafers clapping on the tile. "It's here, please let her go. I'll... I'll give this to you."

The Fourth intercepted him, swiped the page away, and pushed him into the desk so hard he took a seat on top of it.

The Fourth read the Human Resources profile and it filled all of our minds. We'd memorized this city before leaving the fortress, so we knew this particular residence was a few miles east.

"And now we leave—"

But noticed one of our number had remained silent. One of our voices had gone missing.

"Sixth?" we hissed.

The Sixth pressed the woman Rose harder into the wall and made a framed motivational poster SUCCESS go sideways at the fierce motion.

"There is no time to lose," we said. "She is not the Gift. Remember our purpose."

With a quivering gasp, the Sixth pushed down his pants to pull free his sex. His left suspender fell askew over his dense deltoid muscle.

"Sixth!" we warned. "You have forgotten us."

"It's a matter of moments, comrades!" he rasped.

That was it. He wasn't within us. He had broken away, become separate, no longer within the Assembly.

The Tenth caught him at the back of his neck.

"Oh!" He laughed out at first and then screamed, realizing where his brain had derailed from us. "I beg mercy! Please! I just wanted someone while here. We shall all feel it. Let me have this."

"There is no *me*," we told him.

The Tenth hoisted him off the ground.

"MERCY!" he shrieked.

With the loss of connection from the floor, the Sixth's skull caught fire and his skin peeled back like a wind tossed tarp. The exposed skull radiated white amid the flames. The skin shredded and the ends caught with hot embers like thousands of funeral incense sticks. They glowed hotter, slipped down, and surged with red electricity and black smoke. The Sixth's body exploded into spinning silver particles that expanded and pulled inward, into nothing.

There was only silence then. But it was momentary.

With a tremendous ripping sound, a wash of red stretched over the wall. The new Sixth emerged from the corridor shadow. The male body that appeared was larger, with African skin, though no less bloody than the Sixth before him. His gore-oiled handlebar mustache and untamed afro looked reminiscent of the Third Precocious Age, but this one's past was no matter.

We were him.

He was us.

For as long as he could ever dream to be.

* * *

The banshee's scent was stronger coming from another apartment, not the apartment of our Gift, but instead lingering at a stranger's threshold. There was also a dangerous smell, one that bled through all dimensions at once. It would make us lose connection not only here, but everywhere. Sea water.

It was obvious the Gift and the banshee had been in this other apartment as well, and stayed longer for some reason. We wagered the purpose for their stay in the stranger's apartment would ultimately reveal their location. If it didn't, we had little choice otherwise than to investigate.

We would use caution here with the scent of sea water so near. It was nothing to play loosely around. The First and Third took axes from a corridor shadow and went brutally at the door, trading off whacks. Shouts surfaced from the other side, growing louder as large hunks of wood splintered and ripped away.

We consider the smell. It was somewhere low, possibly in the floor, in the worn brown carpet. It's not seen and there isn't much, but the risk of stepping into it would be too high.

"Grab the hooks," we said.

The Fifth cleared the remainder of hanging wood debris. In the apartment a Korean couple hunkered in a corner. Both looked to a hallway, their foolhardy escape plan.

The First pulled a grappling hook from another corridor shadow. We had little time to admire its weight and smell the old death on its steel, and so we hurried to the doorway.

The man screamed an order to the woman, possibly his wife. She protested in their language and shook her head like a stubborn child. He grumbled something and cast his eyes back on us, his bewilderment as to why we hadn't entered the apartment all too clear. We caught the muddled scent of the Gift on one of them.

The Seventh leaned inside, taking the grappling hook from the Ninth. It made us anxious, how exposed we were to the hidden sea water. This might have been a trap set by the banshee. *Caution*. We could only use disciplined caution.

The hook, gleaming, heavy, hypnotic black on black, iron, steel, metal, hated love, we all agreed was and would always be our favorite tool. So many uses. So many beautiful memories. The Seventh cast it out. The married couple tried to run but misjudged the hook's path—it struck the floor just ahead of the man—the Seventh yanked it and swept the man off his feet, catching just below the right knee.

"Bae!" the woman wailed.

The Seventh ripped the man across the room, sending him through a TV tray set up with a bowl of soup. The bowl scattered and broth and noodles rained down on the man as he kicked and clawed at the carpet for purchase. The man wasn't even near us and we could already understand he wasn't the one possessing the smell. It was the woman.

But this was still good.

The Seventh caught the man by his ankle and pulled him into the air, careful not to drag him through the sea water at the threshold. Upside down, Bae yelled to his wife, but she screeched back at him. The Seventh dropped him into the hallway. He flopped there a moment before we pulled him to his feet and slammed him into the side wall.

The First leaned into the apartment, his lips and ours peeling into a senseless grin. He motioned for the woman to come forward. She started to move and Bae reprimanded her—cut off almost at once with the Seventh squeezing his throat between powerful fingers coiled in crusted blood.

"Bae," the woman sobbed, and hurried to the doorway. The Seventh eased his grip and the sound that escaped the man was amusingly melodramatic. We tittered and closed in around the threshold.

The First snatched the woman's hand and pulled it to his nose. The scent there filled all of our nostrils. We detected a similar smell in the room. A laundry basket near the couch. A pile of folded clothes were stacked there, newly laundered but still possessing the smell, if an earthier version. The banshee must have blended out Jared's natural scent and further muddled it with an attracting color. How very cunning of the bitchwhore.

This would take more study.

The First sniffed again, his nose, our noses, going rubbery, and nostrils all flaring with volcanic red intensity.

The man's foot snapped up and his work boot slammed into the First's face. We all flinched, pulled rudely from our analysis. Our hands simultaneously touched our stinging jaws and we tasted murder, enjoyable pieces of pink and red on our tongues.

The Tenth pulled a machete from a slanting corridor shadow and we chuckled at our own breathless excitement.

The First huffed in more of the odor. It was complex but even getting some distinguishing marker would provide a general location in the city. The muddling had been well executed.

Banshee filth!

The Seventh brought the gasping man forward, while we toyed with his wife's body.

"Money!" Bae said. "And let her go from here. Money—"

The Tenth stuck the point of the machete at the man's lower right eyelid.

"In my bedroom. Money. Yours. Please!"

The blade gently creased the skin in a vermillion stroke. The woman's face was locked in a micro-expression, on the verge of screaming. We mimicked her cowardice, the deliciously stupid expression rolling across our ten faces in a cascade. In the next moment we were laughing so hard we almost lost ourselves again. The First had stopped his sniffing. The Tenth carelessly dragged the machete down and neatly split Bae's mechanic jumpsuit, his hairless, pale chest bursting into view.

The sight of bare, clean, unspoiled flesh gave us pause and restored our resolve. The Tenth drew the blade just to the orbit of the man's dark red nipple. The edge rubbed there, summoning blood from below. Bae ground his teeth as the nipple lifted onto the blade. Two picked up the severed piece of flesh and licked it. He passed it on and we all took turns licking it, even the First, between his sniffs of the Gift. A steady stream of blood leaked from the wound, but Bae was brave. Through spit and teeth and burning eyes, he just wanted us to let his wife go. He had no idea the blessed things we would do before we let them both die.

And like that! The First caught the scent and put his fist up and out. He pointed it in the direction of the Gift. Somewhere to the southwest. This would guide us. Not to find Jared but to define the cage we would make for him and the banshee.

The Fourth tossed the nipple at the man and we hissed a serpent's laugh.

We had to leave now. There was no time for further amusement. We had fantasies on the brain though; oh, pleasure, how overwhelming it might have been to skin the couple just to see how pretty their muscle fibers were. Then we could have built a bonfire and roasted the skin. Snacked. Fed it to them as well. Watched the disturbed realization of how flavorful your own flesh really was...

But we could do that with our Gift, for the next hundred years and beyond that if we hadn't grown tired of him. He was ours forever. Ours to share and to have. He was married to us. No moving into the light, no death, no leaving the dungeons of the Deeper Unseen, only bliss with our rotten caresses. All of our Gifts had special chambers in our endless heart. It made us want to revisit the others, the passion clouding our mission.

We could hear the soft whimpers of the couple behind us. They held each other tightly, thinking we'd left them out of mercy. Stepping into this world's dizzying sunshine, we laughed at this idiocy, nearly on the edge of tears.

Chapter 7
Jared

Jared tried to ignore his sore legs. He wasn't used to this much physical activity and his leg muscles weren't the only thing reminding him of that; his heart had done those strange staccato beats a while back, which made him see snaps of light across his field of vision and brought a queasiness into his stomach that stretched to his throat and guts. He wondered if he'd make the entire trip to the beach.

The sun had ascended in the cloudless sky and the day had become ruthlessly hot. The banshee didn't seem to perspire, despite the weather and being in a skintight jumpsuit, while Jared had to knuckle stinging pearls of sweat from his eyes almost constantly. As they passed a pet store and he spotted some aquariums, he thought back to the Kangjuns.

"So salt water hurts them?" he asked. "The Assembly? That's why you spilled the fish bowl, wasn't it?"

"You've finally caught on. Good job, sweets. And let's say salt water slows them down, but no more. They are sensitive to it because if it is, in fact, actual sea water from the Paled Ocean, it's beyond dangerous for them, and me."

"It'll kill you and them?"

"It'll erase us from every possible reality. Even the smell of fish gets our guard up—if we were to come in contact with it, our bodies would break apart as energy and travel on, like all living things. Death for the Assembly happens almost as rarely as for banshees, and most of the time for them it's self-inflicted. I've spoken with banshees that presided over the deaths of Assembly members however." The banshee nodded with some occupational interest only she could appreciate. "Fascinating circuits of energy that release, from what I hear. I'd love to see it, but never have. Sorry, talking shop here."

Jared smiled faintly. "That's fine, Banch. So then, the ocean is my only safety from them?"

"Yes, if you're submerged in it long enough they won't want you as a Gift anymore."

"They'll never come back? The sea water's effects are permanent?"

"Yes, so it is."

"I should be good then, because I've been in the Pacific Ocean before, many times as a kid."

"But you didn't have the mark of the Gift yet," Banch explained. "Any past contact was masked by that. You received the mark a week ago."

"And what if I'd taken an unexpected beach trip before they got to me?"

"They knew you wouldn't visit the beach—they've read the chain of events from the time of the mark until your death, and so did I..."

"Just as well, I don't care for the beach."

Banch lifted one of her pretty glittering eyebrows. "You don't? You always paint the ocean though."

Jared shrugged. "I'm good at painting the ocean."

"And seagulls."

He snorted. "You know me well."

"That I do. Better than anyone."

"Ouch!" Jared bent and rubbed his kneecap.

"Tender?"

"Doing fine." He continued on. "Thank you for protecting the Kangjuns."

Her eyes flitted over with tenuous caution. "I can't guarantee anyone's safety. I can only do my best. I have no idea what the Assembly's next two grants could be. They could ask to kill others, they could ask for any manner of weapon from our dimension, or they could simply ask for passage through a corridor shadow and show up right here and now."

"Why don't they?"

"There's no way to know they would succeed or not. The Assembly rarely does things that aren't calculated for specific results. Right now they don't have a firm lock on your scent, so they would need to guess where to show up and that might waste one of their grants. They won't do that until they're very desperate, which is why the closer we get to the beach, the more dangerous and aggressive they will become in attempting to capture us."

"I understand... but isn't there a way we can take their attention away from other people? I mean, this is about me. Not my friends."

"I'm sorry. If it makes you feel better, I don't see any reason for them to kill anybody." Banch sighed darkly after another moment. "On second thought however, I had no idea they'd do it the first time. That was decidedly unexpected."

"Thanks, I feel way better now." Jared kicked a broken piece of concrete off the sidewalk.

"Well, take it as it comes, Mister Kare. The truth is a bomb filled with either beautiful confetti or rancid manure. And nobody has control of when the bomb explodes."

Jared hung his head and felt even more nauseated than he did a moment ago. If something had happened to his friends, he didn't know if his heart could take this anymore, not after learning about those people at the laundry mat. Not after losing mom. Then dad.

Banch rubbed circles in the small of his back. "I will also say this though: I haven't sensed any changes in the death schedule."

"So maybe the Assembly didn't track us to the Kangjun's apartment?"

The banshee's mouth twisted.

Jared stopped and shook his head at her. "No, Banch, tell me."

She caught him under the elbow. "They need to get to us quickly. I'm certain they have one focus right now. Let's just hope for the best, okay?"

"Bae and Eun Sun..." Jared felt like a zombie as they hurried along past a cacophony of a family pizza parlor, clattering dishes, videogames, and hooting kids.

"Don't despair until there's a reason. Really, you have no idea. Do you know how lucky we are the Assembly hasn't found us—"

Banch threw her arm across Jared's chest and halted him. She studied the distance with dazzling panic in her sapphire eyes.

"What?"

"They've found us," she said.

Down the street a massive pile-up of cars had occurred at the intersection. Jared was about to suggest this might only be a traffic collision, but his eyes tracked another pile-up on the western avenue. He spotted yet another pile-up to the south. He didn't see anybody around the smoking heaps of metal however. Jared tried to second-guess the situation. *How could she be certain this was them?*

"They've sealed off all routes to create a perimeter." Banch searched around frantically. "I can use a Swell. Damn it to hell, but I didn't want to have to do this so soon... later maybe, but good hell, already?" She groaned and pulled him into the graffiti adorned threshold of a long closed medical clinic.

He lowered his voice. "Use a what? A Swell?"

"It's another scream. It's matter-based, not dimensional, so we need to find a better position, and it's toilsome and I therefore need a place to recover. Indoors: this bright sun will make it impossible to regain my strength afterwards. Where does your friend Kaitlin live again? To what direction?"

"I... I'm not really sure how to get there. I usually tell the bus driver the cross streets, Grand and Peyton."

Banch scrubbed at her face and checked the streets again, watching for them. "God, Jared, you've known Kaitlin forever and you don't know the damn direction?"

"I'm bad with that! Sorry!"

The banshee chewed on her thumb momentarily. "Her apartment is near that organic grocery store, right?"

He nodded. "Right."

She stood on her toes, as though it might help her vantage over the office buildings and banks. "I believe it's to the south then. Damn it, shit, I hope it is."

"Wait, we can't involve Kaitlin in this too! We have to do this Swell thing to another place? Can't you take us to the ocean?"

"It won't get us that far and there'd be no place for me to heal."

"Then some other place—"

"Listen to me." Banch touched his face, her hand like warm velvet. "We can't take a chance with someplace random, not after a Swell. I'll be a mess and you will need help while I regain myself. Trust me."

"But—"

"I'll leave something special to protect her, okay?" Just then Banch's eyes went wide with alarm.

A group of individuals slid over the hoods of wrecked cars down the western street. There were possibly six—no, ten of them, as they emerged. All were at least over six feet tall, some nearing seven. At first sight their bare chests looked covered in red-brown camouflage, but as the sun played off their skin, it appeared to be blood, dried and fresh.

Although they were unique to each other, the Assembly felt like one organism sliding up the street. Three of them came forward, shoulder to shoulder, one with the face of a lion and dirty, stringy gray hair, another bald with pointed bat-ears and a blood saturated goatee, and the last with such emaciation his head resembled an alabaster skull with waxy red lips. Beyond them, the next had the look of a rotund Adolf Hitler marinated in gore, flanked at his sides by three others: a spiked red Mohawk man with swirling black tattoos over his lanky frame, a fierce warrior with an overgrown afro and lengthy handlebar mustache, and a man possessing crazed hazel eyes and unruly hair like chestnut stratus clouds.

"Banch?" Jared's whole body quaked. "Is this it?"

"Hardly," she whispered, and pulled him toward an alley.

Before he lost sight of the Assembly he spotted another three figures in the group. The first was a terrifying man with overlarge eyes and unnaturally slack skin from his jowls to his belly, the second had burn scars deforming his face into that of an angry pug, and the last swayed as he walked with the brutish body of a pro-wrestler, yet possessed the shocking facial features of an infant. All of the Assembly dressed in similar dark gray pants with suspenders, yet this one was the only whose size had snapped one of the suspenders and left it hanging.

Jared looked away and made a promise to never look in their direction again. He and the banshee fled down the alley, increasing their speed with every footfall. Out of nowhere, a chain link fence cut off their path.

"It's a dead-end," he said in panic. "Banch! Banch! What happens now? What will—"

She slammed her hand over his mouth and gripped his lips together. "I won't tell you this again, okay?"

He nodded, felt like a scolded child. His eyes lowered to the ground, but he could feel *them* drawing nearer.

"You will live, my love, but not by whining. Understand?"

She released his mouth and Jared took a slow breath to calm himself. He closed his hands into fists. It was so difficult. He was so unbelievably scared. He swallowed and the dryness scratched his throat like a tumbleweed.

"Okay," said Banch with a hurried look down the alley. "What I need you to do—"

Her head snapped back with a sickening, abnormal speed. Down the alley, a scarlet spattered figure had his arm extended. It took Jared a second to understand that the Assembly member had thrown something. A thick piece of steel, like a fishing hook to catch a whale, pulled through a shallow puddle in the storm drain, sending droplets everywhere. Banch clutched her throat, trying to pull air back into her lungs. She fell back and Jared caught her. The hook had smashed her windpipe.

More of the Assembly filled the head of the alley.

"Can you do the scream?" he asked her. "Banch?"

She retched and coughed hoarsely, drawing Jared farther back.

"Release the Gift," all ten of the Assembly shouted, a merged gruesome voice.

Jared and Banch continued to the chain link fence. She held her throat and shook her head. Her eyes widened in pain as she tried to swallow. A wide purple bruise had already surfaced from under her jaw to her collar bone due to the impact of the large grappling hook.

They moved on, the Assembly closing the distance, mouths full of disturbing white teeth contrasted with the dried blood. The giant baby and Mohawk man dragged spiked clubs on the alley walls, and yet all shared the same playfully excited facial expression.

Jared's back met with the fence.

"Climb," Banch rasped.

"What about you? You can't leave the ground."

"Neither can they." She grimaced, hand to throat. "Do it!"

Jared took hold of the fence and started up.

Another grappling hook thrummed down the alley. Banch threw herself in front of it, catching the brunt of the thick metal between her shoulder blades. She dropped at once to the ground.

"Banch!" he called.

"Go!" She was on her knees, fist in her back.

"We'll tear down that fence, bitchwhore!" the Assembly yelled.

Banch stumbled to her feet and coughed. "That's how it is? Really? Well then, come and get some, dog-dicks!"

The Assembly broke into a mischievous stride, adoring every step they took. A rage filled growl followed at Jared's back as he dropped down to the other side of the fence.

Banch looked through the chain link with beleaguered eyes. "Run fast. NOW!"

He put his head down and sprinted. Half way across the alley a sound lifted around him like an indescribable color, the hard essence of everything substantial, ripping and pulling away from its housing of physical material, and bubbling, frothing—hissing—the breaking of waves on the rocky foundation of time and space. It was implausible, dreamlike, and breathtaking, all of those things, and Jared didn't have a moment to even fear for his life. His head turned ever so slightly and he saw particles flowing straight for him. The chain link fence stretched and dissected into silver strings and shrapnel that heated and cooled in micro-eclipses, and Banch's body bonded with those pieces at the speed of a thunderclap, which trapped Jared and absorbed him inside it. But there was no darkness in the next moment, not even when he'd become disembodied, and the city passed beneath, buildings, roads, people, plants, bugs, dust, particles, atoms, elections, the whole of everything passing by—THEN a tremendous tightening of the establishment of all matter made the infinite expansion solid all at once and inside his chest something gyrated and whirled, a rollercoaster heart in a bone cage.

Slowly, the thing among the matter was less than a concept.

It was a man again.

Jared Kare.

His clothes smelled singed and he felt unusually hungry. He couldn't address such bodily impulses though, not in the parking lot of Sprout's grocery store, not with Banch collapsed at his feet, blood streaming from her eyes, ears, and mouth, red tendrils trailing out to meet a small puddle a couple feet away.

Jared took his cell phone out and dialed Kaitlin. His heart leapt when she answered on the second ring.

"Hey, are you done with the audition?" he breathed.

"Yeah, it sucked big time! And—"

"I need your help. Please, you need to come right now. I'm at Sprouts by your place. Are you close? Can you get here fast? How far are you?"

"A few miles away. Jared, what's the deal now?"

Banch's chest hitched and a blood bubble burst at her nostrils.

"It's not about me this time," he told Kaitlin, and hung up.

Chapter 8
Jared

When Jared was eighteen years old...

He carried a spare battery for his cell phone because he'd send Kaitlin hundreds of text messages every day. She answered each one with wit and care, normally within a minute or two of receiving them. Jared needed advice about pretty much everything and she was more than happy to provide that; she'd saved him countless times, from school to friends to family to all things life related. Had their friendship not gone where it had, Jared's mother would have most likely been the recipient of those endless texts, and seeing as his hanging around the office had already gotten her into hot water, that would have made things even tenser at home. Jared's father actually hid from him to avoid such encounters, but his mother couldn't bring herself to do that, and thus got the brunt of it—until Kaitlin. With her there were never any blow-ups or frustrated gnashing of teeth for all Jared's neediness. She dealt with him, always steady, always calm. That put her far up in everybody's book, but when she and Jared kissed one night after watching *Big Trouble in Little China*, their favorite John Carpenter movie, that's when he decided on a list of his favorite people, Kaitlin burst off the page, right from the top.

The kiss sent his boy-heart into motion. He knew things would build, more physical, more emotional, more everything, and he was ready for all of that. He couldn't be a burden on his parents forever—he needed someone like Kaitlin, an able body who actually thrived on walking him through his unreasonable reservations and irresolution. She was his hand-holder, his guide, his soul mate, as far as he was concerned.

The absolute perfect woman for Jared Kare.

For a long while, since before he could remember, he'd thought he'd share a big moment with his ideal girl: they'd hold each other and stare out into the golden distance, into something so much bigger than both of them, and Jared could let out a sigh, not from his mouth, but from his entire heart and soul, and he would say, carefully but without reservation, "I'm finally content."

Kaitlin and Jared went to the beach one cool summer night to make-out. She'd been acting strange the last few dates but agreed to go, so he was certain she wasn't seeing another guy. And how could she? He possessed so much of her time it would be impossible. He told her he'd bought condoms and she'd replied in a text, *"Well good!"* So he was ready to make love for the first time and gaze into that future with all the wonder he'd expected.

So there they were, on his grandma's old patchwork quilt (one of dozens), the invisible but powerful waves crashing around in the dusky, liquid static evening, and the moon a radiant blossom in space, his pants off, her pants off, their kissing becoming a manic lip-dance of the lover's tribe and he was so ready to at last be a man and make Kaitlin a woman. He took out the condom and ripped open the packaging and withdrew it with expert grace (he'd practiced with four others that morning). He began to roll it over himself, when he heard a voice above the waves.

Kaitlin's.

She was crying.

"Jared..."

"Yes?" he whispered, despite the ocean's insistent thunder. "Are you not ready? We don't have to. I can wait until whenever."

"Jared..."

Kaitlin hastily dragged over her jeans and Jared moved away, giving her space. He felt weird being exposed so he tossed the condom into the sand and got dressed too. Kaitlin attempted to say something but couldn't. Instead she held him and wept for a long time. He took her home and they said very little else that night and much of the next day.

They went to their favorite 50's place, Dean's Dinin,' and had an in-depth conversation about how *Gremlins 2* wasn't actually that bad of a film, considering it tried to satire the first film, even if clumsily so. Then a silence ensued after the chuckles died down. Thankfully, or regretfully, Jared couldn't remember which, Kaitlin started talking.

"About the other night."

"You don't have to explain it if you don't want to," he said.

She reached across the table and took his hand. He instantly felt warm from his heart out to his extremities, his head, everywhere. He wanted it to be perfect for her—she'd been so good to him; she was his savior, and she deserved all the perseverance and preservation of dignity he could offer.

"I love you, Jared," she said.

His smile couldn't have stretched any farther across his face.

"But I'm not *in* love with you," she continued. "I've been figuring some stuff out."

His stomach twisted, caught in corrosive barbed wire. "Stuff? What stuff? What do you mean?"

"I liked how your lips felt. I liked kissing you, for a while, but—"

He leaned over his half-eaten Elvis-size chili burger. "Yes, and?"

"I think I... like girls."

"What?"

"Don't be mad. Jared, I care about you so much. Please don't be mad. You're like a brother to me."

The arsenic word touched his lips. "Brother?"

"Please. This was so hard to say. You're my best friend. Don't hate me. I love you."

"Don't say that... don't. But wait, you touched me and kissed..." he lowered his voice, "down there. I thought, I mean—I don't know what I mean."

"I wanted to see for sure. I really didn't want it to be this way. I *wanted* to like you in that way. If I could take a pill or get hypnotized or sell my soul, I would, just because you're the greatest friend I've ever had. It would be perfect but I'm just me. And I realize it more every day. I can't keep it from you any longer. I know this isn't fair. I know I led you on. But please forgive me. I'm not lying when I say I love you. You are the most important person in my entire life."

Jared would have left at that point. He was embarrassed, angry, crestfallen, and jealous of anyone Kaitlin might romantically love in place of him. He'd never learned to drive though, and was too frightened he'd accidently get hit if he walked home across the freeway overpass. He didn't trust himself, and in the diner that night, he hated that self-mistrust more than ever. Since he could go nowhere, since he had imposed his own imprisonment in this awful moment, he sat quietly and ate his chili burger, ignoring the sour retort of his stomach.

Luckily for him, Kaitlin refused to go away. She was his lifelong friend, whether he wanted her to hold that position anymore or not. He learned however that he not only wanted it, but needed it. Her guilt or maybe her genuine love kept her in his text messages for every long day and night leading out of the world of children into the realm of ever-after.

* * *

Kaitlin grunted when Banch sagged under their hold. Jared felt the banshee losing unconsciousness again, becoming heavier around his shoulders. "I don't understand why we can't just *drive* this chick to my place."

"Banch, you gotta help here," Jared said. "We aren't far."

She mumbled and started shuffling her feet forward again.

"Jared, who is she? Why aren't you saying anything?" Kaitlin yanked keys out of her jeans and jangled them until she found the one for her apartment door. "She your new girlfriend?"

"I... uh."

"Okay, so yeah. What the hell is she dressed in? She looks like you picked her up at a comic book convention. Her hair is pretty punk rock though. Wonder what she uses to make those purple and blue streaks look so metallic. It's very cool."

"She's foreign. Europe, somewhere."

"Europe somewhere? What details! You two must have really hit it off."

"Your sarcasm isn't needed."

"None intended. So does the Princess of Transylvania only ride in horse drawn carriages or something?"

"She's frightened of cars."

"And shoes too?"

He had completely forgotten about Banch's bare feet and was at a loss of words at first. "It's... cultural I guess."

"Did you check if she bit her tongue?"

"Huh?"

"During the seizure."

"Oh yeah, I don't think so."

"Has this happened before?" They reached the front door and Kaitlin stuck out the key. "Does she take meds?"

"Don't—I mean, no, no she doesn't. Look Kait, we won't be very long here. I just had nowhere else to turn."

"For her sake, I'm happy I beat the traffic." Kaitlin pushed open the door. The wall to wall bookshelves in the small living room had script pages taped up. Warm sunshine filtered through the far window's white drapes and gave the pages a glow as they fluttered from the ceiling fan. The apartment smelled faintly of weed. Kaitlin always took a drag before auditions.

They passed the short hall with the framed *Big Trouble in Little China* and *The Thing* posters. A vintage *Escape from New York* hung in her bedroom in a more expensive frame her father bought her last Christmas.

They guided Banch over to the eggshell leather couch and laid her down.

"Want to put her legs up?"

"No!" Jared hollered and then caught himself. "That is, no, that'll be fine. She's fine how she is."

Kaitlin bit her lip as she studied him. "Some weird shit going on here, buster. Need to come clean about something to this old girl?"

"I met her online. I don't know her very well. That okay?"

"Jeez. You're *dating* again?" Kaitlin tossed her keys on the glass coffee table with a loud clatter. "Holy wow. Jared Kare. You go. Even banged up, she's pretty damned hot, if you don't mind me saying so. I guess there are all kinds online these days. You totally scored, well except for the epilepsy thing."

He glared at her, but Kaitlin only shrugged. It wasn't in her nature to ever apologize for sticking her foot in her mouth.

"I need some water," he said with a sigh.

"All right."

"No, I'll get it." He started toward the kitchen.

"Impressive! You didn't give me the whole *'I don't know where you keep the glasses'* thing."

"I still don't know." Jared opened several cupboards before finding the tumblers. "But I found one."

Kaitlin switched on the TV and put the volume low. "Did you hear about these Russian terrorists?"

"No."

"Really? You're kidding right?"

"I've had my hands full."

"It happened not far from here. Bunch of people hacked up with machetes. I heard it on the radio. God, when you first called all frantic I thought you might be caught up in that somehow."

Jared filled his tumbler to the point of spilling over. He walked back into the living room and a news report was on TV. A blonde field reporter with bad liver-spotted skin pointed at the laundromat. The footage cut to an alley filled with bodies under sheets, crime scene tape, and law enforcement people scribbling onto notepads. A bulging-eyed old man standing across the street gestured there as he was interviewed. He was shaking his head, not knowing what to think.

"That's near our primary care clinic, isn't it? Holy shit." Kaitlin got closer to the TV as though a better vantage would confirm her suspicions. She looked over her shoulder. "You had an appointment there today."

"No, it's next week."

"I made the appointment for you, dude. It was today. I made you put it in your phone."

"Oh yeah, my phone's been acting weird."

"That's not the only thing." Kaitlin laced her arms together, eying him critically. Banch made a noise and began to stir.

"What am I doing in Kaitlin's apartment?" the banshee murmured.

Kaitlin's head canted. "Wait, how did she—"

Jared knelt at Banch's side. "I mentioned your place was nearby, before she passed out."

"I see. Well, I guess her memory is still fine. Uh, I'm Kaitlin Daning." She put her hand out, all her bracelets noisily clacking together at her wrist. Banch groggily regarded her hand before shaking it.

"Banch."

"Banch what?"

"Like a pop star," the banshee said lowly. "One name only."

Kaitlin chuckled. "Okay, Gaga, do you need pain meds or water or apple juice?"

"You're sweet, but I'd just like a wet towel to clean off this blood. Jared can go fetch it."

Lifting her brow, Kaitlin said, "He won't know which towels to use and he'll just freak out. I'm used to the son-of-a-gun." Kaitlin turned around but Banch caught her arm.

She carefully released Kaitlin and shrugged. "He might surprise you."

Jared hurried off before anything else could be said. If his mind wasn't so occupied on the Assembly he'd have been more annoyed with both women; he wasn't a puppy that needed training. He supposed he brought that kind of treatment on himself, but when it came to him and Kaitlin, there'd never been any discord. She was helpful and he was helpless. It was perfect, although too comfortable to ever get beyond his incapacitating indecision.

He found a red terry cloth wash rag and ran it under the sink with warm water. When he came back out Kaitlin sat in the rocking lounger across from the couch. Banch had straightened from a prone position now. Each woman had intense expressions and for a heartbeat Jared thought maybe Banch had told her everything.

"Why do I need an accent?" Banch asked her.

"Because you aren't American, from all I hear."

"That's correct. I'm not." Banch folded her hands behind her head. She still looked disoriented from the effects of the Swell.

"You speak like anyone who lives in the valley or the hills."

"Well I don't kno' abou' tha,'" Banch replied in a Scottish accent.

Kaitlin smirked. "I can speak with several accents myself."

"That's fortunate." Banch's eyes centered on Kaitlin for a moment before moving to Jared. "Gonna let that thing dry?"

"Oh, sorry." He handed her the towel.

Banch cleaned herself up in a systematic pattern from forehead to nose to cheeks to jaw and neck and then breast plate. The towel was more than spent after she was done.

"Did you deposit my paycheck?" Jared asked Kaitlin, trying to bring some normalcy back into the room.

"Not yet, the audition took all my time today."

"That's okay," he said. "You think you'll get a call back?"

"If I blow the casting agent, and we both know how unlikely that is."

"How bad do you want the part?"

"You're an asshole." Kaitlin snorted and tossed a throw pillow from the lounger at him. Jared caught it with a smile, which faded as she saw Banch carefully watching them.

"Time to go?" he asked. "Do you—"

Banch neatly folded the towel and handed it to Kaitlin. "My thanks."

"Anytime."

"So, are you able to walk?" Jared prodded.

The banshee lifted a hand. "They are far off yet. We have probably another twenty minutes before I can walk well enough. That'll give us time still to keep ahead."

Kaitlin gave a suspicious look and let the towel drop on the end-table. "Where are you off to? Or may I not ask?"

"The beach," Banch blurted.

Jared needed to sit down.

And did.

"Which beach?"

"Seal," he replied.

Kaitlin pressed her lips together and nodded, as though vaguely interested, but Jared knew for a fact she was *very* interested. "Oh okay, well, that's not far."

He let a single chuckle escape on accident and coughed into his fist.

The news changed to footage of the Assembly storming through an outdoor mall. The camera jerked around and the movement of the mall goers was chaotic and disorienting. Jared recognized the grim bloodstained faces and his insides went to ice.

"Can we turn off the TV? It's unsettling."

"I agree there." Kaitlin grabbed the remote and the red wild devil faces vanished from the screen. "You know, you both are welcome to stay over. I don't think it's safe with all that craziness going on out there."

Jared opened his mouth but Banch cut him off.

"You're probably right, but we only have today before I go home... my flight is 5 am tomorrow morning."

"Oh no? You aren't staying?" Kaitlin looked quickly at Jared, concern in her eyes.

"Afraid not, no," said Banch.

"That's too bad, but hey," Kaitlin slapped Jared's knee, "you're both young and if this boy can get his ass on a plane, there's plenty of opportunities to visit."

Jared squeezed the ache forming at the bridge of his nose.

"Right?" Kaitlin cued.

"Right," he said with a faint smile.

"Can I ask a weird question?" Banch said to Kaitlin.

Kaitlin threw her head back and laughed, which she cut off with her hand. "Oh my, please do. I'm OD-ing on normal already here. Bring on the weirder."

"Do you have a full box of washing detergent?"

Kaitlin smirked. "That's the best you can do?"

"Yes."

"I did one load. Only used a single scoop."

"Can we take it?"

"Is it therefore weird to want to know why?" asked Kaitlin.

"It isn't, but I can't answer that," explained Banch. "Sorry."

"Then no."

"Come on Kait," Jared said.

"No, Jared, really. I don't have a bunch of disposable income and I got this European—maybe sometimes Scottish—wonder-woman character asking to take my detergent? I have a shit ton of laundry to do. I was going to spend tomorrow evening going at it."

Banch turned to Jared and tugged her shirt slightly down, deepening her cleavage. "Think it would convince her?"

He waved her off. "Let me handle this."

"Oh, you're handling things, eh?" Kaitlin gave a bewildered half-grin. "Well hell Jared, I tell you what, if you let me in on why you need to run off to the beach, I'll give up the detergent. How's that sound?"

"That's more than fair."

Kaitlin nodded. "So why then?"

Jared stared at Banch a moment and then said, softly, "We want to say goodbye."

Kaitlin's face, a face Jared knew well, didn't betray her true feelings. She wasn't buying everything and yet at the same time she had another layer there. *Pride*. Pride in him. She was happy for her friend, for whatever he'd found, if only as brief as it seemed.

"It's yours," she said.

Jared stood and gave her a hug. "Love you."

"Back at you," she replied, and broke away from him. "Let me go get your box of soap, weirdos."

It was quiet a few beats after Kaitlin left and suddenly Banch said, "Why do you think she isn't seeing anyone?"

"She's busy. But she did have a girlfriend once."

"That was just a fling, Jared."

"Look, you don't know everything about our lives. You just don't."

"I do," snapped Banch. "So shut up."

"Fair enough," he grumbled.

Kaitlin came back with a box of Tide. "You really going to carry this with you?"

"Look at those chicken arms, he needs it, am I right?" Banch offered a contagious smile that captured them both.

Jared patted his bicep. "I'm not that scrawny."

"You're perfect, just teasing," said Banch, before pressing her lips into his neck and instantly setting his blood on fire.

"Get a room," Kaitlin groaned.

Banch smiled crookedly at him. "If there were only time."

He blushed and turned away.

"Speaking of rooms. I need to find the restroom," announced the banshee.

Kaitlin pointed down the hall. Banch nodded and hurried away.

When she was out of sight, Kaitlin asked him, "So what-is-up? Really?"

"Ah, I don't know, Kait. Just trying to figure it out too."

Kaitlin's lips thinned and twitched back and forth. She always did that while considering something meaningful. "I'd be afraid she'd hurt you, only that I guess she's leaving too soon for that."

He nodded.

"She might come back though."

He nodded again.

Banch returned with something in her fist. She approached Kaitlin and opened her hand. There were six spheres of green opalescent there.

"Pearls?" asked Kaitlin.

"These are immature bulbs of a lobe-fern."

"Where are they from?"

"Transylvania," said Banch slowly with a smile.

Kaitlin snorted. "Wait a minute, you were supposed to be unconscious when I said—"

"Place them on the ground if you're ever in real danger," Banch continued. "But don't move. Do you understand? Never, *ever* move, once you've put them down. That would be dangerous, so stay absolutely still."

"Uh, I don't get it. They're beautiful, but I don't get it." Kaitlin accepted the orbs into her palm.

"She's superstitious," Jared offered.

"Ah," said Kaitlin. "Well thanks."

"Promise you'll lay the bulbs down if you are in trouble," said Banch.

"I promise." Kaitlin saluted her and looked back down at the lobe-fern bulbs.

Banch gave her a hug that Kaitlin clearly wasn't ready for. "We need to leave now."

Jared gave Kaitlin another hug as well. Then they headed to the door.

"You mean the world to him, you know," he heard Banch say.

Kaitlin laughed. "No idea why."

Jared stepped onto the porch and glanced into the apartment. Banch delicately patted his old friend's shoulder. "Because you've been his strength, Kaitlin Daning. For a long time, it's only been you."

Kaitlin's face flushed and she looked down at her feet.

As they said goodbyes, Jared hurt inside. He'd never imagined facing a final farewell with Kaitlin. But it felt that way.

Horribly so.

Chapter 9
The Assembly

Things were not as bleak as they could be. We were madly happy the banshee resorted to a Swelling Scream. Yes, the Gift was once more out of our hands, but their course placed them farther from the Paled Ocean. Worse would have been if the banshee used a Swell near the ocean, giving her a tremendous advantage—that, fortunately for us, could not happen now—not unless the banshee wished to almost completely incapacitate herself, becoming worthless to protect the Gift or herself. The dimensional damage she would sustain through a second Swell would require too much recovery and she would fail, no question. And she would not choose this path because of her feelings for our prize. That was our assumption at least. For what else would be the point? Other than to keep our Gift for her own pleasure?

Of course, there were many more tools in that sparkling voice box of hers, but after a Swell most other screams would lose power or potency. So yes, as it was, we still hadn't gained the Gift, and had been damnably so close, and yet we did rejoice that the banshee had just severely narrowed her options and her effectiveness against us.

We had less excuse for failure now.

After smelling and tasting the scorched layers of space-time, we discovered the stream of sonic material containing our Gift had gone in a southwest direction. From our recall of this city's streets, we needed to reach the intersection of Caballero and Valley View to use the most effective location to slim escape routes for our Gift and his harlot. A Lung Spike would be ideal for creating an enclosure. Neither of them would be able to get far without falling prone to its effects. We hadn't had the time to ask the Silent Kings to grant us a Spike before our last encounter, but things were different now, and once again, the Swell was more fortuitous than detrimental; with them farther from the Paled Ocean, we indeed had time now.

Our second grant... we hoped we would not have to ask for the final.

The corridor shadow that could supply access to our arsenal measured by our calculation at a mile's run. No time was lost. We sprinted, shoulder to shoulder, the ten of us a flying wall of strength raging through the city streets. Cars jerked out of our way as we faced traffic head-on. The Ninth and Tenth smashed a bicyclist out of our path—the helmeted man and bike slid over a parked yellow sports car and out of sight.

There was no flaw in our love. We wanted you, Jared. We wanted you like no other possibly ever could. As soon as the flavor of our last Gift had worn off, something like sixty years ago, we started dreaming about who would be the next, our tongues watering, our muscles perspiring, each of our hairs prickling, the hunger in our souls spreading in volcanic contagion. The thought of boring ten holes through your spine to suck out the sweet fluid there, all of us slurping through thin hoses, sharing expressions of deep content, orgasm-eyes fluttering open and shut, open and shut. It was enough for us to groan in splendor and forget all the torturous burdens of stabilizing the dimensions. All the sadness, all the hurt, made sense because you made our hearts feel warmth again—isolated in a universe of ice, a cabin with a handsome woodstove burning bright, and we would open the door and that's your power over us. The ice would melt off our souls... for a time.

We could not be denied our reprieve from the madness of our bodies and the torn fibers of our minds. We deserved this. We earned this. Our pleasure out of shrieking doom.

The shadow came into view: a wilting star stationed just left of a convenience store doorway, above newspaper machines. We went to it immediately. The Third, Sixth and Fifth worked together to pull the

Lung Spike through the red shimmer. Two more of our number helped with the device, a sturdy marshwood make with Beyond-Age design wrought into its golden stress bands at the head, center, and stalk.

An older man of African descent appeared around the building. He stopped short of buying a newspaper, coins poised in hand. He watched us, transfixed. He had not known what to expect turning that corner so quickly and in a few moments fled in terror. This was a lesson to reap here.

Turning corners…

We expected this was part of the larger problem with the banshee. She continued to consider what was around the corner. That's where our failure began. We weren't ready and she always was. As with our plan now, it was likely she anticipated us to use such technology as a Lung Spike, and would try to find a way to deactivate it—such a move would prove risky but would be the only way to get Jared to safety. Then, of course, thinking ahead, the bitchwhore would know we expected her to try something like that.

A better plan must be conceived now, not later. Some of us scratched our chins and those hefting the lengthy Lung Spike mentally did the same.

If we tricked the banshee into believing we had become distracted with something else, it might give her the confidence to make a move. Perhaps we faced difficulties with the Spike itself? A failure of some kind? Once our guard was down, she might think it safe to approach. That's when we could turn the tables.

The banshee knew extremely little about Beyond-Age technology. We could use that to our advantage. By removing a stress band from the spike's shaft, there would be a deal of elemental spillage and sparks, putting on a great, showy display—the centermost band was placed there for redundancy. Removing it would be strident and bright, but wouldn't keep the Lung Spike from functioning at maximum potential.

She would come to deactivate the Spike but would immediately suspect something if some of us were not in view. She'd know it was a trap, that some of us were hiding somewhere, waiting to capture her. It would need to appear that all ten of us labored at repairing the Spike. So in that case, how could we get one of our number to overtake her and get the upper hand?

Tricky, this.

This scene had to be set carefully. We could not flinch. The act had to look genuine. We hoped the cunning tramp would not see around this particular corner. It would be rewarding to see her bones disconnect at each joint and we prayed there would be enough of that voice box of hers to serve ten mouths.

But our fantasies faded as we arrived. The intersection, we found, was not free of cars. We waited, chests heaving, hearts firing with anticipation, and eyes dripping with starving lover's tears. We ventured into the street. Several horns sounded from cars, while others slammed to a halt and departed their vehicles at the sight of us. We paid these things no mind and continued to the middlemost of the intersection.

The sound of sirens from authority vehicles grew louder in the distance. We grunted and lifted the Lung Spike as high over our heads as possible. The sharpness through time-space dimpled the concrete below without it even contacting the spike yet. With a shared roar of power, we plunged the Spike into the ground, sending dirt, rock, and concrete out in an earthen blossom. The Spike traveled down about half its length. The Tenth reached forward with his scabbed fingers and ripped the middle stress band off. Firestars and blue-red-green spurts of light drew forth from the exposed energy seam. It seared off one of the Tenth's fingers, but we only flexed our nostrils in rejoinder to such basic pain. Our hearts calmed.

Down the street, people fell from their opened car doors and clutched their throats. The Lung Spike worked well, as expected, with the superficial wound. Pride fluxed through our Ten. Smiles here, there, there, and there.

"Everyone up against the wall!" an angry voice shouted from behind us. "Now assholes! Right now!"

We turned.

One of the blue uniformed law enforcers had come up the street. His vehicle had two tires up on a sidewalk about fifteen feet down the road. A wiry red-haired man, not fat but paunchy in the stomach, he had his firearm leveled at us. So sweet he was; we cooed at him. He had no concept of what we were. Our bodies had been pressed through collapsing axis hinges—dimensional rivets had passed through our abdomens in endless succession for decades to keep the dimensions from ripping. We shook our head at the silly man, a squirrel trying to intimidate Gods with his tiny acorns? We might have laughed, but recalling the hinges and rivets, we were inclined to a different mood.

The man's arm trembled. His freckled white finger tapped the trigger anxiously. "Back against that wall. Please!" The radio on his shoulder crackled and a woman's voice recited numeric codes.

Four of us approached, arms wide out. The law enforcer backed and his gun went side to side. He stepped inside the Lung Spike's influence and at once began coughing into his fist, his airway constricting. The tension in his lungs caught him by surprise, and with another step he dropped his weapon.

The Third leapt forward and kicked the gun down the influenced street. Bullets would not harm us, but we were not given to invite unnecessary bee stings either. There was nothing to prove. Minutes without physical suffering were ambrosia for us, but never expected.

The man gagged at the threshold of influence. The Fourth and Fifth seized him, but he handled their momentum with expert grace, using one of the Fifth's suspenders to twist away from their reach. It was no matter, however. The Second and Sixth captured him thereafter.

We dragged the man out of the Spike's influence where he could regain control of his body once more. A new plan developed in our minds. This is how we could deceive the banshee. This was perfect! We relished the sight of the red-haired man like a found lucky charm. And with every inch of his flesh, our godsend.

He will do well. Our eyes widened with delight. *Yes. Yes. Yes. Yes. Yes. Yes. Yes. Yes. Yes. Yes.*

YES.

The Fourth ripped at his own left tricep and pulled free some flesh. We gritted our teeth at the sacrifice. The Fourth staggered nearer to the law enforcer and scrubbed the bloody tissue over the panicking man's face. "Stop! What are you doing! Stop!" he cried.

"Welcome to the Assembly," we told the man.

"W-w-w... what?" he gasped, eyes searching everywhere.

The Third unbuckled his suspenders and drew down his pants.

"Take off your clothes," we said to the law enforcer with a mirthful snort. "Time to change uniforms."

Chapter 10
Jared

The box of detergent seemed twice as heavy once they crossed over La Habra city limits.

"Wish we brought a wagon," Jared said, and once again changed the box to his other hand. "Are you sure we need this stuff?"

"Yes, and I told you I could take a turn," Banch replied.

"I've got it."

"I'm stronger than you," she insisted.

"You're already doing enough—how's your eyesight?"

Banch's vision had suffered after the Swell; temporary cataracts had formed in her blue eyes, and their normal sky blue color took the appearance of an overcast winter afternoon. Her mood had been slightly in line with this as well, and despite them being less cloudy now her gloominess continued to prevail. She blinked a lot but her face was otherwise expressionless.

"Banch, did you hear me? Are your eyes getting better?"

She nodded that she was fine. Another ten minutes of silence fell between them. Jared switched hands again with the detergent.

"What's your favorite song?" Banch suddenly asked.

"Wow, where did that come from?"

"You've listened to many songs," she explained, stepping over a piece of sidewalk lifted from a tree root. "I know those songs you've listened to over and over again but there isn't one I'd bet on as your favorite."

"*Free Fallin'*—"

"By Tom Petty?" she asked.

"Exactly."

"I don't even recall you listened to that a lot."

"I guess I don't want to wear it out."

"Would you do that?" Banch nudged him.

"What?"

"Freefall? Skydive?"

"Oh, hell no." He shivered at the thought.

"You could go in tandem with someone. I've never presided over a death from a skydiver. It doesn't happen that often."

"Still, no."

"Well, you don't have much time left in this world."

"Thanks for reminding me," he muttered.

"I'm being serious." Banch glanced over through some swaying purple steel threads of hair. "What would make you happy?"

He shrugged. "I don't ever think like that."

"I know, so I'm making you think that way."

He shrugged again and twisted his mouth a bit. "I'll have to think about it."

"You shouldn't have to."

"I want to live. How's that?"

"Tell me what would have made you happy before you got that news," she said. "I've watched you stare up at your ceilings some nights. I always wondered what you were thinking during those times."

"Nothing much."

"I doubt that."

"Like it or not, sometimes I don't have an answer for your questions."

"I'll remember that next time you ask about the Deeper Unseen."

"Oh come on, you're from a different dimension. Asking that stuff would be natural for anybody," he said.

"I'm just as interested in your mind, as you are my dimension. Okay?"

"Fair enough." He thought about switching hands again but decided to wait it out longer. "So, let me see. When I'm in my bed, usually I'm thinking about how it would be…"

"Yes?"

"To be a different person."

"Really?"

He nodded. "If I were more like Kaitlin. If I were freer, less trapped in myself. I sometimes think I used to be someone else but I lost that person somewhere along the way. I guess I just want the anxiety of life to go away. I want to be at peace with myself and with the world. It's a pretty stupid thing to wish for."

"Not at all."

"Some people would want fame or fortune, but I just want to be rid of my hang-ups. I just don't want to worry about anything anymore."

"They have drugs for that you know."

"Very funny."

Banch flashed a winning smile and pinched his cheek. "I know what you're saying, honey. And if we had more time I would show you how to strip away those layers. I sense greatness in you, Jared."

"Thanks, but I have no idea how you can see that."

"I see it because it's there, knocking on the other side of the door. When you pass on, I imagine your soul's beauty would finally be able to shine." Tears jeweled on her eyes. "It makes me so happy to imagine you separated from all your prisons."

"You want me dead?"

"Shut up, you know what I mean."

He found himself smiling. "When you put it that way, being dead doesn't seem as awful."

"It isn't awful or wonderful, it just is," said Banch.

They came to a crosswalk and stopped.

"We have to press the button." Jared felt his spine go straight and heartbeat quicken.

"Go ahead. You're closer," said Banch.

"Can't you just do it? My fingers are numb from carrying the box."

The banshee lifted an eyebrow and chewed her lip a moment. "Why won't you press it?"

"I just don't want to."

"Really? Come on. It is because of that time when you were a kid—"

"No," he snapped. "It isn't."

"You want to throw off your self-imposed burdens, here's an easy one, buddy. Push the damn button."

"I never go across major streets."

"You are now," she insisted.

"This is bad luck."

"No such thing."

"Fine," he said, reaching over, "but if something happens..."

"What will happen, Jared?"

He pushed the button and she watched him closely. It was infuriating how lovely she remained while making him feel like a cowardly freak at the same time.

"My dear—"

"Don't call me that," he replied sharply. "Call me dead meat. That's what I am. That's what you've been thinking about since Kaitlin's, isn't it? That's why you're so quiet."

"Nice guess, but not even close."

"What are you hiding?"

"No, no, don't twist this up. We're talking about you, sir." Banch motioned to the street. "Light's changed."

Jared carefully stepped into the street, checking that no cars were flying down the road at an unreasonable speed.

"You're going to be okay."

He gave a low growl. "Banch, why can't a person just be uncomfortable with something? Why do they have to be defective? I thought you understood but I guess not."

"Oh please, Jared, are you kidding? Stop feeling sorry for yourself for two seconds."

He went silent and his heart did several of those odd beats. He tried to put it out of his mind like they never happened. They went several blocks before Banch said, "Tell me one thing you're completely comfortable with. Just one."

The answer came easy. "Sketching."

She smiled at him. "I love your art."

"Thank you." He blushed and swung the detergent back and forth anxiously. "It's silly stuff but I enjoy it."

"I always wondered why you never became an artist."

"Not that good and there's no real money in the things I draw."

"*Money makes the fish swim,*" she said.

"Pardon?"

"It's a saying from the Deeper Unseen. Sorry. It's too obscure to explain."

"I appreciate that."

Banch laughed but abruptly threw her arm across his chest, holding him back.

Jared's head spun and mouth went dry. "What is it? Is it them?"

The banshee squeezed her forehead, closed her eyes. "We cannot step any farther on this path. They mean to limit the routes there—yes, of course. I wondered when they'd try this."

"The Assembly? I thought they were far away."

Banch turned to him. "Oh, they're never far, Jared. But don't freak. Just let me think up something."

He looked ahead. Nothing seemed out of the ordinary. "What's the big deal? Why can't we keep walking. I don't get it."

"Take one step in that direction, down that street."

Jared went forward. In the next moment two unseen hands took his lungs and clenched them almost completely shut. He croaked, nearly dropped the detergent, but Banch pulled him back and his lungs released. For a few minutes he violently coughed, his body shaking and eyes watering.

"So now you see, we will be forced to walk the streets they choose for us—all other paths will do this to you. All open streets we can take will lead us right to them." Her sparkling eyes searched to a destination unknown. "I assume they've implemented a Lung Spike—they sometimes use them around their fortress in the Deeper Unseen to corral escaped prisoners."

"That's a horrible feeling." Jared lightly touched his throat. "What's going to happen to people on these streets? They're going to suffocate?"

"No; they'll pass out but won't be deprived of air completely. They'll fall into a coma until the Lung Spike is removed."

"Shit... So what do we do?"

"We cannot be directed by them, obviously, and need to deactivate the Spike. It can be done, but there's a catch."

"Yeah?"

"Yeah. Big, big catch," she said. "Which makes this more difficult and dangerous."

"Are you going to tell me?" he asked.

"Since they are directly linked with the Lung Spike, the easiest way to break their connection will be to disturb that bond. Once that occurs, the device will not be able to have residence here and will self-destruct. That will immediately open up the paths again for us, so we can continue on."

"How do you disturb their bond with the Lung Spike?" he asked.

"I need to physically touch one of the Assembly."

"Touch one of them?" Jared drew back, appalled. "Like with your fingers?"

"Should I use a kiss?"

"I'm not joking!"

"Neither am I," she laughed. "It might be fun to see their reaction."

"Stop it."

"Well, stop asking dippy questions then."

"How will you get close enough to touch them…"

Banch held up a hand. "You're going to help with that. Come on."

She switched directions and headed down the opposite street.

"Is this the area with that Cajun kitchen? The one where you and Kaitlin sometimes go for lunch?" she asked him.

"Yeah, it's a couple blocks up the way. Kind of expensive though."

"Perfect. Do you think there will be a crowd this time of day?"

"People are getting off work. There's a bar."

"But is it crowded?"

"Most times, yes. It's pretty popular."

"This is wonderful." She dragged him forward. "What's this place called again? I never bothered to catch that."

"The Bayou Cat."

She grinned. "Cute!"

"Are you hungry or something?"

"Always, but that isn't why we're going there. We need help with a few items and a place where I can join with my twin."

Jared cocked his head. "*Twin*? You never mentioned her before."

"She doesn't exist in this reality… yet."

"You lost me."

"As it is, just my touching them wouldn't disturb the bond enough. Well, not to the extent we require. The Assembly would fight to retain their bond. There has to be even more dimensional interference. So that's why I will perform a Fusing Scream, which will pull a different version of me from an alternate reality completely—a different set of dimensions."

"I don't follow."

"If your universe and mine were all pages in a book that made up the multiverse, the Banch I will summon comes not only from a different book, but from an entirely different bookshelf. This Banch will have lived her life most likely in an extremely different way than I lived mine, because her reality will be drastically dissimilar to ours. Because you see, Jared, that even though I come from another dimensional space, our worlds do share the same reality. We are, in fact, in the same book."

"Can I just go on record to say that's very, very weird, Banch?"

"While my twin resides in this world, anything we come in contact with long enough will cause the object to aggressively disassociate from reality, since dimensional logic breaks down, you see. The Assembly will have to struggle to stay resident in this reality and in order to do that, they will be forced to let the Spike go."

"Then what?"

"This is where you help. I need you to escort my twin back to the *exact* place I Fused. She'll be nearby somewhere and I'll show you how to find her. After the Spike's destruction, dimensional logic will restore itself. My twin and I will both return to where we came from, but only if she shares my same space at that moment." Banch looked at him with surgical appraisal. "Let me say that again because you looked out to lunch. *She has to share the same space with me at that moment.*"

"I heard you the first time," Jared grumbled. "But okay, I'm going to pretend I understand all of that. What if I can't get her back to the place where you Fused?"

Banch pressed her lips together. "We will Self-Destruct along with the Spike, I imagine."

"Are you kidding? That's friggin great. How will I even get to your twin with the streets choking the life out of me? And how will you get near the Assembly without them seeing you?"

"I'll worry about that, and as far as getting through these streets, that's where this place comes in."

They stood outside the Bayou Cat. The host, a tall bald man in round spectacles, opened the door with a big grin, "Hi folks, coming in? Table for two?"

Banch slipped her arm through Jared's. He switched the detergent to the other hand and put it behind his back.

"Yes, for two," he said, and then followed the host into the black-lit innards of the restaurant. The host sat them at the far back end of the building. Kaitlin would have asked for a different table, since it was so near the kitchen and clattering dishes unnerved her. Banch, on the other hand, was all smiles, almost giddy. It was the best mood he'd seen her in since the Swell.

"Your server will be right with you," said the host before departing.

Banch nodded and picked up her menu. Jared studied her a moment. Her full lips parted as she took a breath and held his hand.

"Wh—"

A sound came forward and Jared saw everything masked in gold for a flash. It happened so fast he didn't have a chance to be frightened.

"Don't worry," said Banch, cutting off his question.

"I wasn't ready! Was that a Fusing Scream?"

"No, calm down," she replied with a wink. "We're not ready for that one yet."

The waiter came up and blinked at them as though freshly awakened. "Whatever you need," he said with an unnatural smile. "Tell me what I can do for you both. *Please.*"

"Why thank you, sir," Banch said. "We need you to find who has the fastest car in the parking lot. Oh and a Self-Contained Underwater Breathing Apparatus."

"At once." The waiter bowed deeply and hurried off.

"The hell was that?" asked Jared.

"It's long for SCUBA."

"I know what that is! Why was that waiter acting like a slave?"

"The Gilded Scream," Banch replied. "Everyone in the restaurant will do what we wish them to now. They'll also offer blindly to give us presents—"

A young brunette woman approached their table with a sheepish grin. She opened her purse and fished around for something. She withdrew her cash and credit cards and set them on the table. Then she reached up to her necklace, but Banch stopped her. "No darling, we don't need any of this. We want privacy right now. Can you please let everyone else know?"

"So sorry, yes," the woman replied and quickly gathered up her items. She went from there to a table nearby and shared the request. Then moved on to the next table and worked her way through the restaurant.

"How long does this last?" asked Jared.

"Forever," Banch explained. "But you can send them away for good if they bug you."

All eyes in the restaurant focused on them, neediness welling in every pair.

Jared's insides chilled. "They'd fight for us too, wouldn't they?"

"Yes," said Banch. She studied him a second. "Would you use them that way?"

"Absolutely not," he replied.

"Good. Me neither. It might needlessly change the death schedule anyway."

Jared couldn't help the smile forming on his lips. "So this entire restaurant—everybody in here is our slave?"

"I think a few people in the kitchen avoided the effect—the Swell has made my range more limited. All of my screams will be less effective for a while. Hopefully those few unaffected people don't own the fastest car in the parking lot. You'll need a high performance machine to drive through the choked streets."

"But—I can't drive. I don't drive. I never have."

"You will today," Banch said simply.

"I can't."

"It's only for the first leg of your trip. The rules still apply to my twin. She can't break connection with the ground. Once you find her, both of you will need to return on foot. It won't be far, but it certainly won't be easy coming back on foot. The SCUBA gear will provide you enough air to avoid the coma though."

Jared sunk in his chair.

Banch glanced at the menu. "Oh look, fried okra!"

"Maybe this is too much."

She dropped the menu on the table. "What?"

"This, all this stuff we have to do." He threw his hands together. "I'm gonna die anyway, Banch."

"We've covered this. The Assembly is worse."

"I know, but if more people get hurt—"

"We aren't going to let anyone get hurt." Banch grabbed his hand and squeezed it. "We're going to get you to the ocean, remove the mark of the Gift, and your soul will be spared. You think this is difficult? You don't want to look back on this moment until the end of time and wish you'd fought harder. Believe me, Jared Kare."

He rubbed at a small headache forming in the center of his forehead. "Will you go back to the Deeper Unseen after the beach? You'll still be my banshee, right? You'll be there for me... when I go."

She gave him a faint smile. "Certainly."

"You promise?"

Banch sighed and crossed her heart.

It was difficult holding a conversation with every person at every table staring at them with expectant, hungry gazes.

"You said the Pacific Ocean shares space between our dimensions. Back in the Deeper Unseen, do you ever swim its waters?" he asked.

"The Paled Ocean? I have a few times. I can feel this world in its every drop. I adore this one beach near a free-zone called Mazanyia. It's a peaceful place that the Silent Kings don't control. The city is known for its fine parchment and textiles. Quaint yellow and white cottages built into the sapphire moss covered cliffs. You would like it."

"I bet." Jared noticed he still had his fingers looped around the detergent's handle. He moved the box between his feet under the table.

The waiter showed up at his side with two men. "I've brought these two gentlemen for you. Jason here has a Mustang Shelby 2014—next was a supped-up Camry, but I think we have a winner."

"Sounds perfect," said Banch. Jared swallowed uneasily.

A tall, handsome, nicely dressed Mexican man with a shaved head pressed the keys into Jared's hand. "It's at half a tank. Do I need to get it filled up?"

"No, we'll be fine, thanks," Banch told him.

"Are you hungry? Want dinner? The prime rib jambalaya is awesome. I'll pay of course, and how about some hurricanes?"

"Maybe later," Jared said. "Thank you. I'll try to be careful with your car."

"Do what needs to be done, brother. It's your car now." He patted Jared's shoulder and jumped up with childish delight, so happy to have provided for his masters.

"This is Kyle," the waiter introduced the other man, "and he dives and snorkels all over the world."

The deeply tanned man's heavily stoned eyes peered out behind his long shaggy golden hair. "My gear's at home, but I'm less than a few miles from here. I can hurry."

Before Jared could answer, Banch said, "Yes, please do."

Kyle charged down the aisle and sprinted the length of the restaurant. He slammed his shoulder into the front door rather than opening it and took off running outside as though on fire. Everyone at the tables stared on in envy. Jason and the waiter bowed and left Banch and Jared alone once more.

Jared looked down at the keys. "Haven't driven since I was sixteen."

"I remember," said Banch. "But you'll do fine."

"How do I know where to find your twin?"

"You've been with me long enough now—up in the sky you'll notice a crease in time-space. Follow that and you should find her."

"Will she cooperate?"

"Yes."

"How do you know?"

"Because I've Fused with other Banches from different realities before."

He absently jiggled Jason's Mustang keys, a Corona beer bottle opener with a half-naked lady swung from it. "Boy. Different versions of you. That's crazy."

"Not really. Not when you've gone through time as long as I have."

"How old are you then?"

"Screw you, Jared."

"Whoa sorry."

She faked punching him in the jaw and laughed. "Okay. We've wasted enough time. I need to begin Fusing. You'll notice the choked street will erupt in steam once the Lung Spike is destroyed. If my twin isn't sitting in this chair very soon after that happens, we will fail. Be careful and be quick."

Jared knuckled a cold bead of sweat off his brow. "Okay. You be careful too, I mean, with *them*."

"Don't worry. They'll not see me coming."

"What if they do?"

"My twin will vanish... and you'll know that you're on your own. That will be your cue to get into your new muscle car and floor it all the way to the beach. The Assembly will most likely use one of their grants and head you off at the beach. If you can avoid that and get into the water, you'll be lucky."

Jared sighed through his nose.

"Okay," said Banch. "So, again, no more talking. Time for shit to happen."

Jared wanted to hold on, had a dark feeling this would be the last he saw of her, or at least this version of her. The sound that came from Banch made the insides of his ears itch—maybe even his brain tickle—bizarre, but more bizarre was the feeling of rain coming down inside his skull.

The banshee rested her head down on her slender arms and slowly faded—translucent, transparent, and then gone.

"Bye," said Jared. He took a breath and looked at the empty chair for a long moment. "I love you. God help me, but I do."

A hand dropped on his shoulder. Kyle, clearly out of breath but very happy, held out a SCUBA mask. The tank was at his side. "Hey man, it's yours. Full tank too. Just filled it for Catalina, but whatever. I love that I can give this to you."

"Thanks, I appreciate it," Jared told him. "Sorry you'll miss your trip."

"Nah! Anything else you need?"

"This will do. Oh, well, you could tell everybody in here to hang tight until I get back. It's dangerous out there."

"Absolutely."

"Thanks." Jared took the mask and tank and headed out of the restaurant, all eyes on him. Once outside, he saw the silver crease running down from the sky in the distance.

"There she is," he whispered. *The twin.*

The Mustang Shelby was parked out front, black and red paint job, like a robot black widow. Down the street by the bus stop, a man and woman screamed at each other. Their little girl cowered beside them, hands up to her trembling mouth.

It wasn't the type of image Jared wanted to absorb before climbing into the driver's seat of a car for the first time ever, feeling like a kid himself all over again, but he had to do this. He had Banch to worry about now. She wanted to save him, but he actually thought, for maybe the first time ever in his life, that he didn't want to be saved.

He put the keys in the driver's side door and a sad thought settled on him. With all the banshee had asked him about what he wanted in life, he hadn't done the same for her. What would make Banch happy? What did she need?

Jared hoped there was still a chance to find out.

* * *

When Jared was ten years old...

His mom and dad argued more than ever. Had he not been so terrified by the prospect, had he not been so terribly young, had he not thought himself the defective piece of the machine that needed fixing, he would have embraced a divorce.

It was only a few days after his birthday and he was trying to ride his new bike. He didn't have much experience without training wheels, but was happy he could ride on his own now. He took a spill and cut up his elbows earlier that morning, after which his dad kept at his side and wouldn't let him pedal off alone—at first Jared loathed this, but then decided the extra attention wasn't a bad thing.

"Bob," said his mother from the front porch. "Why don't you just let him go? He's fine."

"If this bike wasn't such a hunk of shit, I might."

She folded her arms against her pale green house dress. "You helped pick it out."

"Yeah, from the rest of the used crap."

The insinuation was clear. Jared's father always griped that his mother needed a better paying job.

"You're a prick," she told him, and went inside.

His father just waved this off, but later, after they finished going up and down the block on his bike in awkward silence, he stormed back into the house. His father's hands were plunged deep in the pockets of his jeans, which always meant he was pissed beyond all belief. His mother was taking out a casserole dish from the cupboard when he started in.

"You know that kid is the only reason I stay with your abusive ass. After you went out on me with that, that, *waiter*. I think you forget about that."

His mother gently set the dishware on the sink. "You've reminded me enough these past six years, so how would I ever forget? Why not give it a damn rest? How about that?"

His father took a deep, exasperated breath and scowled. "Jimmy called me up the other day and asked if I wanted to play a little softball with the guys, like in the old days. But I couldn't do it. I'm too afraid you'll take the opportunity to go off and hump someone."

His mother's eyes glittered with a special kind of hate for her husband. "You are so childish it makes me sick to my stomach. Really, you do."

"Oh, *I'm* the disgusting one?"

"What about Jared, you selfish asshole?" She pointed at him and Jared almost felt the sharpness of the gesture in his gut.

"And I'm also the selfish one? Wow, this is so eye-opening! I had no idea it was me fucking everything up. Well, let me let you in on a secret, Mary: Jared will be fine. A lot of kids have to live in two places. A lot of kids are completely happy that way."

"Right."

"I don't need this crap anymore. You're ruining all of our lives!"

"Why?" His mother slammed a fist into a cupboard. "How? Tell me! By just existing? You miserable bastard!"

Jared ran out then. His mother had never been so loud and his father had never sounded so *sure* about something in his entire life. Out of the door in a flash, Jared grabbed his new bike, hopped on, and took off. He pedaled down the sidewalk like he was going for warp speed, like maybe he could time travel somewhere in the near future when this fight had simmered.

His front tire hit a deep crack in the concrete and he flew over the handlebars. In the remoteness, his parents were screaming, and above the sky also screamed, but with light blue and dark gray words. Everything ended in painful strobe lights. The breath had been knocked out of him and it took a few attempts to regain it. He rubbed some grit and pebbles off his cheek and saw his parents slowing down, winded and white-hot concern in their faces. He rolled over and his left leg cramped and made him cry out, more in surprise than in pain. His parents' arms were disembodied things that stretched out for him, and he avoided their touch like poisonous tentacles from the deep. He broke away from them and ran for the house. Once he got back he shut himself in his room. They came back into the house a few minutes later. He could hear his mother slamming things in the kitchen and his father going on about the "piece of shit bicycle" again.

Jared hurried to his closet, thinking he'd take all his clothes and run away to show them, to make them feel horrible for this, but instead he rested his head against the closet door and gently pounded his skull there. "Don't," he whispered and pounded harder. "Don't," he said again. Harder. Thump. Thump. Thump. Thump.

"DON'T!" He roared and slammed his head into the wood. *Don't*. Thump. *Don't*. Thump. *Don't*. Thump.

He couldn't tell when they came in, but he remembered his parents pulled him away from the closet before any real damage could be done.

"Don't leave me," he cried. "I need you both. You have to help me. Or something bad will happen again, like when I used to go to Bella's."

"Baby," his mother began.

"No!" he hollered. "Don't divorce! Okay? Don't divorce. Don't divorce. Don't divorce. PLEASE!"

Jared sobbed for a long time, both his parents hovering protectively over him, and when he finally quieted his mom or his dad, he couldn't recall which, said, "Of course we won't do that. Of course honey. We'll always be here together."

Of course.

Chapter 11
Jared

Jared had one moment of joy, though brief, about being in a Mustang—he'd really feared it would be a stick shift and if that were the case, the trip would have been near impossible, but the Shelby had a six-speed select shift automatic transmission. The driver could choose manual or automatic. This being the case, he gladly let the car shift for him.

The black leather and silver interior reminded him of something inside a Star Wars spaceship and it might as well have been, for he'd never bothered to pay attention to gauges and buttons in a car. That was the driver's responsibility.

Now, he was the driver.

He checked the pedals. He was pretty sure the brake was in the middle. That's how he remembered it, but hell, that was half his lifetime ago.

It will be half your lifetime forever...

"Shut up," he told his brain and turned the key. Fear fell on him, heavy, cloying, dark, and unjustified. He imagined most people would enjoy sitting in a car like this, but its superiority petrified him. His heart thunder-trembled at the sound of the engine turning over. He took a couple deep breaths and wrapped his hands around the sleek steering wheel. It felt really good, much better than his Dad's old station wagon.

He tapped the first pedal and heard no sound. *Good, that's the brake.* Outside he checked the sky again for the crease. It made sense to drive the way he was pointed, whatever direction that was, and then he would turn left and keep going until the crease got larger in his view.

He placed the scuba mask over his face and tested the tank, which he'd leaned against the passenger seat. Air flowed out with a low hiss and he twisted the valve shut.

A couple cars passed by and it made him think about the world that had become involved in his and Banch's problems. He wondered if telling the people to stay at the restaurant had been a good idea. What if he didn't come back? Would they wait there forever?

And what about the rest of the city who happened to find themselves blacking out for no reason? What could they imagine was happening in these choked streets? The end of the world?

"You're stalling," he told himself, and placed his foot on the accelerator. The engine made a tremendous sound of effort, but nothing happened. "Oh, stupid." He dropped the gear into drive and pressed again. The car lurched and a thick grating sound came from underneath. *Now what?*

Realizing the cause, he shook his head in self-reproach and put the parking brake down. "Great, this trip is going to be just... splendid."

The car moved forward and a thrill went through him. He was doing it. He was driving. He checked the mirrors, which he'd toyed with first and had them perfect. No other moving cars were in sight, which made things somewhat less stressful, he supposed. The light ahead turned red and he slowed to a stop.

He almost heard Banch in his head. *There isn't time to be law abiding, dummy—go!*

Unconsciously, he stomped the gas pedal and the car roared ahead. He busted through three red lights, not even watching for cross traffic. He checked over his shoulder and the crease had changed position in relation to him.

"Okay, left," he said, and put on the blinker.

He turned left and built speed. Thoughts of crashing immediately went away as something sucked the breath from his lungs. He pawed open the valve on the oxygen tank. When he didn't feel much air he turned the valve some more, but the flow was as free as it was going to get. His lungs just weren't opening all the way.

He squinted at the path ahead, feeling faint. Shapes lay in the street. He tapped the brake. The world wobbled; the planet was a balloon ready to fly away and get caught around the neck of a carousel horse, the universe one giant merry-go-round. Vertigo gripped him tighter. He feared he might vomit into his scuba mask.

That'd be pretty.

He tried to focus again. The shapes in the street looked like clothes. He shrugged and pushed the gas.

Then one of the heaps of clothes lifted and he saw a young woman's face, her mouth going in and out like a wounded trout washed ashore.

"Oh shit!" He jammed on the brake with both feet and the Mustang fishtailed with a screech of its tires.

Silence and jagged heartbeats. Hisses of stale air. The engine's slow purr.

He wanted to feel victory for stopping in time, but he'd almost killed someone. His head fell against the steering wheel and he blacked out. He came out of it right away though and searched around in a panic. Twenty or thirty people were scattered around the street. They must have left their cars and collapsed. There was no way he could drive around them all, even if he knew what the hell he was doing behind the wheel. He'd have to change routes.

The car had stopped diagonally and he had to crank the wheel a bit to turn it—the cranking reminded him of his dad driving—he'd seen that before, that cranking of the wheel, and wondered how it might feel. Now he was doing it.

"I'm *doing* this," he said. A smile almost formed on his lips, but then his lungs collapsed in even farther and he wheezed.

He took a side street ahead and floored the gas until the next crossing. Took a left and moved around parked cars with caution. Some affected people lay in the street here too, but most had made it to the sidewalk before subsiding. Jared kept driving, grateful for how wonderful the car handled, not that he had anything to compare it to. Impulsively he made another left and came back to Valley View Street. It wasn't as bad over here. He looked at the sky and the crease had grown larger, gotten closer.

Jared screamed.

A plastic garbage can splintered and flew into the sky as though fired from a cannon. He'd veered off the road, and then overreacted and jerked the wheel. The tires skipped along and the Mustang went sideways. He righted the path but went into another left turn.

Was that a mistake?

He scanned dizzily outside. The air from the SCUBA burned his nostrils. Once again he wanted to throw up but the crease loomed over him now and that gave him focus. He sped up, made another harsh left, the car skidding, the engine growling.

Then all at once he couldn't see the crease anymore.

He jammed on the brake and nearly smashed headfirst into the steering wheel. He tapped the buttons on the door handle, searching for the driver's side controls. The window made a futuristic humming sound as he rolled it down. The silver crease, like a metallic spinal column of some invisible Godzilla sized robot, hung directly above this area. He breathed out in relief and also noticed his lungs felt full. Everything around him increased in color and the dreamlike state vanished. He was in a safe place, off of the choked streets. He'd soon have to return to them though, without the luxury of a car. *This is only the first leg of your trip*, he remembered Banch telling him.

With that thought of her, he spotted her twin.

The banshee sat against an old brick building with real estate signs plastered all over its façade. She pushed up from the wall and marched over to the car. It was Banch all right, but at the same time it definitely *wasn't* her. Jared had to look away to keep from staring too long. This Banch had no hair and most of her scalp ran with waves of third degree burn scars. She had no eyebrows and her uniform looked different. The outfit was more revealing than his Banch's, but in a sad way; her breasts were hardly covered in some type of quasi corset, and she had a black tutu on with silver glitter in its folds. She came to stand in front of the car, an unceremonious slump in her posture.

"Are you my guide to the Fuse?"

Jared swallowed, tried to keep direct eye contact, though it was extremely difficult with her bleak, bloodshot gaze.

"Yes I am."

"I cannot step inside the vehicle. I'll lose residence in this dimension."

"Oh yeah, duh, sorry." Jared popped open the door. "I have to get the air tank because the streets—"

"I know the situation, human," the twin cut in. "The other and I shared some thoughts for a few minutes during the Fuse. Hurry on with your equipment."

"That makes this easier, I guess," he said shyly. This version was intimidating for completely other reasons than what he had grown accustomed to.

"She's getting closer to the Atmosphere Javelin."

"What? Oh, is that what you call a Lung Spike where you're from?"

The twin leveled her hard gaze. "We must go."

"Right." Jared ran around to get the tank. He hefted it out of the car, got down on his knees, and strapped it onto his shoulders. It was heavy enough to make him wobble a bit during the process. He attached the hoses and pulled up the mask he'd left hanging around his neck. He smiled at the twin, feeling goofy. "Lead the way, Banch."

"Who?"

"Oh, right, nothing."

The twin squinted as she started off. "Wait, you have given me— *her*—a name?"

"Sort of, yeah."

The twin nodded in mild approval. "Nice. Too bad it's a horrible fucking name."

Jared laughed and followed her into the street. His lungs tightened and he reached back to twist the valve. When he turned he noticed the twin studying him with her cadaverous eyes.

"I remember you," she said.

"You do?"

"Keep walking, human. Quickly now."

"Sorry."

"You were the kid I had to make a call for when you were ten. Your babysitter, Bella Boyd, got drunk and hit you with her car when you ran off to feed some stupid pigeon or something."

"What?"

"The sitter got twenty-five years in prison. You hung in there for another five years but you were paralyzed the whole time. Then I had to make the call. Your folks were rightly insane thereafter as I remember it, but they weren't my assignments, so I'm not sure what became of them."

Jared didn't want to think about their fate, but couldn't help wonder if his parents were still alive in another dimension, perhaps many different dimensions. They could have gone on to live longer without him. Conceivably they had a divorce and found someone else and they were happier without him. Or they actually loved each other in these different realities.

"So I really died? That young?"

"Almost twenty years ago now," she said. "I'm glad to see you again, grown up. I remember thinking you were a nice kid, going after that chicken or whatever the hell it was. You actually cared. A lot of people, man, they just couldn't give a shit about such things, even at five years old."

"Fatso," Jared said through his mask.

"The bird? No, you called him Feathers."

"If you say so."

This is beyond weird. Jared had a disturbing thought then. "Was I the Assembly's gift at that young age?"

"Gift?"

"Yes, you know, how the Silent Kings allow them to take a gift every hundred years?"

The twin shook her head. "Where I come from there is no such Kings. The Assembly rules all of the Deeper Unseen."

Jared's blood went cold. "Really?"

"So I suppose you could say that *everyone* is a gift for them."

"I'm sorry."

"It's life. Nothing to be sorry about, Jared Halte."

"It's actually Kare."

"If you say so, human," said the twin Banch. A smile touched her gray lips.

Chapter 12
The Banshee

Banch crouched at the dumpster and surveyed the scene around the Lung Spike. She moved her eyes to each of the Assembly, counting all ten. What was so important that they were standing around idle? As an answer, a wave of purple and cerulean sparks showered the air around them, all bursting forth from the spike.

She grinned. "Technical difficulties, boys?"

This was a good development. She observed the sky. Her twin could be felt but it made the situation more reassuring to see it with her own eyes. The crease had not moved much, which meant Banch needed to hang back for a while. It was fine though. The Assembly were having so much trouble with the Spike, she could hold out a bit longer and that would give Jared and the twin more time as well.

But she'd need a better vantage for when she made her move. Turning, a flash of silver washed across her line of sight. Out of instinct she swayed back and a long sting went through her shoulder. The fabric of her uniform split down to her bicep. She protectively grabbed her arm and moved back.

Standing behind her, one of the Assembly lifted a machete with a debase smirk on his waxy red lips. His pale body was wiry muscled, not in pants and suspenders as the others but naked as birth.

Taking another backward step, Banch stole a glance over her shoulder. The other Assembly members broke away from the Spike with unsettling ease, as though it was never a concern. One fell to the ground, so much useless meat. He moved his head and she saw that his face looked too fresh, not imbued with the toiled misery of the Assembly.

Because he's a decoy. They've set a trap and you were the fool to fall for it. Banch retreated more and thought of possible screams to use — none of them would be powerful enough though after the Swell.

The nine others drew closer. Banch could see nowhere to run. She was surrounded. The naked Assembly member's lips moved but ten voices filled the alley with what he said.

"He's ours, banshee. You will *never* have him again."

Ten grins peeled back.

Chapter 13
Jared

Jared's face slammed into the brick wall. His jaw buckled and teeth lathed across each other. The air tank clanged loud enough to bring him back into consciousness. Someone caught his shoulders, yanking him upright.

"You have to knock this off, human!" Disgust layered the twin's voice.

Jared tried to regain himself. The world flexed, expanded, dropped in and out, a mockery of what his lungs should be doing.

"I can't... help it." Ripples of vertigo swelled through his head. The banshee wouldn't allow him to stop, but he just wanted to pass out like the other huddled masses in the streets. He kept burping, trying to settle his stomach. It tasted like Eun Sun's cold cucumber soup from breakfast.

"Here." The banshee shoved him into a cross-street. His lungs sorely ballooned and he bent forward, hands on his knees, enjoying the pull of oxygen into his unhindered core. "We can't stay long," she said. "Get your head on right."

He nodded. "Guess you probably don't see the point... saving me. In your world I'm long dead."

"You're talking, so you're ready." The twin tugged him back into the choked street.

Jared coughed, gagged, and stumbled along. It couldn't have been even half a mile since they left the car, but felt as though he'd been air deprived for hours. This Banch was even less forgiving and she'd not let him get away with any other resting so far. His brain kept chanting: *How much farther? How much farther?* After a while it became a twisted cord of nonsense sounds saw-cutting his mind. *Howucharther? Howucharther? How-we-tar-ouch-ouch-ourch-far-far-far-terth-terth?*

"No!"

The twin stopped and put a hand over her heart. Her grim face managed to dial in something even darker.

Jared couldn't ask what had upset her. He swayed there and checked the valve on the air tank—he'd been doing this habitually, although it never amounted to any new discovery; the air was flowing as it always had, but he just wasn't getting enough of it, simple as that.

The twin slowly edged forward, checking the sky.

"The other has stopped moving."

"Who?" Jared was able to get through his mask.

"*Banch*," said the twin, giving him a sidelong look.

"Why?" he wheezed.

"I don't know, but I'm still here, so she is too, let's go." The twin pulled harder at his underarm, almost making him trip. Her footsteps slowed and she shook her head. "Oh shit…"

Jared groaned. "Please tell me."

"Something's really wrong, human. She's in very bad trouble."

"We… help… her?" Jared said through grunts.

Once more the twin led him on. "I have to get to that Fusing location. That's all we can do for her, besides hope… damn it all!"

Jared hated every word this banshee said, but right now he couldn't resist or voice any objection. Everything pitched sideways, a deity grabbing the earth and twisting it like a doorknob. *Where does the door lead?* He blinked and tried to focus.

"You're okay, you're okay," the twin whispered, almost sympathetically. Her tone wasn't normal; it was far too reassuring and patient. Perhaps she knew the end was near and, like most people, thought if she was kind she might bypass a worse fate.

Banch! thought Jared in a panic. *Banch, you can't do this to me!*

Their pace had slowed again. He lifted his head, fighting the shifting, gyrating, colliding distortions of unsteadiness and nausea. Before them a six car pile-up sealed off the road. The path had no openings through, at least none that the banshee could get over. It would involve climbing, which she couldn't do, or trying to move the cars, which there wasn't time for.

Hopeless and pointless—all of this!

Jared fell to his knees. "Sorry," he muttered.

"Get up."

He pressed his hand over the burning in his chest. "It's done."

The twin pinched the flesh at his tricep and he winced. "Up!" she shouted.

Jared scrambled to his feet, but he spread his hands out at the futility. "Why? What for?"

"Don't piss me off. Come on."

"Can't."

For another time that day, Jared's jaw buckled. This time it was because the banshee had slapped him.

Very hard.

His face mask went sideways but she quickly adjusted it so he could look at her in the face. "Human," she told him, eyes fiery and clear, "you don't ever get to use that word again. *Can't* is not part of your vocabulary."

In another moment, they were moving again.

Chapter 14
The Banshee

Banch couldn't turn this around, but hadn't accepted it yet. It was both good and bad the Assembly knew not to get too close to her. She could avoid some of their thrown machetes and rocks, but she couldn't get close enough to touch any of them and thus destroy the Spike.

Infuriating to her. Fun for them.

They'd won and knew it, so why not chase her around and scare her, throw rocks and daggers and machetes? And then they brought out ball and chains. One of them impacted her lower back and sent her sprawling. There were so many angry thoughts racing through her mind. How could she let Jared down like this? This outcome had been expected, but not here, not now. At the beach she wouldn't have felt so surprised.

She tasted blood on her tongue. It was saltier than what she'd tasted after the Swell. That had been old blood—this, well, this tasted closer to the vein, a bitter, cold, iron, copper tickle.

The bowling-ball sized end of the ball and chain smashed into the concrete near her face—she realized then she'd fallen and lay completely prone before the Assembly. Chips of concrete bit into her face and she pushed up, startled and overcome.

A chorus of laughter.

For her pain.

And humiliation.

It didn't change her mood. She knew how they were. She knew what they were.

She struggled but got to her feet. They wouldn't take her lying down like a weakling.

Jared, I hope the car gets you to the beach—I hope the Silent Kings don't grant them a direct corridor shadow to head you off—I'm so sorry. Why did I not approach you sooner? Why did I not do so many things differently?

Because I wasn't meant to win, I guess.

That's okay though. The universe works that way. I've tried many times to Fuse only to find out that me, the so-called Banch, never existed. Because in some realities, the Deeper Unseen is missing, and there are no transfers of energy after death—in those places, when the soul dies, the body still remains, a living dead, and those concepts are the implanted memories of such worlds in our dreams—and nightmares—for those realities are closer than we think. I know you cannot hear my thoughts, Jared Kare, but if you could, I would implore you to fight, because you are still here, in this world. You're still alive. Hear me.

On the second impact, the ball and chain dislocated Banch's shoulder. The pain made her sick to her stomach but she ate it and refused to change her expression of defiance. In the distance she saw a foggy red-scored figure drop the ball. With a tall red Mohawk and a scandalous, hungry leer, he stood off the sidewalk in a planter full of only dirt. The ball struck the ground and a dust cloud lifted around him like honey vapor. The chain cinched up and rattled, and she wondered if it happened across all realities because it seemed SO LOUD.

She bit her lip.

Maybe she was wrong.

Maybe the other Banch would remain here.

And get him to the beach.

You're fooling yourself. You know how it works. It's done for you and the twin.

The ball smashed into her stomach and the impact made her think of puking out her organs. Her head slammed to the ground and she heard her own scream, but it was magic-less, only filled with pain instead.

But she stood again.

Damn it.

She got up, ignoring the growing ache through her side, because the hell with them. They would not do this easy!

The Assembly giggled. It still didn't bother her. She kept her face locked in one expression for them: *end it if you like, but I'll be here until then.*

The ball flew out again. Banch saw it clearly. Black, spinning, final. She raised her hands, opened her fingers and caught it. Mohawk man's carnage-caked brow lifted in shock.

"Come here, bitchwhore!" Banch cried, and yanked the chain hand over hand.

The Assembly member staggered off the planter and fell into her from his momentum. She threw her arms around his body, *tight*. He squirmed, fought, but it only took a few seconds. The other Assembly scrambled for cover but it wasn't soon enough. The Lung Spike's spilling of sparks increased tenfold and the entire length of the shaft shattered into fine emerald and sapphire shrapnel that stretched out in a ring. The Assembly shot into the air and lightning threaded through them in a blink—they were caught from heel to toe in florid flames and slammed to the ground. Immediately some of them rolled around to smother the flames, to no avail.

Banch grappled with the spinning world around her and crashed into a dumpster. She licked more blood off her lips.

"So much easier calling deaths," she mumbled.

Glittering cinders fell from the sky onto the passed-out Assembly members. The streets suddenly erupted in steam, every single shadow becoming the mouth of a smoking volcano.

Banch checked the sky for her twin's crease.

It was still visible. And wasn't near the restaurant yet.

"We still didn't make it." She lowered her head. Her lips trembled and eyes welled. She hated that lack of control but let her pretenses go. Banch took a breath and closed her eyes. Accepted what would come for her. But not for Jared.

Chapter 15
Jared

When Jared was twenty-two years old…

His mother Mary died of breast cancer. It had claimed her in less than a year, even after a partial mastectomy. Jared had written something to say at the service but didn't have the courage to read it once the time came. He didn't feel as bad, though, once his father made it known he wouldn't be saying anything at the service either, except to thank everybody for coming. Listening to other accounts from friends was hard enough, but saying something about Mary was just too much for them to take.

The day was still clear to him. Jared looked down at that cold sheet of printer paper with the laser-inked words for more than an hour. His mother had bought the paper at Costco. His mother likely had bought the ink cartridges there as well. That was her favorite place to shop. She loved shopping. Loved spending money. It relieved stress for her. In fact, his earliest memory of her was a shopping run to a grocery store. Two and half years old and he'd been sitting beneath the shopping cart. He preferred the solitude down there instead of facing the cart-pusher. She let him sit beneath unless she had cases of soda or bulk items to buy. One day he'd gotten his finger pinched while exploring one of the spinning wheels. The pain was erased from his memory now, but seeing his mother bend under the cart, parking lot sunlight and shadow crosshatches over her sweet face, and her kissing his wounded finger, that was an image that never left him.

He recalled shopping with her for much of his life. With her gone, she'd not be that person holding such mundane household duties. No paying bills, cleaning, cooking—god, her meatloaf, Jared's favorite, and he'd never thought to ask her how she made it, had no clue if she wrote the recipe down somewhere, but that hardly mattered since he couldn't cook to save his life. Even though he'd known she was dying, he wouldn't let such questions cross his mind.

His eyes went to the words he'd written about her:

"...she was my best friend. I spent most of my childhood with her. She even brought me to her job when I was too afraid of babysitters." His eyes filled. *"She loved Science Fiction movies, the campier the better. I admit she liked them a whole lot more than me, but I watched them with her every Friday night, she with her blush wine, me with my diet Dr. Pepper, and tons of microwave popcorn. I asked her once if there were really creatures on the moon. Mom just laughed and told me the moon was nothing more than big rock stuck in the sky, nothing special, but to her make-believing was still fun and worthwhile."*

There was one more thing he'd wanted to add but hadn't. *I'm sorry I made her life so hard and I'm sorry she could never be happy because I needed her so much.*

Jared wadded up the paper and let it fall to the hardwood floor of his bedroom.

He glanced at his shoes, still untied. For so many years his mother would shake her head, kneel down, and say, "They'll just come undone that way. You didn't tie them correctly," and then she'd untie and retie them. And she was right; his shoes felt more secure, like they belonged on his feet when she did, opposed to when he tied them, his shoes felt borrowed and the world that much more chaotic.

So he stopped tying them and would find his mother every morning to get them tied correctly. It was a ritual he enjoyed. It was attention. It was safety. Even as a young adult. His father hated it and his parents argued over the matter often enough, but his mother relished taking care of him—to her, it probably meant her baby wasn't really growing up.

Jared's father knocked and cracked open the door. "You good?"

"Yep."

Bob entered, hands deep-deep in the pockets of his black slacks. "You ready to go down and talk to the fam?"

"No."

His father nodded and glided a hand over the shiny dome of his bald head. "Me neither, I guess."

For a minute he stood there, not saying a word, just glancing around at all the art and movies posters on Jared's walls like cave writings of some alien race—no matter how hard he tried, his confusion and the awe of this dark moment ran so much deeper than pockets would ever go.

The silence ended with broken sobbing. Jared didn't look at his father crying, wouldn't face seeing something akin to the sturdiest fortress walls crumbling down. For his mother and for this, Jared's eyes spilled too; he couldn't and wouldn't stop it from happening.

Taking a knee before him, his father tied Jared's shoelaces. Once finished, he wiped his nose with the sleeve of his suit coat and sniffed. "How's that?"

Not as tight as his mother used to tie them, or at least it seemed so, but Jared wouldn't have dreamed of critiquing at that moment. "Good, Dad. Very good. Thanks."

"You're welcome, son." His father pressed his lips together, face muscles twitching as he fought another crying spell.

"Do you think I made her do too much?" Jared asked.

"What?" His father now looked straight at him. Jared had never seen his eyes so swollen and red, except when his seasonal allergies kicked in.

"Did I run her down? Make her sick? She did so much for—"

His father held up a hand. "She did a lot for both of us, but that has nothing to do with it." He shook his head passionately. "It was goddamn cancer. That thing doesn't care if you're lazy, tired, or have all the energy in the world. It just *is*."

"I know, but do—I mean, did I make your marriage harder? I did, didn't I?"

A look of fear bloomed in his father's gray, bloodshot eyes. "You must never think that, okay? Please. Okay? Say okay."

Jared nodded. "Okay."

"Your mom and I didn't get along. I always believed I could be the right man for any woman, that I had a lot to give, but sometimes you'll never be content with yourself and that gets in the way, makes the other person feel like you don't want them either. I understand now that I wasn't the right man for your mom—"

"No, Dad."

"Just let me finish, son. I wasn't right for her, but *she was right for me*. We stayed together because you were right for both of us. I might have said some awful things to your mom, and she may have called me names, but we didn't hate each other." His voice broke and he cleared his throat. "She may have tolerated me, but I loved her more than I could ever explain. Please always remember that before anything else."

Jared bowed his head. "I don't know how I'm going to get through this. I need her, Dad."

"I know son, but I'm here to take care of you now. Not to mention your girlfriend, Kaitlin."

"She's not my girlfriend. I've told you that before."

"She's downstairs bringing food to everybody right now. So at very least she's a damn good friend."

"Agreed," said Jared.

"We'll get through this together kid, you and me."

Naturally his father had a rough go of things that year. Lots of drinking, lots of bad cigars, and plenty of shouting matches with televised sports. Jared couldn't talk to him about anything. He didn't know how to be there for his father. Some of the players from the softball league finally came over one day to try to cheer them up. Then they started coming by every Thursday to play poker and drink microbrew beer. His father wasn't as alone. Things started turning around after that, but with his wife gone, life was always fighting upstream for Bob Kare, and Jared took that battle with him too.

* * *

What will I do now?

Jared's heart raced. His cell phone vibrated in his pocket, syncing with the blood pounding in his face. The Bayou Cat was in sight but as they headed into the street, massive gouts of steam lifted all around them.

"Shit!" the twin yelled and pointed. "Is that the place?"

"Yes, yes," he said, coughing, the sudden air in his lungs overwhelming.

He turned to the twin. She held his hand but her body stretched a mile away into colorless stands that bunched and unbunched. In the next second the strands all pulled back together into a human form. Her molecules were unstable, thinning out to nothing.

"Hurry, I'm

dis

associat

ing

from

reality."

Her voice was a metal machine echoing in his mind.

After that, the next moments were dream. The door to the restaurant opened. He pointed to the back. People stood at their tables like obedient lap dogs welcoming their masters. Jared crashed into a few chairs with his air tank. The twin transformed into a kaleidoscopic swirl that drifted apart in grains of molecules, only to pull back together in a temporal version, a fainter variety of herself. They were in front of the table and he could see her screaming at him but bewilderment had his tongue numb.

"Which seat, Jared? Hey? Snap out of it? Which seat was yours?"

Jared stared at the table. He pictured Banch in one seat. He pictured Banch in the other seat. He stared back up at the twin, sounds through the breathing apparatus the only reply he could offer.

The twin's body scrambled, the particles hovering a bit before sticking back together.

"Jared! Which goddamn chair?"

"He sat there." A waiter pointed to the chair on the left.

The twin lost no time and dropped into the opposite seat. A blinding flash expelled from her body, followed by a darkness that contracted and pulled inward.

Banch.

His Banch.

Just as she had before, she sat at the table, head resting on her arms, eyes clamped shut. Jared stripped off his face mask and dropped to her side. "Hey," he said, patting her shoulder. "Hey, please wake up. Wake up!"

Her eyes fluttered and she gave him a drowsy stare.

"Are you okay?"

"That was... too close," she said and licked her lips. "I'm starving."

Someone in the room gasped for joy and cried, "SHE WANTS FOOD!"

Everybody jumped to his or her feet, rushing for the kitchen, tripping and clamoring over each other.

A Samoan guy shoved someone to the ground. "Wait your turn assholes, I said I got this!"

"Be nice! Be nice!" Jared hollered.

The crowd stopped, almost in a comical impersonation of a freeze frame. A multitude of apologies slowly filtered through the people. They detangled from each other, a couple friendly pats on the back here and there, and they headed to the kitchen in orderly groups.

Banch pushed up slightly from her arm and wagged her head. "Damn. That was a split razor on the aperture."

"Huh?"

"Another saying of ours—any longer and the disassociation would have been irreversible. What about you? Are you okay?"

"Am I okay? Banch, you and the twin almost went out, like a puff of smoke."

"Oh, believe me. I get that." The banshee pulled down her torn uniform at the shoulder to reveal a colossal blue-brown bruise.

"Did... they?"

"Don't worry about them," she said pointedly. "They'll be scraping their asses off the ground for a few hours would be my guess. That gives us time to eat and then head to our next stop. It's not far. Remember our detergent."

He took off the air tank and gradually sat into the other seat, his legs burning from fatigue. "Did you get a look at the twin? How she looked, I mean?"

"Why?"

"She said you shared thoughts for a while."

"That's true, but no, I got no image of her."

"I see," said Jared.

"Why do you ask?"

"Nothing."

"What did she look like?" Banch narrowed her eyes and folded her arms neatly under her breasts.

Jared took a much welcomed breath of fresh air and smiled. "She was beautiful, just as you are."

Banch's lips twisted and she hummed. "Be careful talking that way, charmer—if I had more strength I might jump your bones right here."

"Oh, well then lucky for me."

Banch tossed a linen napkin off the table at him. He caught it at his chest and laughed. His phone vibrated again but he couldn't imagine picking it up right now. He was just so happy. So happy, beyond happy, that he was sitting across from his banshee once again.

A pair of bickering people brought forth steaming bowls of gumbo and set them down.

"There's bread, too," said a dazzled-eyed business woman with her hair chopsticked in a bun.

"Want a Caesar salad? Seafood salad? Coleslaw? Cajun style?" said the other, who Jared recognized as the sleepy eyed surfer guy who'd given him the scuba gear.

Jared glanced at Banch, but before she could answer the surfer said, "Well dumb of me, of course you want some."

The two hurried off, once again arguing the finer points of what he and Banch preferred. As the swinging double doors of the kitchen closed behind them, the woman said, "Did you see their faces? They have no interest in salad and—"

A second later the doors opened again and more people emerged bringing platters of fried foods and shell fish. Banch started on her gumbo and eyed the other plates, which became increasingly copious and had to be placed on an adjacent table: boudin, jambalaya, red beans and rice, crawfish Étouffée, and several different sugary sweet manifestations of the beignet.

"Can I just get a muffuletta sandwich?" Jared asked. That was what Kaitlin always ordered for him. He hadn't tried anything else on the menu.

"Like a huge one?" someone asked in the crowd.

"No, normal size, please."

"How about a beer? Red Stripe? Purple Haze? Black Voodoo?"

"Diet Dr. Pepper or Coke."

When they were alone again, Banch asked him, "Why no beer? I recall you trying wine once, but never beer."

He shrugged. "I need the right occasion for one."

She smiled. "You are living on borrowed time, my love. I don't see when there's a better opportunity."

He offered a small smile of his own.

"Sorry," she said. "I shouldn't have brought that up."

"It's okay. In some realities, I went out of this world a long time ago."

Banch stared at him with delicate eyes. "I'm lucky to have met you. Until I end or time does, I'll never forget you, Jared Kare."

"Ditto."

"Well," said the banshee. "With that said, I'm getting Purple Haze when they come back."

"Have yourself a ball."

His phone hummed again and he slapped the rectangular bulge in his jean pocket. "Fine," he sighed, and dipped his hand inside to retrieve it. He checked the screen.

Kaitlin.

He considered whether he should answer it, then relented.

"Hi, Kait."

"Jared," she said, sounding panicked. "Where are you?"

"Why? What's the deal?"

"The deal? Aren't you seeing this shit on the news? Those guys from earlier are terrorists or something. The reports say there might have been a bunch of chemical weapons used in the city. People were out there suffocating in the streets—they're bringing in the National Guard right now. Are you crazy? You really haven't heard about any of this? Where are you? It isn't safe out there."

"I'm just with Banch."

"At the beach?"

"No, not yet, we—look Kaitlin, we're fine. Really."

"This is too weird. I'm gonna bite my fingers off at the knuckles. Tell me where you are so I can pick you guys up. Seriously."

"I said we're fine. Kaitlin, just, I'll call you some other time."

"Oh, what is this? Big man with a new girlfriend? I'm telling you there's some crazy shit out there and if you care at all about Banch—"

"We're FINE," Jared said, so loudly Banch blinked and self-consciously took another sip of her soup.

"Here's your muffuletta," said a woman, and she proudly set down a plate with the biggest sandwich Jared had ever seen. "Thanks," he whispered to her and cleared his throat. "Hey Kait, I'm sorry for raising my voice."

But the call had ended. Kaitlin had hung up. Jared's hand dropped to the table.

"She's pretty mad?" asked Banch.

"Yeah, pretty."

Banch reached over to the other table and grabbed a plate of blackened shrimp. "No doubt, you're being a jerk."

"Pardon?"

"She was just looking out for you. Try and have more patience when you talk to her."

"What for?" He took his sandwich in hand with a sullen shrug. "I won't be her problem for that much longer. Remember?"

Banch paused, shrimp halfway to her lips. "Yeah," she replied. "I do indeed remember, Jared. But never forget, a best friend is the greatest kind of problem to ever have."

Chapter 16
Jared

When Jared was fifteen years old...

He met Kaitlin for the first time. It was in a state of crisis, which would from there prove an appropriate symbol of their relationship.

Jared followed a rigid schedule every day. He got up the same time every morning, showered, dressed, ate Wheat Chex, brushed his teeth with cinnamon toothpaste, and went to the bus stop for school. The stop was just two blocks down the street and there were no traffic lights, so he walked it with little trepidation. It was a straight shot and no big deal.

The morning he met Kaitlin, however, it wasn't a straight shot. The night before his dad had some of his friends over to watch the Dodgers game. It ended up sucking—a boring pitcher's duel—so the guys got restless, drank way too much, and started joking around. His dad's friend Tom, who usually traded such TV parties for long nights at nudie clubs, brought in a Hustler magazine. The guys played drinking games, betting on whether they'd get little boobs, big ones, blond, brunette, red head, race, and so on. Jared's mother ushered him into his parents' bedroom to watch sitcoms.

The next morning he found more magazines near the couch. Tom must have brought in more later on that night and forgotten them when he left. Jared knew how to play this without attracting undue attention. He took one magazine, choosing a cover with the largest breasts, and then he hid the forbidden object in his school binder. He showed his mother where the rest of the magazines were, which promptly set off a fight with a hung-over version of his father, who hardly recalled where the magazines had come from in the first place.

On the short trip to the bus stop, Jared flipped through the pages, growing more excited and fascinated by the stark truth of the female form.

"Holy shit! Whaddya got there?" a kid yelled across the narrow street. Jared stuffed the Hustler away and acted casual. He'd seen this guy before: a total hybrid type student, a star football player and also a math genius. Obviously despite his stunning display of worth, he still possessed the same teenage mortal weakness as many.

"Bring it out man. I want to see that shit. Was that Penthouse?"

"It's an art book," said Jared, hurrying on.

"Of course it is. And I wanna Jackson Pollock all over that chick's labia."

"You're gross."

"And you're stingy," the guy pointed out.

"Leave me alone."

"Nope. Too much at stake. When else today am I gonna see that shit? Calculus lab is all morning."

"Sorry to hear that, but it belongs to my dad's friend."

"Which totally stopped you, right? Come on. I'm just gonna hound you all the way to school. You know that right?"

"Well..." Jared thought a moment. "I'm not going to school."

"Oh really?"

Jared turned up the street. He'd walked this way with his mom before. He could cut over and walk back down to the bus stop from the other side and hopefully keep his distance from this spoiler of dreams.

"Come back man," the guy called, throwing his arms up. "I'll give you my lunch money to borrow it for just today."

"Thanks, no." Jared quickened his strides.

"You suck!"

Jared never recalled the kid's full name. It might have been Matthew... something. Evidently he got in a car crash on a canyon road in his early twenties and couldn't play football in college. He went on to be an engineer though and did well for himself. Jared learned this later from Kaitlin who had the interest to actually attend their high school reunion. He always wondered how things might have went that day if he'd just shown Matthew the Hustler and been done with it.

The walk up the street turned out to be longer than Jared expected. His thoughts wandered to the type of high school category he fell under—he was decent at whatever he applied himself at, which usually extended to computer programming and science, but he still wasn't a genius in those disciplines. He loved movies but couldn't hang with novels or lengthy historical accounts. Jared pretty much was a mediocre person on all fronts.

But I have this. He unfolded his binder and got a gander at an Asian woman with an unruly undergrowth of pubic hair. He flipped the pages until he arrived at a photo of a woman with bigger breasts. He had no idea at the time that a certain banshee watched him and took notes about his preferences in anatomy.

Jared glanced at his watch. It was a quarter till and he wasn't even to the main cross street. He broke into a jog. The road stretched and the distance became more apparent—he'd never thought of it before, but this was way, WAY out of the way: he ran faster but the bouncing landscape in his vision, the jumping trees, the quaking streets, all dancing to his quicksilver breaths, never opened up to the bus stop. And when it finally did, the bus resembled a bright yellow model down the road, in the distance. Gone.

He got to the corner and dropped his folder and his backpack fell off his shoulder. He screamed. He felt terror then like he'd not felt since that time he was five and walking to feed Fatso. He dropped to his knees and bit his fist. He knew he shouldn't be carrying on. He knew he looked like a scared little wimp, an annoying crybaby, and maybe he shouldn't even exist in such a hard world, but he couldn't help being scared and wimpy, and he couldn't help being that purveyor of "oh please, this shit again?" to his friends and loved ones. That's who he'd become.

Slow footsteps dropped behind him and he looked over his shoulder. That was the first time he ever saw Kaitlin. He quickly stood and tried to look more formidable.

"Damn, missed the bus again," she muttered with a telling smile.

She reminded him of Daphne from Scobby Doo, but a little heavier, which was a good thing, a really, really good thing to his breast-happy eyes, not to mention he'd always found Daphne very pretty for a cartoon. But even the presence of a real life girl his age could not stop the terror from rising inside him. Jared needed to just cry his eyes out. He looked to the road and he held back a scream. This wasn't happening. He couldn't miss school. Things had to happen the same as they always did or things might fall apart at home.

Kaitlin headed down the sidewalk, touching her violet comb barrette holding her red locks back. He accidently let out a shudder and she glanced back. "You okay guy?"

He nodded. Closed his eyes. Shook his head. "Supposed to be... on the way to school."

"Aren't we all?" Kaitlin pulled out a pack of gum from a side pocket in her backpack. "Want some? It's grape."

Jared said thanks and with a trembling hand took a piece. He just held it though—his mind went too fast to think of chewing something.

"You sure you're okay?" Kaitlin asked. "You're as white as a ghost. Not to be rude or anything."

Jared tried to breathe normally. "Never... missed the bus... don't know what I should do."

Kaitlin chuckled. "How about head home? You got a key right?"

"My parents are still there. They'll get mad and—" Jared's muscles went limp. He dropped his binder. The Hustler spilled onto the ground.

A redhead on horseback aimed her naked, heart-shaped ass straight for Kaitlin.

"Yuck!" She kicked the magazine away from her. "Pervert."

Jared went stiff as a board. "No—I found that on the way here, in a bush."

"Bush is right." Kaitlin rolled her eyes and started away.

Jared fell against a no-parking sign post and held his face, stick of grape gum still wedged between his fingers. He didn't want to cry anymore—the pretty girl would hear him, so his body quaked instead. When he was able to get control, he lowered his hands.

Kaitlin was still there though, checking him out. "Panic attack?"

"No," Jared snapped. "I'm totally okay."

"You look totally un-okay to me."

She retrieved the dirty magazine and handed it to him. Jared slowly hid it back in his binder.

"I lied," he admitted. "It belongs to my dad's friend. I swiped it this morning."

Half her mouth lifted in a smile. "Curious, huh?"

He shrugged.

Her half-smile became a full one. "You're cute, guy. Definitely not a pervert. What's your name?"

"Jared."

"Mine's Kait—well, Kaitlin."

"I've never seen you at school before."

She grinned and gestured to the empty street. "Not many have."

Jared coughed out a laugh. It surprised him he was capable with how on-edge he was.

"I've only been in the Hills for about a month now," she said.

"Oh."

"You really want to get to school, Jared?"

He nodded hopefully.

She blew a purple bubble and crackled it between her lips. "Cool. That was a good bubble."

A faint warmth entered Jared's core. He immediately trusted her, and had no idea why.

"Tell you what." She pulled out a cell phone. "My friend Stacy's grandpa is a nice man. He'll give us a lift no problem. He only lives on the other side of the park."

"I'm not supposed to go in cars with strangers."

"He's seventy-two years old, Jared." Kaitlin scrolled through her phone contacts. "If you and I can't take him, we deserve our fate."

"So you're coming to school now?" he asked.

"Yeah, why?"

"It seemed like you didn't want to."

"I didn't have a reason to, but now I do."

"What reason?"

Kaitlin held the phone to her ear. Then she pointed.

To him.

He was the reason.

And Jared would always remember that.

Chapter 17
Kaitlin

Kaitlin couldn't help but grumble. It had taken her longer to get to La Habra than expected. Streets were barricaded and traffic accidents were numerous and grew scarier with each new one she saw. There wasn't a single clue in her mind as to what to make of any of this, but it seemed like an invasion or some unseen disaster on the horizon. Jared had picked a fine time to fall in love again. Such huge events on the world scale and him in the mix? She doubted his stress load could handle it. And yet he'd seemed so damn sure of himself, and *snappy*. Where the hell did he get off? After all she'd done for him, this was the kind of treatment she deserved? He'd never been this way before. That Banch woman couldn't be the cause—unless she was pulling the wool over their eyes. Kaitlin had been fooled by people before, but by all appearances that gray-eyed beauty was an absolute sweetheart.

Well, these ponderings were pointless. Jared would need to explain himself when she got to the Bayou Cat. Kaitlin was certain that's where he was. On the phone call, the voice in the background clearly said "muffuletta," and there wasn't any other restaurant nearby that served those sandwiches.

Another roadblock came into view. Police cars. Uniformed men impatiently directing traffic around blockades.

"Fudge," Kaitlin muttered. If she missed Jared she'd never forgive herself. After a quick reroute down the street she found a parking spot along the curb. Quickly she grabbed her purse, killed the engine, and got out. The weather was peculiar, damper than usual. Faint traces of steam wiggled up from cracks in the sidewalk. Kaitlin got a bad feeling all at once and considered, for the first time, whether coming to look for Jared was a good idea. After all, wasn't it always the person trying to help a bad situation the one who ended up stabbed or killed?

Keep scaring yourself, but you know you won't leave him until he's safe, so might as well knock it off.

She slowed down for a family arguing near the bus stop. The man had a bloody gash, which the woman tried to delicately inspect.

"Goddamn it, I said don't touch it!" The man shoved her away. "I told you I'm fine. I couldn't breathe for a second and now I'm fine. Shit! I'm not a kid. You always treat me like a goddamn infant."

"Go to hell, Frank. I was checking because I care."

"Get off my dick, you nag. Go and take that rat-faced daughter of yours with you."

The little girl stuck to her mother's leg and buried her face in the flower patterned folds of her dress. The woman's mouth was open and quivering with shock and rage. "Don't talk to her like that. What in the hell, Frank?"

Kaitlin gave them a wide berth. "Excuse me, sorry," she said in a low voice.

The man and woman remained quiet as she passed, but as soon as Kaitlin got a few steps away she heard a growl and a scuffling of feet.

"I said leave me alone!"

He pushed the woman and child back. The little girl dropped to the sidewalk and the woman crashed into a chain link fence.

Kaitlin whipped around. "Are you kidding me?"

The man's pale eyes burned at her. "This is private. Go on. We're done here. Take that fake ass red hair with you."

"Fake?" Kaitlin almost lost it. She was always accused of that, but her scarlet hair was natural. "You need to leave right now buddy, or I'll call the cops."

"Oh," he said, taking a few steps toward her, throwing his arms left and right. "You may get one to come calling in say... uh, a *few weeks*, but go right ahead and call, sugar-tits."

Kaitlin met the end and did it without thinking. Her purse flew out, and perhaps halfway there to its mark, this guy's big stubbly stupid shitface, she regretted her choice.

But.

It was already done.

And maybe, not such a big regret.

Her strike connected and the man's head twisted around and his body followed in a punch-drunk ballet. The purse's center seam split and everything spilled out. Compact. Wallet. Grape bubble gum. Lip gloss. Tampon case. And something opalescent—when it struck the ground, two honey colored roots burst free and anchored into the concrete. A flake of stone nicked her arm and peeled some flesh away.

"Ouch!" she yelled.

The man staggered back, holding his swollen eye. "Goddamn ouch? *Ouch*? I'm gonna yank your head off, woman."

The bulbs Banch had given her—something Kaitlin had planned to eventually throw in her dish of rocks and pebbles at home—swelled with orange and green stalks that shot up and shoved the man into the woman. Both flew back to sit on the sidewalk with the child.

"The hell?" the woman shouted.

"I don't know!" the man shouted back. "Let's get!"

The trees grew around Kaitlin in a ring shape. Her impulse was to throw her arms up, but the trees weren't really growing, but instead *appearing*, and as her hand lashed out in front of her, the trees formed around it—she pulled back but two fingers caught inside the trunk. The inside became denser, squeezed her ring and pinkie finger with an ungodly strength that became something evil—it hurt so bad she chewed into her lip and couldn't even wail. The flesh, bone, and muscle blew up inside the tree and grisly bits spattered at her feet.

Kaitlin smacked against the other trees forming behind her. She held up her hand and saw the torn, bloody sockets where her two fingers had once been. The air blazed with midnight diamonds and dark starbursts that connected, married, and brought complete black.

Her blouse bunched up her back as she slid down the tree trunks and passed out.

When Kaitlin opened her eyes her gaze was pointed at the redness of bone, blood, and sinew on her shoes and the concrete sidewalk below. She tucked her bleeding hand under her arm and felt faint.

Banch had told her to stay still when using the bulbs, hadn't she? But Kaitlin didn't—wouldn't—have ever believed those bulbs magical. She thought Banch was giving her some kind of mystical hippie meditation instructions or something. What in the world was going on here?

"There is no magic," she said, in spite of the foreign trees flexing around her. It was obvious she'd inhaled some of that toxic gas the terrorists were using—it must have been that steam she saw wiggling up from the sidewalk. *You're a first-rate fool, Kait.* This was a convincing hallucination though—as well as the pain pounding in her exposed knuckles. Maybe she really had been injured, just not in the fashion she'd seen?

She bent closer to look at the pieces of her fingers on the ground and without any warning the red and pale bits burst into flame. The fire was aggressive, like it had met with gasoline, and it expanded from where the mess had been and reached the perimeter of the trees. Kaitlin grabbed onto the trunks and started to climb. Her gory, shattered hand painted the beige bark as she went. It hurt like nothing she'd ever experienced before. She locked an arm around one of the thin trunks and peered down. The fire climbed with a steady flow of licking blue and white flames.

If this is a hallucination, I can just fall into that fire—it can't hurt me.

Heat waves blew back her hair, beads of sweat immediately covered her forehead, and she shook away that thought. "Hell with that," she said, and climbed higher.

Something struck her shoulder and pushed her down. She fought to keep hold on the trees. Looking up, she saw several other branches snap off as the trees grew together at the top. Four other branches fell down past her. She tried to flatten her body but couldn't—they struck her—she slipped—her legs dropped into the fire.

"No!" she wailed and scrambled up. The fire made a tremendous fluttering sound, as though it might die out, but instead it resumed its climb toward her, this time faster.

Another branch dropped and walloped the top of her head. She got a view of racing silver streams of pain and the accompanying fire below. She realized she'd let go of the trunks completely and held on with only her thighs. She started to slide and threw her arms back around the trees. Her legs stung as though badly sunburned, but not horrible considering direct exposure to the fire. She could deal with that pain, but as she scaled upward, the agony in her injured hand became a person of its own: raw, unrelenting, vindictive, and incapable of caring.

She was more than half way to the top now. A voice jabbered on from just outside the ring of trees.

"Well, how do we get in? There's smoke!"

"It's a chemo-dimensional reaction. She must have moved before it was done. Why did she use the bulbs? The Assembly isn't even here!"

It sounded like Jared and maybe that Banch woman. Kaitlin's mind, again, was probably doing naked jumping jacks, but still, she played along, even if this was a hallucination. "Jared? Is that you? I'm almost to the top!" she cried out.

"Keep going!" the woman's voice replied.

Kaitlin craned her neck and was slammed in the face with another falling branch.

She lost hold and fell.

Fire engulfed her completely. But something tingled around her body, especially in the two open wounds in her fingers—they pulsed in the bare sockets almost like an SOS and suddenly the fire sucked into the ground and the trees vanished.

Kaitlin stood there on the sidewalk, clothing lightly singed and her skin feeling like it'd spent the day at a nude beach with no sun block. The air around her hung with the odors of burnt paper and sweat. She hadn't realized it until now, but she was weeping. Jared bounded over and caught her.

Then everything went dark.

Chapter 18
Jared

The people affected by the Gilded Scream had to be shooed away. They set up a makeshift bed for Kaitlin with t-shirts and black fabric cushions from the bench in the restaurant's lobby. All were arranged on the sidewalk with exacting care. Many offered to drive her to the hospital, but one man insisted on calling his brother-in-law who drove an ambulance for a living. Other emergency calls were placed too. The bleeding in Kaitlin's hand wasn't completely under control at the moment, but much better than before. Thoroughly cleaned and bandaged, one of the gilded now kept her hand elevated.

"How did she not catch on fire? Those flames were so intense." Jared moved some crimson locks of hair away and touched his friend's flushed face. She slept a restless sleep.

Banch watched the street like an indomitable hawk. "The fire wasn't completely resident in this world. The chemo-dimensional reaction occurred by the coupling of her flesh and the trees. Two different groups of matter shared the same residency. She moved into the trees' space and that set off the reaction, causing a fire, which then lost all residence when she fell into it. It could have started a minor disturbance paradigm, but thankfully it did not."

"Makes sense," Jared muttered, shaking his head.

Banch silently said something—it sounded more like whispered singing than just mere words.

"What are you doing?" he asked.

"Since we've lost time and our edge with the Assembly, I'm working out one of the new screams I learned from my twin."

"I can take the car and drive to the beach," Jared told her. "I just need to make sure Kaitlin gets on her way to the hospital first."

"It wouldn't matter. The Assembly will be reestablished very soon. You would have to leave right now and there's still a chance of them intercepting you at the beach. Assuming they asked the Silent Kings for the Lung Spike as their second grant, their expense account has not run out. They still have one grant left, and I believe they'll use it for direct access to the beach through a corridor shadow. They've been avoiding going anywhere near the beach since the water scares them like nothing else, but they'll face their fears if they know they're going to lose you."

Kaitlin stirred and Jared leaned in closer. "Easy Kait, easy, we're getting you help."

"Knew the fire... was a hallucination," she said and smacked her dry lips. "Sucked in poisonous gas. *Terrorists.*"

"You're safe now."

Banch resumed practicing her new scream. The ginger-haired accountant holding Kaitlin's wounded hand in the air winced and supported his arm with his free hand.

"I can take it," Jared offered.

"No!" the man said, his eyes wide with disappointment behind the lenses of his glasses.

"I got this. Trust me. My muscles are only a bit tired."

"You've held it a long time. Let me take over and you can come back in ten minutes." Jared noticed the man's reluctance and added, "I don't want you to drop it."

In sullen agreement, the accountant nodded, and Jared gently took Kaitlin's wrist.

"I'll be back soon," the man said. "Going for Motrin in my car. Do you need anything?"

"No thanks."

He got up, and with one more thoughtful look back, shuffled across the street to the parking lot.

"Who were you just talking to?" Kaitlin asked. She had come more fully awake now.

"Oh," said Jared, "just someone who helped us out."

Her eyes darted around. "Don't see anyone."

"Kait," he said softly, "why the hell did you come here?"

Her eyes narrowed. "What has gotten into you, Jared?"

"Wait up, let's talk about you. Coming out here and almost getting yourself killed. What? Just in the name of babysitting me? You wouldn't have gotten hurt if you just listened to me and stayed put."

Kaitlin closed her eyes. For a few minutes he thought she'd slipped off again, but when her eyelids drew up once more, clarity was there, greater than it had ever been. "Jared, you're my best friend. I love you more than most of my own blood relatives—"

"STOP IT!" he shouted, and Kaitlin flinched at his volume. "You will *never* love me. Okay? You've only made my life harder."

"Just calm down for a second—"

"Just stay out of my life from now on," he said, looking her levelly in the eyes. "I don't need your help anymore."

"And how about her?" Kaitlin looked to Banch, who was doing a poor job of appearing to not listen to their discussion. "That's how it is?"

Jared seethed. "I need no one, okay? Nobody."

A moment later the whine of an ambulance rounded the street. Dozens of the gilded came out waving their hands and pointed at Kaitlin, making it impossible for the ambulance to miss her.

Jared didn't say anything else to Kaitlin. He spoke with the paramedics and gave them her purse, but that was all. In his mind the same idea kept repeating, *goodbye, so long, farewell, later...* His eyes watered at the insistent mantra. As the EMTs put Kaitlin into the ambulance on the stretcher, he saw her eyes watering too. It wasn't like her to cry.

Better to hurt now, my old friend, my first love, thought Jared. *If I escape today, I'll be gone in a few months, at best, and this will be easier.*

The doors of the ambulance shut.

Forgive me, Kaitlin.

Jared watched the ambulance hurry up the street, cars pulling to the side of the road. Banch rested a hand on his shoulder. "I'm sorry that happened."

He whirled around. "Nobody else was supposed to get hurt. You said that. How can I trust you now?" He pressed a fist between his eyes, shaking his head. "I'm just going to wait here. Screw this. Let them have me. I'm done. My knees are about to give anyway."

Banch thoughtfully pursed her lips momentarily. Over her eyes, a few flags of metallic magenta and brown hair rippled in the steady breeze. "Did you know the Assembly has a machine in the fortress that smashes a prisoner's groin with an anvil attached to a counter-weighted pendulum? The process goes until they decide to stop it. How do your knees feel now?"

"God…"

"And I might add, this is the machine the male prisoners often hope for after suffering other devices. It's the most forgiving of their toys."

Jared felt his muffuletta start to rise.

"I know why you told Kaitlin what you did, believe me I do," said Banch. "But whether you know it or not, I've been with you longer than her and you can't push me away so easily."

He folded his arms and sighed. "Fine. Then what the hell next?"

"This."

Banch opened her mouth. Something like a harp of gold lit inside her throat. All colors around them, on the ground, in the distance, in the air, began to separate and drift in different directions like strands of fog. The sun flickered overhead. Then, so suddenly, there were two suns—twelve—two-hundred—too many to conceive, and in the next blink the sky fell to night and the moon came out in a similar fashion, spraying multiple versions of itself across the heaves. Ghostly images of people flashed all around them, some with archaic clothing going back to the 1800s and beyond. The weather went from hot to cold to rainy to windy in seconds. Banch closed her mouth then, and the world at once returned to how it had been before. The glowing voice box in her neck quieted in intensity until it could no longer be distinguished.

"What… did you do?" he asked warily.

She rubbed at her throat a little. "That was the Chronos Scream. My first invocation but it seems to have worked, though if I hadn't stripped out my voice on that Swell, it would have worked better."

Jared noticed everybody frozen in place on the sidewalks. A pair of birds overhead appeared stuck in the sky. Even the cars in the street had halted.

"You've stopped time?"

"Not stopped, slowed it down. We have about twelve hours that will roughly translate into five real minutes. Had I more practice and less wear on my voice, I could have made this last for days, maybe weeks."

Jared's heart rocked violently in his chest, suspended on fraying wires.

"What is it?" she asked.

"Just this chest thing. I'll be fine." He glanced down the street in wonder. "We'll definitely make it to the beach if we have twelve extra hours. I think it's probably only about a few more hours of walking."

"Indeed, but I wanted to buy us more than just certainty. I want to spend some time together, resting," said Banch. "If you die today, before the scheduled date, the Assembly will claim you through a different banshee. You'll be like a special delivery package that goes immediately to their feet. All of this will be for nothing."

Detergent in hand, he limped along with her for a moment. His knees burned and shook. "That could happen? I thought it wasn't my time to go yet."

"Well, this day technically wasn't supposed to go this way for you. All this stress might invoke something earlier. We have to be careful."

"I'm not opposed to resting," he admitted. "If it's safe, I guess."

Banch took out a business card. It was for the Marriott hotel. "Remember when all those gilded insisted you put their contact information in your phone? Well, I got to talking to one of them while you were doing that. Apparently he operates several of these hotels. His office is located at one of them just a couple blocks away he said. He set us up in a suite while you were taking phone numbers."

"So you planned on this?"

"He offered without asking and I didn't bother saying no. But now it makes sense to take him up on it, right? It was meant to be. Let's take six hours together for ourselves, before moving on."

"I feel like we're still pushing our luck here."

"If you feel like leaving earlier, we certainly can. Let's at least rest your legs some."

"How could I say no to more time with you?"

She grinned. "There is a clothing store on the way. I want to change out of this uniform, okay?"

Jared reached out and took the banshee's hand. "I guess it's a date."

* * *

When Jared was twenty-five years old...

He went with his dad, Bob, on walks in the park. They were often the same route as those walks Jared had taken with his mother when she was still alive. He had grown used to them and his day became dependent on having a stroll after work.

It was spring and the world made that clear. Butterflies found purchase on the wind. Plant life restored to vibrancy. His father's hay fever was at two hundred percent. They both enjoyed this time, even though they rarely said much together. Bob sometimes talked about crucial Dodgers decisions in management or lamented about not being able to make it to spring training, but that was normally the extent of the discussions. So when he started talking about the weird sensation in his chest one afternoon, Jared almost paid it no mind; he was accustomed to tuning his father out.

"Hold on, hold on." He took Jared's shoulder. His face seemed to collapse under a tremendous weight and his eyes went glassy.

"Dad?"

"I have medication." Bob fell forward and Jared held him. His father wasn't as big as he used to be. He'd lost a lot of weight after his wife died and Jared held him easily. "In… the glove compartment."

"What do you mean? Medication for what? What's happening?"

Bob sank to his knees and Jared dropped down with him. "I can't find the car, Dad. I need help. You know that."

"We come this way every day!" Bob shut his eyes, his voice disgusted.

"Is it over there, that way?" Jared pointed. His heart pounded in his throat. His hands trembled fiercely.

"I have to lie down." His father curled into a fetal ball right there on the grassy hill. He dug into his pocket and handed Jared the car keys.

Memories of the next moments had a painful razor blade quality to them; they stuck finely in Jared's mind, but each moment was its own and nothing connected it.

He got lost trying to find the car.

He ran into a nice couple walking their dog.

They helped him find the car.

He got lost finding the right hill again.

When he did find him, his father was still coherent and took the pills.

The medication worked but Bob was admitted to the hospital that night. Jared recalled very little of that evening, except a moment where they quietly watched the full moon out the hospital window.

"I wonder how many people are staring at it like us," his father said.

Jared shrugged. "A lot, probably."

Jared remembered how his mother had called the moon just a big rock in the sky, nothing special. He didn't want to bring that up though.

"How many dreams and wishes are aimed up there, right now?" Bob scratched the top of his bald head with the tip of the heart monitor on his finger. "It's a magic thing, the moon. I've always thought so."

"I guess it could be."

"Oh, it is." He nodded, taking another long look at the radiant sphere. "And you know why I know that?"

"Why?"

"Because I don't understand its power over me, and that's real magic, son. It makes me happy sometimes when I can't for the life of me find anything to be really happy about. Such power there. So, so powerful. It's a wonder and it belongs to us all."

Jared continued to watch silently.

Two days later, Bob Kare passed away. Jared, Kaitlin, and his estranged sister, Jared's aunt Becky, were at his bedside. Natural causes were cited. Jared never learned what his father's medication had been for. The events were too blurred together and his emotions too out of sorts. He wasn't in a place to care about the cause. His dad was gone. The last piece of his protection blown to bits. His desperation kicked into high gear.

After they were led out of the hospital room, he remembered Kaitlin slipping her hands around his waist and drawing him close. He got an erection, and hated himself for it. This was supposed to be a solemn time and here he was getting hard. He prayed she didn't feel it. If she had, Kaitlin must have been so disgusted, not just because she wasn't interested but because it was awful timing. *Awful.*

But she held him tighter. Closer. The air became her perfume 212. He loved her... so much, it was stupid. He had to be mental. The only way he could get past this moment was through her and yet he knew he'd hold her back, just as he had with his parents, until their deaths. They died unhappy because he wasn't brave enough to take care of himself.

It was inconceivable. He couldn't believe his father was gone. His grandfather had lived to ninety-two years of age. This genetically didn't compute—plus his father had taken his meds in time. Hadn't he? Had Jared's taking so long and getting lost contributed somehow? Or had it just been a matter of time?

At the wake, Jared heard nothing said. People actually stood and clapped after Kaitlin's speech, but Jared had heard none of it. He could only think of his first memories of his father. He must have been around three or so. His dad needed to go into the gas station to pick up cigars. He'd pointed at the gear shift and said, "Don't mess with that. I'll be right back."

Jared recalled a sense of indignation. Here was a grown-up trying to keep him from something interesting. He moved the stick into neutral. The pick-up truck rolled back. He remembered seeing his dad hauling ass to catch up with the vehicle before it dropped into the street and into oncoming traffic. Somehow he caught up with the truck, opened the door, and threw the parking brake.

Jared's next recollection was crying into his dad's shoulder. His father wasn't angry, even though Jared assumed he'd be. Bob hummed a song, the bass vibrations going through Jared's chest, calming every wicked, sharp-toothed beast gnawing from within.

That day, when he realized his father was gone forever, Jared longed to feel that humming again, that gentle sound flowing through him.

But that was done, over. He was alone, in silence.

His father's favorite mechanic, Bae, and his wife, Eun Sun, visited Jared every day that week and the week after. The visits became steadier and more frequent, until they were incorporated firmly into his existence. The Kangjuns and Kaitlin, from there on out. He loved them, and Jared would always know, without a doubt, that he owed them his life.

Chapter 19
Jared

Jared was surprised how quickly Banch found something to wear in the department store. She went into the changing room with black boots, a white off-the-shoulders mesh dress, and knee high stockings. She came out happy and didn't need to try anything else on or vacillate between wardrobe choices. Perhaps just being in clothing other than her uniform was enough, but it was definitely a different experience for Jared. His mother, and even Kaitlin, as tom-boy-indifferent as she was about clothes, had always made the women's department a trial of forbearance, and the boredom of waiting around through countless changing room visits and then to not buy anything at all—well, it used to make Jared wish for an immediate store evacuation switch.

Earlier, while waiting for Banch in the changing room, the other shoppers moving so slow they might as well have joined the mannequins, Jared's thoughts had turned to Kaitlin. It hadn't been the goodbye his best friend deserved. He hoped, so, *so* badly, she might understand why he pushed her away. She deserved much more from life. He'd relied on her just like he had on his parents and he'd stifled her happiness with his weakness. It made him sick with grief, but strangely happy he'd finally set her free.

In the end, all she had to lose were a few fingers.

He'd flinched at the thought.

A moment later, Banch slid out from behind the door's white curtain and his heart just about seized. It could have been any outfit. It could have been any moment. But this outfit and this moment conjured its own unique electricity. Beautiful. The word didn't service the person who stood before him at all. Not in the least. Everything about her spoke volumes of femininity, but there was also such power there, nothing fragile or vulnerable. Where she stood was the center of Jared's universe, of every universe; all else became lonesome planets revolving around such a pure focus, and he was grateful for orbit, for the warmth of this sun.

"I want make-up," she said.

"Are you kidding?" He laughed incredulously. He was still stunned. The smoothness of her legs, neck, and the slope and divide of her breasts. Her hair, while a bit messy from the day's travels, still draped over her shoulders in ribbons of delicious color that his eyes could happily devour for days. "Like you… even need make-up. You don't, Banch. You really, really don't."

"I want to try some. Can your knees hold out or do you need to find a place to sit down?"

"Oh yeah, yes, of course. I'll be okay. Let's go check it out." He searched around and spotted a glassy, well-lit area across the store. "That's probably a good bet. I think the stuff is over there."

She slipped her arm through his and Jared warmed from his chest all the way to the ends of every hair on his body. They walked not far before Banch stopped at a kiosk with themed stationary. She picked up one with seagulls and the ocean. "We'll be at the beach soon. Hey, does one of these remind you of Fatso?"

Jared chuckled. "Sure. My first good friend. Silly little boy that I was."

"You were sweet. You still are."

He bowed his head in embarrassment while she took out one of the card stock and ran her thumb over it in circles. "These are nice. In the Free Zone, when I was sent on an errand for the Assembly, I visited the parchment maker Felderman. He showed me his process, and I had the privilege of handling some of his new products. You can taste and smell the ideas printed on his stationary, almost *feel* them in a way. I think you'd like the experience."

"Sounds like dropping acid or something."

Banch hummed in agreement and put the box of cards back. "I suppose it would! Only the senses aren't really confused by chemicals. In the Deeper Unseen they are united in a most natural way."

"I wish I could go there."

"Only some places," she pointed out. "And you would have the same problem I do here, which is you'd need to keep close to the ground or risk losing residency."

"So no road trips in cars for me in the Deeper Unseen, I guess."

"We don't need vehicles. Traveling is a matter of touching the world with your eyes."

"Okay."

"It's not something you can easily understand."

"Agreed!" Jared grinned.

Banch smirked and bumped him playfully with her shoulder.

"Are you worried about your other assignments?" he asked. "All those people you should be sending on their way to the Light right now? Leaving them just to come help me?"

"There are a lot of good people," she replied. "And plenty of good banshees as well. I'm not worried. They've taken up my other assignments without reservation. My kind treat our job like a necessity of living, like a biological process, not an obligation. One doesn't curse the thin air in the mountains; you just breathe deeper and move with more purpose. I would do the same for any one of them, and have, many times."

"So if your honored job is that second-nature, why didn't you just send me on my way, as planned? Why not let me get taken? I'm just one of many. What for, Banch?"

"Why?" She raised an eyebrow full of glittering stars.

"Yeah, why?"

"Because this." She pulled him over and crushed her lips into his. Jared held her and ran his fingers down to the small of her back and gripped there as she hungrily sucked his lips and tasted his tongue. When she drew away, nothing existed around him except their eyes locked on each other. It was a brief moment, them staring at each other, but he was fine with that. More than fine.

"So, okay?" she said.

He smiled. "You're crazy, but okay."

"I know, right? You *so* aren't worth it."

"Hey!"

She pulled him along. They passed a couple mannequin sets and he noticed Banch slowed at each one before stopping to study one particular lingerie piece. She shook her head. "You humans sure do love your tits, don't you?"

Jared shushed her and she gave him a sly glance. "Uh, time's nearly at a halt, nobody's going to hear us, Uptight Timmy."

"I know." He shrugged. "But still, come on."

"You aren't such a prude at home watching on the computer—"

"Buhbuhbuhbuhbuh," he shouted and put his hands over his ears.

She giggled, tightened her grip on his hand, and dragged him forward. He couldn't help himself and had to ask. "Did you... really watch every time?"

"Yep!" she said proudly.

Jared grabbed his face in shame.

"Oh, now this I can get behind though," said Banch.

He looked up at an ad poster: a woman's mouth with dark purple lipstick at the partition of her lips.

"The mouth and tongue. Now those are truly amazing things."

Jared snorted. "So is that what your kind obsess over?"

"No, it is the music that emerges from the mouth. The meaning of the sound, the feeling derived there. The voice makes it."

He cleared his throat. "So what's your taste in voices? Bass?"

"Oh, that's personal."

"*That's* personal?" he asked, amazed.

"Yes sir."

"Alto?"

"Personal!" she reaffirmed, and put a finger to her lips. "I remember before your voice changed. I still hear that little boy sometimes when you speak. And I can also hear the man you want to be."

He grew uncomfortable and gestured to the counter. "Okay, enough picking on me. Here you go. Make-up galore."

She went to the racks and searched around. Behind the counter a woman with a retro rockabilly hairdo pointed somewhere to another customer, a woman in her fifties wearing a beige pea coat. Banch took in the range of cosmetics before her.

"Anything strike your fancy?" he asked.

She shrugged. "I'm not certain. I don't know what would look good. Can you pick something?"

Jared backed up. "I don't—"

"Stop being so damned scared about things. Pick something!"

He chose a brownish red lipstick and handed it to her. She gazed at it for a long while.

"Different color?" he asked.

"No, I just... what if it makes me look ugly to you?"

Jared straightened. "Then I'm an absolute dick. Ain't gonna happen though."

The banshee smiled, but set the lipstick back on the counter. "On second thought, I don't want to be different to you. I want you to remember me like this."

"Okay, Banch, okay. Like I said, you need nothing."

She held up a hand. "Let's go on to the hotel. I want to lie beside you in a place where lovers go. This is a gift and I want to enjoy it as long as we can."

Jared didn't have a chance to answer before she was heading for the exit. Quickly, he swept the lipstick off the counter and stuffed it in his pocket.

* * *

Jared fiddled with the hotel's computer and hoped he was making progress. It was difficult leaning over the receptionist with her hands poised over the keyboard; he almost sensed her fingers creeping toward the keys at a snail's pace.

"Wish there were just real door locks like back home," said Banch. She leaned against an ornate stone fireplace in the lobby.

"I almost got it," said Jared. "Nice. This is the only suite they have on the first floor. What name did you give him?"

When she didn't answer, he looked up. Banch was grinning ear to ear. "Betty."

He chortled. "Really? Betty who?"

"Kare, of course."

"Of course," he replied and shook his head, smiling. He pulled up the reservation and it prompted him to swipe a card for the room.

"Boy, I wish you'd known this scream from the beginning… takes a lot of pressure off us."

"You and I both. My twin didn't know the Swelling Scream—I wonder if she'll ever apply it?"

"She comes from a hard reality. I'm sure it'll come in handy."

Banch said nothing and it wasn't the first time he felt small compared to her wisdom. She could have pressed him to know more about the twin, but she didn't. He always asked a million questions, but sometimes silence was called for instead. He wanted to learn that, even if he only applied it for the next few months before it was done.

He just wanted to be a person like Banch.

Jared searched for the key cards and found a box under the desk. Swiped one. Room 125, the screen declared. He held the card up dramatically. "I've done it!"

Banch pushed off the wall and slapped both of her hips. "Never doubted you!"

The room was a short walk past the elevators, with only one turn down a T-section hallway. He had to turn the card over several times before he managed to engage the lock. Upon opening the room, he felt a gust of frigid air coming from the air conditioner. Someone had set it very low. They walked in and both took a look around. It probably wasn't the hotel's nicest suite, but it didn't bother Jared and he doubted Banch cared either. The size of the space was impressive though. Several cylindrical ceiling lamps hung over the vast ceiling like glowing paper sushi rolls. A chocolate egg-shaped table sat in the center of the living room area with burgundy couches surrounding it. The walls were painted dark brown and the carpet, with its kaleidoscopic designs, had gold and rust colored fibers. Several trays of complimentary cheeses, crackers, hard candy, and assorted flowers had been brought in and set around the room.

"I like it!" Banch cried out and clapped her hands. "Open that champagne, unless… do they have beer? I never got one at the restaurant."

Jared searched the fridge. "No, just the bubbly. What a jip!"

"Damn. This would have been a good occasion for you to have a beer, don't you think?"

He shrugged. "I don't know. I guess so."

"You *guess* so? Come on, Jared! You haven't had sex in ages."

"What? We're, you, me, we're? *What?*"

"Don't be dense. We could have *rested* anywhere. Isn't this what people do? Go to hotels? When did you last lay with someone? That Denise woman with the kids?"

Jared sighed. "I keep forgetting you know everything."

"Saw everything, but I don't *know* everything. Big, big difference."

"Okay." He set the champagne down on the kitchen counter.

"Sorry." Banch batted her eyelashes. "I won't mortify you anymore."

"Thanks."

"Can I ask something though?"

"I think you will, no matter what."

"Why'd you leave Denise? I never understood that. I know you say you aren't into kids, but from an external view, it seemed like you really cared about her and would have been willing to do anything to make it work."

Jared bowed over the kitchen drawers to look for a corkscrew. "The kids were nice. Michael and Michelle. They were actually better than nice—great, as children go."

"Am I ruining this?" asked Banch. "You don't have to say anything, if you don't want to."

Jared found a corkscrew in with the oven implements. He waved it at her. "Absolutely not. It's fine."

He stared at her, unblinkingly, and then had to remember what he'd been trying to do. He hurried to the champagne.

Banch picked up on this and her mouth hitched at the side in a devious fashion. "So you want me pretty bad? Don't you?"

He squeaked, "I don't know... what you mean."

She threw her head back and laughed. "You gonna break open that bottle or stand there clutching the corkscrew?"

He returned to the bottle with focused diligence, and began stripping off the black foil wrapper over the cork. As he embedded the corkscrew's point, he had a few flashbacks to his parents. His mom always had him open her wine for her. The secrecy she shared with him, and the secrecy his father shared with nobody, gave him pause.

"Denise..." he said, not looking up from the bottle, "was a wonderful woman. She only wanted someone to love her in the way she was prepared to love. Her kids came first but she was dedicated to making her partner a top priority as well, one of the treasures of her life."

"Then what happened?" Banch slowly approached, arms folded over her chest. "Even Kaitlin was fond of her, from how I saw it. And she's pretty critical."

"Yeah, she definitely was." Jared tensed. He wanted Banch so bad and felt he might undo everything in only a few sentences, speaking of someone else he once had feelings for. "Remember when I lost her son Michael at the park that one time? I'd been the one watching him."

The banshee stood behind him. Her breath on his neck was gentle. She glided her hands over his shoulders and hugged him around the neck. "Yes. You were scared when he went missing."

He turned to face Banch. "It was more than that. I loved that kid. That boy, his sister, and their mother… and even though it wasn't a big deal, I knew that somehow, in the future, I'd lose one of the kids again. I knew I wasn't enough. I would fail them. Being a father wasn't something I was born to do, I guess."

Banch pressed her lips together thoughtfully and then said, "And now Denise is remarried."

Jared's eyes warmed. "Yep," he replied.

Putting a slender finger under his chin, Banch lifted his eyes to hers. "You poor baby. Do you need me to hold you?"

They embraced. It was different than in the department store. Jared's emotions raced ahead of his body. Holding her was more unreal than anything that had happened today.

"Do we have to… be careful? I don't have anything with me. I just, I mean, oh God, sorry—"

Her moist, hot lips touched his neck and sent a thrill through him. "Thank you for asking, but though I have a human form, I cannot bear children."

"Why is that?"

She squeezed him. Her entire body fit into his and both their hearts thundered together, his with its unnatural, awkward rhythm, and hers with pounding strength.

"The old Kings, when they still used their voices, spoke of humankind often and it affected the Deeper Unseen. The human form, the body, was a motif there, from buildings, to biology, to the cosmos. This was no exception with my kind. We are born from

Symphony Roses, and when the wind howls through their flute shaped blossoms at the exact, perfect pitch, we begin to grow within them. We spend our childhood snuggled in the petals, suckling nectar, learning the billions of strings in our throat, practicing like a musician might for the performance of her life. Once we find the ending of every progression, every chord, every emotion contained therein, the ending of what we are, the Divine note, we can crawl out of the rose's cup—the Mother's Cup—and that's the day we commence our duty to the dead."

"Do you have a belly button then?"

Banch tittered at his unexpected question and took his hand, placing it up under her new blouse. "Why wouldn't I?"

His finger traced the circular knot of flesh in her abdomen.

"You weren't born from a human body."

"That doesn't matter. When the Old Kings thought of our kind, at our inception, they imagined a woman who nobody would fight death over, someone a soul would willingly surrender for. Some see us as mothers, some see us as lovers. But all are taken with us."

Jared took a trembling breath in. "They did a good job with that."

"I'm glad you approve." She drew away and stared him in the eyes. "We can't go on the bed. It's elevated."

He took her behind the neck and felt his hunger build beyond capacity. "We wouldn't make it there anyway."

He brought her face into his and they consumed each other. After kissing, becoming so dizzy, they collapsed near the couches. Banch's mesh dress stretched and ripped and all her new clothes, along with his, ultimately went to all corners of the room.

She was above him when she climaxed.

He had been in another place.

Another time.

Floating.

And he didn't realize at first what had happened, and what the sound leaving her luminescent throat would end up meaning.

She'd accidently let loose a Divine Scream.

He sobbed into her shoulder after his own release. Banch whispered an apology to him and then passed out, for which he'd always be grateful, because the Divine Scream had changed everything all at once and now he knew he had to get moving. He had to leave her here and go out on his own. Never before in his life was Jared Kare so certain of what needed to happen next.

Chapter 20
Jared

Banch had lied to him. She hadn't made the painful trip to this world because she loved him. That might have been part of it, but it wasn't the real reason. It certainly wasn't her original intention. Jared knew this for certain because of the Divine Scream. Its power had put details into his mind that were like scripture from Banch's heart and history. Other than the Swell's impact on her power causing fragments here and there, making the whole story somewhat incomplete, he knew almost every emotion she'd ever possessed in her long life, and he knew most of the thoughts leading up to those emotions. Likewise, he knew about the Deeper Unseen, almost like a map of the dimension had been emblazoned into the back of his mind.

The Divine Scream was one of the few physical response screams, not like any other she'd performed that day. In her ecstasy, she'd let it slip and the very last recorded feeling that surged into him was the self-hate she felt for allowing it to happen. She knew her secret was out now. That's why she'd apologized before dozing off; from what Jared understood about the Divine Scream, Banch would be out for several hours. Sharing your soul in that fashion took everything from you. This was fortunate, however, because it gave him enough time to do what needed to be done.

He put his clothes back on and went to the bathroom to wash his face. It was terrifying to have so much new information inside him; he felt as old now, possibly, as Banch did, having memories of so many experiences and locations. Helpful to his plans now, but still intimidating to possess such a wide breath of knowledge and understanding of life and death and the dimensions. Jared's mind connected with various locations of corridor shadows throughout the city. He was sure he could find the correct one long before Banch awakened. He imagined he'd be ruminating on her history the whole way there.

Over the last two centuries, Banch had become quite disillusioned. She lost every sense of time and her belonging to the multiverses. No other banshees understood her sorrow or her love for humans and they referred to her sometimes as "She with an error in the heart." After a time Banch wouldn't even bathe with her sisters in the velvet ponds or go into the diamond gardens to feast. Banch became a lonesome creature who worked ceaselessly, taking on more assignments than any other before her.

Then came Martha Peters, a favorite of Banch's. She was a young single mother taken in a horse carriage accident after leaving off her children at the schoolhouse. Banch sent the call, but before Martha could embrace the light, corridor shadows split the main road of Woodward County and the Assembly came crawling out to claim their gift. That was not long after the turn of the century, but Banch, being tied to this assignment, kept her mind's eye on the Assembly's exploits of Martha for decades to come. Feeling helpless, she elected to do something no other banshee before her had: she moved into the Assembly's fortress so she could be near enough to help Martha whenever possible.

The Assembly gave Martha children. They raised their spawn to become her own private torturers. So wicked and cruel were these children, other prisoners in the fortress referred to them as the Grim Three. They enjoyed finding new ways to make their mother scream. After their maturation the fortress became a place of endless suffering, for even when the Assembly departed to keep the dimensional structures intact, the Grim Three remained to savage their mother and other prisoners. No doubt, they would join the Assembly someday when positions became free. In the meantime though, they spread enough chaos in that place to almost rival their fathers.

Something had to be done, and so Banch made the first of two infiltrations of the lower dungeons. The initial descent was to save Martha from her new ghastly children. Banch would make the call again and let Martha's poor soul finally go on to rest. But despite the difficulty and danger in reaching her, when Banch offered an escape the woman would not take it. She refused to go. The savagery in the fortress often infused a prisoner's heart with dark love and Banch couldn't convince her to walk into the light. None of the prisoners would ever go willingly, from what she discovered. They loathed and loved their horrid existence.

Banch went on after that episode not knowing if she could continue her duty. She confided in her own banshee, but the concept of abandoning their role could not be fathomed, and she gained nothing from that conversation other than to reinforce how alone she really was in all of this.

The Assembly got accustomed to Banch's presence in the fortress and they imposed work on her. When not calling souls on, she ran errands for them across the Deeper Unseen. Some of the tasks were loathsome—such that Jared didn't even want to think of them.

Just last year, Banch finally broke and resolved to end her existence. The only way she knew how, since banshees were immortal in the Deeper Unseen, was to find a lasting way to disconnect from reality. There were certain screams she could have performed but they would have likely caused disturbance paradigms that may have harmed others. The safest way would be to manifest in the human dimension and throw herself into the Paled Ocean, which would negate her existence.

So the second time she infiltrated the lower dungeons of the fortress, she sought to locate the Assembly's map of corridor shadow routes. She could memorize them all in an instant and then know the correct pathways to become *mostly* resident in the human world.

In the dungeon archives, however, she found more than she bargained for. A missive from one of the Silent Kings named Jared Kare as the next gift. Banch had known he was scheduled soon but had never anticipated him being the gift. In fact, she had already taken solace in the fact that she wouldn't be around anymore to make the call on his life. He was her favorite assignment in this era—she might have even fallen hard for his sweet odd ways, if falling in love was even possible for her ancient mind now.

Then it came to her. The perfection of it all. The Paled Ocean would set both of them free. She would get to visit the human world in the flesh and get to meet an assignment face-to-face without calling their death. And in the end she would be wiped off the slate of all known universes and never need to witness Jared's or any other person's passing again.

The Assembly would likely go after them, but if she managed to get her and Jared to the ocean right away, perhaps with a Cosmos Scream, she would have some time to hold them off with a Swell. If they killed her, or the ocean killed her, it all worked out the same way. Jared had nothing else to lose. It was worth a shot. Not even the worst people deserved to become a gift and she couldn't leave without knowing she'd tried to save him from that. Then, of course, the paradigm formed and the trip became much longer than she'd planned for. She got more time with Jared though, and she didn't regret that.

Jared knew now, also, where he would die—at his office desk, suffering from some sort of attack, clutching a scrap of paper with his handwriting on it: *Schedule with Doc*. The details surrounding it were foggy; again the Divine Scream's potency had been hindered by the Swell and some memories lacked clarity or conclusion. That wasn't completely a bad thing though. Banch's heart had a lot of memories of death and people to share, so Jared was glad he didn't have it all.

Trying to be quiet, he located the box of detergent sitting near the door. Banch intended to use that to cause a chemo-dimensional reaction in a series of corridor shadows, making it near impossible for the Assembly to take a direct route to the beach. The shadow where it needed to be dumped was about a mile from the hotel, but Jared had other intentions now. He'd pour this stuff right into the heart of their fortress, into the chamber where the Grim Three slept. The Assembly would need to return there to deal with the chemical fire and save their children. Banch would have time to escape into another shadow, most likely near the border of the Free Zone, and Jared would get his chance to bathe in the ocean. The most unfortunate part was Banch would never be able to return to this dimension, not in that territory; there were no corridor routes in the Free Zone that would give her so much physical residency as she had now. That was the price. But she could still live, if she chose to.

Jared thought a moment. The shadow leading to the fortress would be backtracking a bit, but with time still slowed down there was nearly ten hours left. The sleeping banshee stirred a bit under the comforter on the floor. He'd propped her head up with a pillow and it was a breathless display for him. He wanted to admire his lover forever. This would be his last time laying eyes on her. He prayed she took this chance to escape and continue to live, but he could only control so much.

With some hotel stationary he wrote a note to her:

Dear Banch,

I'll never, ever forget you. I know you don't want to go on, but I can't see you die. I can't. So please go to the Free Zone. I'm setting fire to the central chamber of the fortress. The Assembly will go back, if not for their kids, for their prisoners. You know they will. I may be important, but I'm just one gift of thousands.

In the Free Zone, you will still be obligated to call deaths, but you will have another chance. You will be ALIVE. Forgive me for being too selfish to give you what you really want. I can't. I'm in love with you. Please take this, and always remember me and our time together.

--J

Jared set the tube of lipstick on top of the note, which he'd placed across her dress on the coffee table. His desire to kiss her one last time was intense, but he could not risk waking her. He would remember every one that came before though. His one, perfect girl. He felt so fortunate he'd had the chance to meet her in this dimension. He wondered if any other Jareds had had that chance. And if they did, could they have remained together forever?

With that he left the banshee sleeping there on the hotel room floor.

He closed the door, without looking back.

Chapter 21
Jared

He'd never known such peace. His knees creaked, legs burned, heart rattled, and lungs wheezed from the stresses suffered earlier, but Jared could not help but admire the serenity of a world in freeze-frame. He kept watching the faces of people—caught in mid-expression, some were comical and others were honed on boredom, joy, sullenness, or anxiety. He was walking through a photograph, through an instant in so many lives, and despite time not being completely stopped, this was only a matter of micro or nanoseconds to the people on the sidewalks; the birds stitched into the air with invisible thread, their wings holding the wind at the peak of every feather; the rows of palms with fronds flared, making the vaulted trees look like giant flowers.

He took a brief rest on a bench to give his knees a break. Once he poured the detergent into the shadow he wondered how long it would take for the fire to catch in the Deeper Unseen. Time had slowed everywhere, he presumed, so he might be at the beach well before the Assembly even discovered what he set into motion. It was difficult to get all this stuff straight, but the only thing that really mattered was buying Banch enough time to escape to the Free Zone.

If she listens...

But he got this idea from Banch's memories, after all. She'd originally thought this a viable option in dealing with the Assembly, but decided the path would take them farther from the beach and they couldn't risk the extra time. Those thoughts were made well before she learned the Chronos Scream however.

"Whole new world now," Jared muttered.

On the sidewalk ahead he spotted a man howling with laughter, his hands planted on his knees. A younger man had his head thrown back, laughing too. Something obviously was pretty hilarious. Jared wished he knew what it was.

Jared reached down and massaged his kneecaps. Not even a half marathon in distance and he was giving out like an old man. What if this had something to do with his condition? He ran his wrist over his sweaty brow. He knew one thing now. He would be taking a bunch of time off from work. He'd be damned if his last days were spent wrangling data and messing with accounting spreadsheets.

A scrap of paper flashed in his mind.

Schedule with Doc.

Some of the fragments of information regarding his death had finally settled in his mind, or at least how everything had been expected to happen. Jared would learn of some ailment and have to schedule a follow-up with a cardiologist. Kaitlin will get the part she auditioned for and have to fly out to London two weeks from now. The Kangjuns will leave to visit family in Busan.

They are still in Korea and Kaitlin is still in London when Jared dies. *Nobody will be around. You're alone when it happens.*

"And now Kaitlin's hurt, and you were an asshole to her," he whispered. His eyes warmed with regret. "You're such a jackass. Always, always."

Trying to put that out of his mind, he dragged over the box of detergent. He would be grateful to shed this extra weight. He eyed the auburn shadows randomly located throughout the city. He could un-see them if he chose, sort of like letting your vision go loose and blurring things together. Because he had so much of Banch in him though, his own mind was connected to the other dimension. His connection was limited only to the sense of sight, which he'd now learned was the most inferior of all senses. It was still a pleasure to behold these shadows and their depths.

He mused on how many other people had ever glimpsed into the Deeper Unseen. No such instances were recorded in his banshee's head. Most of Banch's memories involved normal, everyday people meeting their end, peacefully, violently, or anything in between. In every circumstance, she made the call and a tremendous ocean of light flooded their way. All they had to do was take a step into it. Nobody, outside of those in the fortress, had ever refused that light. Banch and the light were too much to resist. He understood now why she'd rather him go there than stay to be the Assembly's plaything for eternity. He loved her even more for trying to spare him that, and with her past recollections he realized Banch could easily end up back there, under their order for trying to save him. Then she would never have a way out. She'd need to perform her morbid duty until the end of time.

An awful taste flooded Jared's mouth. Suddenly he felt bad for resting so long. His legs shaking and his tail bone on fire, he stood with the substantial detergent box, the plastic handle eating into his palm. He thought about the Kangjuns and hoped they were doing okay. He knew they were alive but hoped those blood drenched monsters hadn't made a lasting wound in their minds.

Jared grinded his teeth, feeling responsible yet again. He tried to push all the guilt far from his mind. Then push all the deaths a banshee had to endure out too. He could switch it off, but the rub was not being close to Banch. Going through her emotions and scattered memories was almost as intoxicating as spending time with her. Shutting it out made him feel cold.

When *the* corridor shadow came into sight, he couldn't help himself and started running. The slanting bloody splash leading to the fortress sat just left of a Chevron gas station, along the wall, near an air compressor. Jared ripped the cardboard band and pulled it around the detergent box. He opened the lid and took a smell of the white and blue crystal powder. It made him smile, the thought he would be cleaning the fortress of its filth.

"For the Grim Three. I hope you burn and all the prisoners escape." He carried the box to the shadow and lost no time overturning it there. Everything dumped out and disappeared inside. After a couple minutes all that persisted was a sweet, chalky cloud as a reminder. Feeling slightly victorious, he dropped the empty box with an immense sigh and took a step back.

Footsteps fell in a normal rhythm on the sidewalk behind him.

* * *

Jared cautiously searched around, looking down different alleyways. After a few minutes he hadn't found anyone but the sound of falling footsteps grew louder. He began thinking he might have imagined the whole thing, or maybe it was some sort of weird echo effect from pouring the detergent into the corridor shadow. Everything was still moving at a snail's pace, so it couldn't have been somebody walking nearby. It had to be Banch. But how had she recovered so quickly?

Then a person appeared before Jared, only a few feet away.

And it wasn't Banch.

It took a moment to recognize the teenager. He wasn't dressed in a Varsity football T-shirt and jean shorts and his hair wasn't buzzed. The guy hadn't aged a day since Jared last set eyes on him, but he now wore more mature attire: a powder blue polo shirt, brown slacks, and loafers. His hair was styled. The world had not resumed its normal speed and yet this person, whose name still escaped Jared, moved through time just like he and Banch did.

Jared pointed at him, too dumbfounded to ask a question. "You... we went to high school together."

A small smile.

"I can't remember your name."

"My name doesn't matter, Jared. What I am does, however," he said.

"How do you—wait—"

The teen held up his hand. "My kind normally don't reveal ourselves, but in this case I couldn't just subtly dabble in your life. There is often a misconception. You see, our silence isn't particularly not using words or making sounds, but rather that our identities are silent from all known worlds."

"How did you get here?"

"Strange that you and I always meet when you've chosen to do something foolish, or I daresay brave, for someone like you anyway. But, alas, this time the stakes are a bit higher than missing the school bus."

Jared blinked as the memory returned more fully. Yes. The day he'd met Kaitlin. "You're that kid who wanted my nudie magazine."

The teen snorted. "I only wanted to distract you, and set you on a different path. You had to meet Kaitlin that day. At least, in this reality. Oh, and by the way, that wasn't your magazine, Jared. That was truth in *all* realities."

"Tell me what you want with me."

"While my Assembly keeps the dimensions separate by physical application, that separation is *not* enough. Events within dimensions should never flow in similar directions. We cannot afford intersections to occur. My work is done in quiet secrecy. I'm in everyone's life. I'm the person you hardly recall, but never truly forget."

"Didn't you become an engineer after a car wreck... or something?"

"To some," said the teen. "To others I've been ruling the Deeper Unseen."

Slowly, Jared swallowed and his heart trembled. "You... you're one of the Silent Kings, aren't you?"

The teen nodded. "But I cannot remain silent at this stage, not with what you've just done. My intervention here must be loud."

"Why now?"

His pale pink lips twisted. "You should have studied the corridor shadow routes better before you went dumping hazardous dimensional compounds down them. The banshee had a better grasp of the routes and what you've gained from her through the Divine Scream wasn't enough to truly recognize all the potential paths. You've screwed up here, Jared. Royally."

"That route went right into the fortress," said Jared, his panic rising. "I saw it clearly! The inner chamber where the Grim Three live."

"Do you know," the Silent King said, stepping forward with a casual kick of his loafers, "that your chosen route branches off in three directions? And that the force of airflow is greater through one route than the other two."

"So what? They all end up in the same place!"

"No!" the Silent King shouted and pushed a hard finger into Jared's chest, making him stumble back. "One route goes straight through the inner chamber, with more force, and spills into the fissure where the Assembly performs their essential duties. It's called a *dimensional hinge* and the greatest chemical reaction will spread from there, not in the inner chamber."

Jared swallowed. He knew enough about the instability of the hinges to know this wasn't going to be good. "What will happen?"

The Silent King's blonde eyebrows lifted in amazement. "Such a fool... you've just instigated the largest disturbance paradigm *ever known*. And despite the banshee's decelerating of time, the disturbance has already started to evolve and spread."

"I—"

"Oh shut up, Jared Kare. You do know I have to spoil your playtime now? I must sever the remaining effects of the banshee's Chronos Scream. The chances for the dimensions to survive this paradigm will greatly improve if I intervene in this way. The destruction suffered while time drags on would be far greater. It would end *everything*. I've only dropped in to tell you this so you stop messing with things of which you have no understanding!"

Jared lowered his head. It wasn't fair. His plan should have worked. How could he have overlooked that corridor's destination? *Because your insight into Banch's memories is limited.* Yes, the Divine Scream hadn't given him every significant detail, even though he thought it had.

"So the fortress... will it still catch fire?"

The Silent King folded his arms and shrugged. "The paradigm will shift everything around. Some places will catch fire, and some places will explode, but not just the fortress." He pursed his lips in thought. "I've got my fingers crossed the Free Zone goes up in flames. That would be nice to see those jackasses scramble for a change."

"No! It can't! The Free Zone is too far. Isn't it?"

"Not with what you've done, Jared. Everywhere and every soul will suffer for your actions." With an agile turn of heel, the teenager started off. He lifted his hand and made a cutting motion in the air.

The next moment cars sped past, birds fired suddenly through the air like bullets, and people walked on unhindered. Time had resumed to its normal progression and the world became incredibly noisy all at once. The Chronos Scream's effects were over.

Jared stood there, too numb to form a coherent thought. The ground trembled underfoot. It was building, like a massive train rocketed underground through the soil, set for exploding through the upper crust.

"How can I fix this?" he yelled. "Please, you have to tell me!"

The teen gave him a pinched, disgusted look that seethed with impatience. "The Disturbance Paradigm is ready to take hold. I cannot give advice, but my Assembly has awakened now as well. This normally means a whole lot of running the hell away, for most wise people."

Jared broke off down the street, his feet flying beneath him.

The Silent King shouted through his hands, "See you in the fortress, my friend! *Soon!*"

Chapter 22
The Assembly

We had to push ourselves up. We had to reach our feet. Stand. That was foolish of us to risk the banshee's touch. She was stronger than we could ever know. We had to remember she believed she had more to lose than we did—such false conviction make a soul's fire burn higher and fiercer, and unexpected strength therein follows. But we'd known that! And should have remembered! We must have been blinded by the Gift being so close. It was impossible to help our elation sometimes—every hundred years seems to feel longer, each gift seems sweeter but less sustaining, and all the while, holding the dimensions apart becomes crueler, more painful and insane.

Writhing around in the alley, in the debris, we attempted to regain ourselves. Something strange had occurred, as though we'd held our breath for a long time and were now finally allowed to breathe.

Time has been played with.

For a few minutes we picked free metallic splinters from our bodies, but only those that pained us to move. The other shards would remain until we had more time to remove them. The Eighth had femoral bleeding from a collection under his thigh and the Second had a particularly nasty, lengthy shiv pushed through his jaw to the back of his ear. We all shuddered as he pulled it out.

A corridor shadow widened on the wall of a building. That would only occur if a being from the Deeper Unseen had the correct route, which was coveted by someone of great power. That knowledge made us shrink back. The shadow spread across the building, darkening a banner of obscene blue-white-orange graffiti painted along the bricks and then rippled across rusted iron bars covering an old dirty window. The auburn depths of the shadow cascaded to the ground and a rotting wooden palette that had rested against the wall fell momentarily inside the shadow before a loafer kicked it back out into the alley. A figure emerged.

"Yula'deem," we greeted, as the light clarified his features. We hadn't expected to see this Silent King. We hadn't seen any of them outside the fortress in around four hundred years, but that was a short time considering the familiar fire in his young eyes.

"Enter," he bade.

Some of us limped forward, while others braced against a dumpster for a moment before moving, but we obeyed.

We always did.

There wasn't a choice.

He was a vital organ for us...

All the Kings were. And one didn't argue with the demands of his liver or pancreas. You allowed them do their work and keep you alive. You trusted them with everything you had. That was how the Silent Kings were. We loved them, but knew, oh we completely understood to our marrow, what they were and what we meant to them. There was no shortage of true nothingness to define their indifference for us, and yet we hoped they'd love us anyway, just like our Gift had hoped his parents would love him. It was silly, but it was an unstoppable need.

We filed into the corridor and staggered out onto the fibrous, opalescent firmament. The fibers flexed underfoot, the artificial wind flowed on, and silver-gold-rust particles surged down the hall, which to an outsider might have been as alien as a god's esophagus. Only halfway to a junction, the Silent King stopped us.

"We are distressed."

"Why, our King?" we said, all of our heads bowing in shame.

"You've stocked too much interest into this Gift. He's only one in so many."

"One?" We gasped. "But he is ours."

The Silent King nodded. "Indeed."

"It's time. We want our gift so much, our King."

"You will have your gift—when have you not?" he nearly growled.

"You are a gracious, loving, cherishing, uplifting, beautiful, kind, tolerant, and worthy King."

We meant it.

Every word.

Every.

Word.

The scent of sharp electrified steel bit into our nostrils. We stumbled back. Linen. Soap. White resolve. Blue crystal death. It went up in the air, everywhere. To the top of the ceiling, to the lowest crevice of the floor. The fire. The flesh. Then the rendering of fat.

"What has occurred here?" we asked.

"A massive undoing," the King answered.

We already sensed that. The Silent Kings would not reveal themselves for a lesser cause. "How large is the Disturbance Paradigm, our King?"

"Four times the size of the unhinging of 1734," he whispered.

"*Four* times?" Our voices flared in the sliding darkness and dust.

"You will need to see to the hinges and help the effort to restore the separation."

"At once," we replied, and followed out of the corridor into another. We walked on, heads buzzing with the same question: what did this mean for our gift? Would we lose him? That couldn't happen. That shouldn't be *allowed* to happen. "Was this the banshee's doing again? How did this paradigm conceive?"

"Ignorance and haste," said the King. He took us through the last sweeping corridor into an inverted room. Bricks bled into each other and super-heated inside like cores of magma burned within. It took us several moments to realize we'd come to one of the inner chambers of the fortress. The Disturbance Paradigm had reconfigured the shape of the room and made all the stone brick unstable, volatile. Our mouths dropped open in shock.

"It wasn't the banshee who caused this," said the King. "It was your beloved gift. He did this while you were sleeping off your failure." All the remaining slivers of the Lung Spike embedded in our skins stung deeper at that moment. The King beckoned us on. "I will lead you to the hinges so you can begin your work."

Hollowness expanded through us like a soul-devouring disease. After an anxious rush down several more warped passageways, the Silent King, not breaking stride, spoke again: "Before you enter the Space, I want you to consider something. I will make an exception this time and your third grant can be a new gift. This Jared Kare and the rebel banshee have caused more disruption than they are worth. Once the Paradigm is handled, I can send you another gift—male, female, young, old, or in-between. That will suffice your needs, I'm certain."

We bowed our heads in thanks. We would not risk going the next hundred years empty handed. This was a generous offer from our King.

We continued toward the space when a voice hailed from a hall filled with pulsing orange-red rubble.

"Fathers," the voice said.

One of our children. Amaen. Flesh a ghostly white, he was so bloodied and disfigured we might not have recognized him but for his voice. Dirt and crumbles of mortar caked his wounds. A large one in his neck coursed with fresh scarlet spillage. We rushed to his side, the ten of us surrounding him in a protective circle.

"There is no time for this!" the Silent King hissed.

Amaen choked on some blood. "My brother and sister are dead, Fathers. The walls folded and chopped them into..." His voice broke at the word. "Pieces."

Our bodies trembled. We didn't know what to say, what to do.

"Before it got very bad, I had time to check the prisoners and oldest Gifts. They are frightened with the size and scope of this disturbance, but they are alive. Some are trapped behind walls, but they are alive and still serviceable... we didn't fail you Fathers... we didn't fail."

With a violent twitch, Amaen clutched the Fourth and the Seventh's wrists and his body twisted for a breathless second before the last of his life poured from his neck, and then he went still. We could say nothing. We could feel everything. It had taken several miracles to bare children in the Deeper Unseen. Now all three were gone.

"Stand and continue," ordered the Silent King. Tears bloomed in our swollen eyes and the King noted this with an impatient sigh. "You may have other children. Take another woman as a gift this time. I will let you choose anyone. I will even alter the schedule once more so that can happen. But you must obey now. Tend to the hinges and take your new gift after this resolves."

Quietly, we resumed our trip to the Space.

When one dies in the Deeper Unseen, banshees from another territory lead their souls onward. Had this not been the case and we could see the one who came for our Amaen, we would have ripped her throat out on the spot. We could do nothing, however, except brood and cry and feel sick at the stomach from the faint sweet smell of the unseen banshee's breath on the air.

"I know you've suffered here." The Silent King's voice softened. "But I don't wish to create a new Assembly and waste more time... so hurry your steps."

We all looked back to our fallen child. The death of our other children had not yet hit us. We weren't choosing to let it have access to our minds. Many assumed we were grooming our three offspring to join us someday. Even perhaps *the children* believed that. And yet, such a notion couldn't have been farther from the truth. We wanted them to have real lives. The Assembly would never lack members. If all ten of us fell, another ten would soon rise up. As we traveled these bending halls and corrupted rooms, the job ahead of us already penetrated our minds with a complete and absolute dread.

First would be the pressure. All of the hundreds of thousands of times we stepped into the Space, there was no becoming accustomed to the sensation that an organism must endure there. The skin becomes a brittle paper stretched over miles. The muscle, organs, and bones become water and the blood becomes a noble gas—inside our veins would be a highway of emptiness that provides no relief for the crushing forces above, beneath, front, around, back, and inside. When a physical life form forces itself between the hinges, only the nerves have tangibility.

And they are all boiling in acid.

They are all on fire.

They are all frayed.

Cut.

Ripped.

Shredded.

Raw.

Second would be the madness. What holding the hinges open does to our minds, if one can imagine, is really a sense of ultimate love lost. It is beyond even the loss of Amaen, Raithy, and Dureen, our young ones. There can be no explanation of the heartbreak experienced in the Space; one had nothing to direct the feelings to, but it was there and it was very real. Love attained by the void and love lost simultaneously within it. We've long called this "falling for the ghost," because it seems like something real—it made our hearts warm, it made us quiver with desire and hope to nestle it within our arms like a superb lover. But we couldn't. It didn't exist. It has NEVER existed. The whole sensation of adoration and the need for utter devotion was a farce. In the Space, holding the hinges apart, keeping the dimensions from colliding, this and this most of all, wore on us; that feeling of perfect happiness, of being content, once and for all, was so elusive, it was enough to make us sob in the abyss and hope for more. Always more.

Third, and lastly, would be the soul. Our job imparted another pain on us, beyond the physical and the emotional. The next ruthlessness was something few could understand because in many dimensions few believed such a thing existed... but the soul can suffer the worst. Some might mistake this as a projection of emotion, but they would be wrong. The soul was something more meaningful on a cosmic scale and its relationship to the universe was at stake and what caused suffering. The way ones might appreciate their "grain of sand" status in the universe, but have no idea the millions of nuances beyond that, no idea how large they really are compared to nothing. Physical matter can be cut in halves forever and a soul can go forth into the light and become energy, which is useful, purposeful, and necessary. But to be reduced to nothing? Zero? Nil? Less than dust? Holding the hinges apart brought one closer to realizing that bleak concept. One became the void. You aren't a particle. An atom. An election. Proton, neutron, lepton.

You were the emptiness.

All that mattered was the tangible, what was left behind. Like fingerprints in setting concrete, these would be indicators of your fight, your life.

Children were like this. A reminder of your *once upon a time*.

As we approached the opened area of the fortress, which was so different from how we remembered it, this truth sunk in and vengeance clawed to the surface.

We wheeled around on the King, surprising him. "No!" we all said in a unified roar.

His irritation with us found a new pitch. "What?"

"We wish for direct corridor access to the beach, where we will collect our gift, Jared Kare. That will be our third grant."

He anxiously waved his hand to move along. "So be it, but you cannot be certain you'll reach him in time, Assembly. You might end up with nothing."

"You are right in that, our King, but the risk is worth the prize. He's the only one we want. The only one we can have. Nobody else will do. He is the Gift we will have."

The Space between the dimensions opened.

The Silent King watched us rush into the vacuum. "This calamity is partially your fault. So I ask that you keep the amount of lives lost unexpectedly to a minimum. I principally don't wish to change the schedule for millions of people. If you succeed, your grant will be given on your return."

We gave our thanks, but it was silenced by the chaotic scream of oblivion and its forever war on all of existence. A moment later, we became that war.

Chapter 23
The Banshee

Like a heavy hand on her throat, pulling her from the realm of sleep, Banch flew up into a sitting position, a soft comforter slipping off her naked body. She let out a squeak of bewilderment and immediately felt rawness throughout her neck. She recalled, though she wished she could forget, letting free the Divine Scream. While it wasn't a scream she'd done many times, she knew it shouldn't have caused the coarse feeling inside her mouth and down her throat. This was a backward sensation, like using a muscle in reverse, an against-the-grain uncomfortableness.

A scream had been negated, and she was unnervingly certain she knew which one. Some force had literally reached inside her and plucked the many strings of her vocal cords to counter the effects.

Few beings could control such things.

"The Kings," she whispered, wincing at the pain that came with her words.

Jared!

Kicking the beige comforter off, she scrambled to her feet, head filling with leaden heaviness (*now* that *was an effect caused by the Divine Scream*). She'd never had such a failing of control. Never shared her entire self with another soul in such a reckless fashion. It was the first scream a banshee learned before leaving the Mother's cup; it was the scream that defined you, made you relive your entire life, like how people used to do with slideshows or photo albums, but this was *experienced* by another person, all in one orgasmic blink.

After sharing herself with only two other long forgotten souls, Banch had never expected to use that scream again. It had happened almost involuntarily. She'd only slept with a few men in the Deeper Unseen, and for how old she was, that practically made her a virgin in the cosmic scheme of things. But Jared was no different in that way. He was very inexperienced, and yet, they had been perfect together.

But Jared wasn't here. He wasn't in the bedroom and the bathroom was empty.

What have you done, Jared?

She could almost hear the stern lecture from a sister banshee. *Don't be dense, Utumm Resona, you know what the human has done. He felt your plans, the fatigue of going on, when the light is so close at hand and yet you've never yourself stepped into it and left all the suffering of the worlds behind. He knows your intentions now and he means to stop you, because he is in love with you.*

Banch grasped her forehead. It ached with questions. What had he gone to do?

He cannot bear knowing you'll be gone forever.

Her eyes warmed with tears. "No!"

Time had resumed. That meant the Assembly would recover soon and Jared would be powerless. It was inconceivable to imagine his torture in the fortress, being able to do nothing to stop it. She breathed in silently, feeling so small and powerless—if he was taken, she had no choice but to go on with her plans—the Assembly wouldn't allow her to return to the fortress and they certainly wouldn't allow her to provide Jared any sort of reprieve. They'd make sure she would never get to him again.

She went to find her clothes and discovered them neatly spread over the coffee table. Banch picked up the note. Read it. Read it again. Closed her eyes. Opened them and picked up the tube of lipstick.

Oh Jared.

No.

How would she know if he'd made it? She had no clue how long she'd been out before the Chronos Scream was canceled. Why had the Silent Kings intervened in the actions of another? The Assembly couldn't have asked for this as one of their grants because they were in a state of suspension like the rest of the world. That meant the Kings had to consciously meddle in her affairs. They wouldn't even do such a thing if it meant their own safety. It was their choice to let fate unravel on its own.

Unless the universes were at stake. That would be the only cause.

Quickly, Banch got dressed. Her skirt fit a little looser now after being torn off. It was impossible not to feel like an absolute fool now for getting… so caught up with her lover.

The TV turned on and startled her, blouse halfway dragged over her head. She pulled it down and watched a sandy-haired news anchor. The camera tilted at a strange angle and suddenly the news desk sat in a meadow full of wildflowers. The anchor stood up and looked around, mouth agape and his blue eyes wide.

The walls shook in the hotel room, sucked inward, and an awful noise surged from below.

Disturbance Paradigm.

"Oh damnit!"

Banch ran for the door and slammed into a beveled stone wall that appeared from nowhere. The opposing force threw her back into the armrest of the couch. The black fabric in the couch quivered as though it had become a living beast. Its molecules were destabilizing. She couldn't believe the disturbance had reached into pieces of furniture. This was something unlike she'd ever seen. This was awful. Many people would die if this thing wasn't righted. The Assembly had its work cut out for it.

The lights in the sushi roll lampshades flickered in different shades of color. Burning red. Radioactive green. Molten orange. Soaring blue.

It wouldn't surprise her if life itself ended for everything in a matter of seconds, but she wasn't waiting to find out. She found an opening between the shifting walls and squirmed into the hotel hallway.

The carpet rumpled under her feet, bunching together. She tripped and slammed to the floor on her elbows. The jolt got her teeth clicking. In the hall the canned light overhead continued to pulse in unnatural cadences and colors. It disoriented her but she staggered into the lobby. Beyond the reception desk everything rolled off into a cobalt abyss of streaking starlight. It almost reminded her of the light the dead would venture into, so calm and vast and embracing.

She shook her head of the thought. *Focus*. She had to reach Jared. There was no telling how he'd deal with this. The dimensions would right themselves. The only way out of this was letting the Assembly do what they did best. More people would be hurt, there could be no doubt, but hopefully the casualties were low, as well as any pain and suffering.

Banch charged out into the sinking street, and hoped such a scenario would come to be.

Chapter 24
Jared

On his best day Jared had absolutely no sense of direction, but since the Disturbance Paradigm had set in now, he had no clue even what planet he was on. Terrain stretched, morphed, rearranged. This had been the beginning, but now buildings seemed affected as well—they almost unfurled and grew like organisms. Streetlights whipped about, made of concrete licorice. Manhole lids expanded in wrought iron orbs as though some giant sewer creature with powerful lungs blew air up into them like bubble gum. Jared saw one lid rupture and scatter shrapnel through a barbershop window. The glass shards twisted in the air, suspended there, rather than falling to the ground.

Everything was nuts, and he'd caused all of it. Just because he wanted to do right by Banch. Now he might be responsible for the destruction of this world and all other variations of it. He'd always known he was better off receiving help than giving it and this brutally proved that theory for all time.

As surreal as these things looked, they were only too real and that was the hardest part to process. Jared's mind felt like it was rebelling. His insides tickled. He glanced down to his arms. His skin flickered, losing color and regaining it like a television image on the fritz. With each change of hue he got a long chill down his spine that pooled in his calves and shot down to his feet, into his toes, then burnt his toenails. He hopped about like walking on hot coals. His tennis shoes burned and he worried they might catch fire. He had several horrible notions race through his mind: what if his frightening thoughts became true just by thinking them? Or worse, something unimagined?

What if something had happened to Banch while she slept? He'd seen so many buildings collapse, implode, reconfigure—he'd be responsible if something bad happened to her.

He stopped short in the inhaling, exhaling road. It was like being on the belly of a slumbering dragon. He shook away the unsettling thought and returned to Banch. There would be no way to find her. The universe either ended or this thing resolved, but there would be no navigation through this bizarre maze. Especially for someone as helpless as him.

He stood on a bus stop bench and tried to get a bearing on the ocean. From here he believed he could see something. The sky bubbled off into a froth with no other indication of water beyond it. The ocean could no longer be seen.

A piece of steel from the bench's armrest slithered up and Jared caught it in his fist, the silvery dough wiggling between his fingers. He squeezed. And squeezed. So hard. He was so impossibly angry. How could he let this happen? He'd asked himself that a million times since his encounter with the Silent King and yet asking the question a million times wasn't enough. His intentions had been pure. He'd wanted to be the hero. He wanted Banch to wake up with a clear choice before her—life or death—but the person she'd chosen to save from damnation cared more about her than any lover or friend she'd ever known. He was already high up in her mind, God knew why, but he wanted to punctuate that with something noble— maybe it would change her mind, make her want to live.

Jared splashed the metallic grease onto the sidewalk.

Or maybe it wouldn't have changed her mind.

He inspected his hand and there was no residual. Other pieces of metal from the bench slithered up like chrome cobras. He jumped off the bench to the quaking ground and headed left—just because, no real reason; he knew he had to choose some way to go. He walked toward a building in the center of the road. Cars were parked around it in a circle with odd uniformity. The vehicles shook, experiencing an earthquake rendered just for them. The Disturbance Paradigm was doing its best to make him second guess his mind again.

He started around the single story building, which looked like one of those community center buildings circa 1985 with a wooden beam frame around its perimeter—the office of either a dentist or a realtor.

A shadow fell over him. He craned his neck and his body went stiff. A larger industrial warehouse bent toward the smaller one, looking like its concrete had turned to taffy. He tried to hurry past before the other building crashed down, but then he heard the screaming and froze.

On top of the smaller building stood a young blonde with her hair in a bun, a young boy clutched to her side. She wore a torn pants suit dyed with blood at the various tears. The boy appeared unhurt, but his eyes suggested terror beyond anything conceivably possible.

"Help us! Please!" called the woman. "We don't know how we got up here!"

Jared was locked in place for a spell as he watched the larger building become ghostly and fade out of sight.

"It's going to come back!" she called. "It already disappeared twice and it gets closer every time."

"I—uh—I mean, hold on! I'll get you down!" he shouted.

What? Exactly how will that happen, you jerk?

His eyes darted around. The roof wasn't too high. The frame flexed in and out repeatedly, though, and was far from reliable enough to climb. There was a small palm tree however, and it grew only a couple of feet from the building in a planter of island bush poppies.

"The air conditioners want to eat us!" the little boy yelled.

"Hold on. I'm on my way."

He clamored up into the planter and jumped onto the palm tree. The world pitched and he almost slid back to the ground. Somehow his hands wrapped around the thin trunk and he got a great hold on it. He hadn't climbed a tree since childhood—maybe since his days spent at Bella Boyd's when he'd been more adventurous. Now he tried to tackle this problem like an adult version of that same child. *You're bigger. Stronger. More capable. Right?*

He dug his feet in. His knees still ached and his legs had little strength left in them but the solidness of the tree was reassuring in this strange new world.

"Hurry!" the woman called.

"Trying!" Hand over hand, he kept pushing up. Every grip got sweatier, felt less likely, but he slapped his palms against the tree to make it work. He got a rhythm, even though he acknowledged it as an unnatural one, probably coming to pass because of physical laws being moot—but who cared, whatever worked—and he made it to the roof with only a couple feet between the woman and child.

"Give me your hand. You can hold onto me and we'll slide down."

The woman nudged the boy forward.

"Come on," he said. Jared extended his hand. "Let's get down. Okay?"

Visions of Denise's kids flashed through his mind. *I could have been their father if I hadn't been so scared.*

The boy grabbed onto Jared's hand.

"Gotcha," he said, and pulled the boy closer to him. Hot, feverish breath blew down his neck, probably with the same cadence of a young, stressing heart. Jared tried to ignore the beating because his own heart felt very near absolute failure. His forearms shredded against the coarse trunk as they slid down. His feet met the ground and he had a simultaneous sense of trepidation and excitement at the prospect of climbing back up.

The boy caught onto Jared's pant leg. "Don't leave me!"

"I'm not! I gotta get your mom."

"She's not my mom!"

"Well shit, kid, I don't know! I gotta get that woman. Let me go!"

"Will you come back?"

"Sure I will. I totally will."

"Promise?"

Jared threw himself onto the palm tree. "Cross my heart," he said in a diffuse bass tone he hadn't intended. The bark's texture felt different this time. His hands connected with something mushy and dense like putty—then softer like pudding—then jello—then air—it was holding, gripping, clutching to nothing and the lack of sensory input drove him into a panic.

"I CAN'T do this!" he screamed.

"What?" said the woman above.

"What?" said the boy below.

"Nothing..." He hugged the tree to rid himself of the falling sensation in his guts. Only two more pushes and he would reach the top of the building. "Hang in there," he said, and throttled up to the very top.

The woman hesitated, eyes going left and right, then she stuck her hand out. Jared enclosed his hand in hers, hard, and pulled her forward, taking her into his arms. The palm tree went rigid, snapped, and splintered, a dusty cloud of wood exploding underneath.

"What's that?" said the woman, panicking. "That sound?"

"It's nothing," Jared replied.

The tree slid apart into two pieces and dropped.

"Okay, it's something," muttered Jared. "Hold on."

The woman sunk her fingers into his shoulders. The tree halted at a slant, caught in a splintery mess of its own pieces.

"Let go," he told the woman.

"Like hell!" she yelled back.

"Look, it's not that far of a jump." When Jared glanced down it looked way farther than he himself would be willing to jump. "Damn it..."

The tree broke and swayed closer to the ground. Jared rocked his shoulders to free the woman's grip. She instinctively tried to hold on but he thrashed her away. She dropped and landed on her side in the planter below.

"Asshole!" she cried out and held her hip. The young boy hurried to her side. "Come on! Get me out of here!"

Jared saw them for a blink before the tree catapulted him over the roof. He flung his hands out to grasp something and met a circular vent, which slashed through his palms. He landed on his ass and a knife-like pain went up his tailbone.

The larger building suddenly loomed over everything again, but now it appeared all around the smaller building, with Jared caught inside it. Then, in only a few seconds time, it vanished again.

However, with it having come so close, sharing the space, something about the smaller building had changed. Jared sat there in shock. He'd glance at his hands, cut and bloodied, and then he'd glance around the roof. Although part of him understood what was happening, the larger part of his awareness could not.

The single-story office building actively grew taller. It rumbled and stretched skyward, on and on. All he could do was hold on. He began to cough when the air was thinner. He wondered if this eccentric new skyscraper would penetrate the atmosphere and reach into outer space. But after fifteen minutes of dizzying movement, wood clicked and flexed beneath him as the building's expansion halted. He spotted a 747, maybe only ten thousand feet above, flying sideways and looking oddly like a boomerang.

He was still able to breathe, thankfully, and from his earlier experience today with the Lung Spike, he could do so in a surprisingly efficient manner.

You've come a damn long way since the doctor's office this morning.

Suddenly his cell phone rang and scared the hell out of him. The ring tone had a hellish timbre to it, definitely not the one he'd chosen. He fished the phone out of his pants pocket, his bleeding hand stinging terribly.

"Hi, Kaitlin," he said when he saw who it was. His voice startled him; it sounded like a man's voice. It didn't belong to him; it *could* never belong to him.

"Are you okay?" she asked.

"Are *you* okay?" he replied.

"I was in the ER, hadn't been admitted yet."

"Where are you now?"

"I think... I'm still there. The curtains around my bed turned solid—they're like plastic walls. I can see people's shadows behind them, but the curtains are like a foot thick now. What's happening to me? I thought my hallucinations were over."

"Just a while longer." Jared's eyes filled. "Just sit on your bed and wait. Things will go back to normal soon."

"The walls are closing in, I think."

Jared searched around helplessly for a moment, unsure what to say. Kaitlin saved him that and spoke again. "You hate me because we couldn't be together, don't you?"

As he stared up, the sky became a glassy blur from his tears. The plane was no longer in sight. Not even a cloud remained. "No, course not." He sniffed and wiped his nose. "I hate *myself* for that."

"Will I ever see you again, Jared? You and Banch—"

"Banch is gone forever," he cut her off. "But so am I."

"Why Jared?"

"In a few months' time, you'll understand. Be happy, okay? It's tough to come by, but it has to be possible. I think so anyway."

"What are you—oh, the walls just moved again."

"Stay on the bed… okay? Kaitlin?" Jared waited a moment. "Kaitlin, are you there?" He checked the phone.

CALL LOST.

He called her back but it went straight to voicemail. Quickly he stuffed the phone back into his pocket and painfully got to his feet.

His heart twitter-thumped.

He walked to the edge of the building and peered down. A sloping wall of tinted windows flared out the side, running away to blue sky nothingness. In the vast empty space, a couple of birds attacked each other and then dove out of sight. He wouldn't be climbing down *that* anytime soon.

And like an answer to this, the roof tiles started dropping through the floor, one by one. In the square voids they left behind, Jared only saw darkness. The tiles underneath him quivered. He moved out to the sloping ledge and climbed a bit farther out onto the slick surface of the windows. In no time the roof had become nonexistent, just a long dark drop into infinity.

On the ledge there was no place for his hands to grip. He would have to wait, crouched there, extremely careful not to move. Hopefully when the Disturbance Paradigm ended it would correct all the structures it changed.

It had to.

Had to.

He had to wait it out, or climb down. That was that.

His tennis shoes squeaked on the glass, and gradually his body slid down the glass surface toward the edge.

Chapter 25
Jared

When Jared was twenty-eight years old...

He'd never been so alone. It had only been a month since he'd broken it off with Denise, and he'd managed to finally delete all of her and the kids' pictures from his phone. Kaitlin had been going out a lot with some casting agent named Janice and was only around to talk at lunch time. He relied more on the Kangjuns than ever before, and although he loved them, he had an idea that staying over at their place to watch the late shows every night might be wearing out his welcome. After all, they were married and needed *some* kind of time alone together.

It was difficult to be completely by himself. Each night he turned on the TV in his living room and bedroom just to hear human voices. Watching movies without Kaitlin seemed a betrayal so he'd put on documentaries, music video programs, or reality shows. He regularly would sketch or ink late into the night rather than really pay attention to the TV. In those moments of creation, his mind would flux between the task and to Denise and the kids. When he got that processed, his thoughts would settle on familiar old territory:

Kaitlin.

He wished she would understand him—not just how he felt about her, but his *entire* life, every little thing he'd gone through that made him afraid or unsure—made him who he was. She knew most everything about him but she'd never experienced it. She didn't know what it really meant to be inside his skin and see the world through every shade of anxiety and doubt. Maybe that knowledge for her would transcend sexuality? Maybe she would fall in love with him, or at very least understand him better?

But what would she really do with such insight into him? Would she try to fix him? She'd always been trying to inject him with courage, but with knowing his heart maybe she'd have a better route planned. Or what if she just thought him hopeless? What if she quit on him? It was hard for him to speculate.

One evening, just as he'd put his inking pens away, his phone rang. He had dropped down on his bed and planned to just lay there, think, and lock eyes with Uma Thurman on his *Pulp Fiction* poster for a bit before changing out of his clothes. It was early for him, only 8:45 pm, but initially he was a little peeved someone would call so late.

He couldn't be peeved anymore when he saw who it was.

"Hey Kait—I thought you were at the beach."

"The beash?"

"Uh... yeah." Jared turned on his Chewbacca lamp. "On a date with, what's her name, Janet? Janice?"

"Hey guess what?" Kaitlin cried, the previous question unanswered.

"What?"

"Holy shizzlins... I'm... I'm coming over. Right now."

"You're—huh?"

"Takin' a cab. Left my car somewhere. Anywhere. Nowhere. Shit if I can find it."

He couldn't help but chuckle, even though he immediately became worried for her. "You're drunk."

Kaitlin blew out a raspberry. "How the hell can you say that? You don't drink—you got no clue, muthafucka!"

Now Jared burst out laughing. Kaitlin seldom swore at people. Inanimate objects, yes; people, no.

"Okay, well excuse me. When can I expect you?"

"Esspeck me? Fuuudge, if I know. Hold on." Her voice dropped at first but then it suddenly bumped in volume. "I SAID WHEN ARE WE GETTING THERE, *DUDE*?"

The cabbie murmured something in the background. Kaitlin barked at him about something but it was indiscernible.

"A day? A goddamn day?" There was a pause. "You said twennie-four hoursh." Another pause. "Bullshit, you said twennie midgets. *Minutes*. Ha. Midget—that was pretty funny."

"Hey Kaitlin," Jared chimed in.

"Eh?"

"Stop talking before you get your butt kicked out on the road."

"He wouldn't."

"He could," Jared pointed out.

"Akmal, would you kick me out?" A long pause. "Oh!" Kaitlin's voice went an octave higher. "Why didn't you just say something? It's all fun and fun stuff here tonight!"

"Text me when you get here," Jared told her. "Okay?"

"Yes mama!"

The call ended and Jared shook his head. A smile was on his face though. He'd seen Kaitlin drunk only a few times before and she was a handful, but he welcomed the company, as well as something he couldn't yet put his finger on.

When she got there, he had to pay the cabbie and then almost drag Kaitlin to his apartment. He asked her a few times what happened on her date but she thought the "Life's a beach!" pun was too hilarious and much more relevant. From what he gathered though, the date had not ended well.

He got Kaitlin to the couch and let her rest there while he went to get some ice water. "Don't break anything," he told her.

She tossed up her hands and gave him a look of astonishment. "Is—are you kidding? Don't talk to me like that. This is *my* house."

"No, it isn't," he laughed, and went to the kitchen. He took out a glass and went to the Arrowhead water cooler. As the water poured out he heard something shatter on the fireplace.

"Shit!" Kaitlin yelled.

"What was that?" He accidently got water on his hand and flung off some droplets.

"Who put glass figgers—figgereens where people can bump them?"

"On the mantle?"

"On the mantle. Christ!"

Jared walked back out to the living room. Kaitlin was on her knees by the red brick fireplace, staring in dismay at a small explosion of crystal scattered there. She turned her bloodshot eyes up to him.

"Was that my seagull?"

She lowered her head and shrugged. "That's what it was?" Her hand moved to her face and she clutched it, moaned miserably. "Why's everything moving?"

She poised over the glass, oblivious to it being there, like she wanted to lean on the fireplace for support.

"Stop!" he said. "You'll cut yourself!"

This frightened her and she drew her hand up. "I need—to be sick."

"Come on then. Bathroom."

"Nope!" She jumped to her feet, staggered, and then ran into him, almost knocking the glass of water from his grasp. Her face was so close to his, her lips only a breath from his own. "We should watch Gremlins 2," she suggested with a goofy smile. Her long crimson hair hid one of her pretty, wild eyes.

Jared gently pushed her away. "It's too late to start a movie."

"Oh bull pucky!" Her head jerked left and right, eyes searching the room like a mad woman. "Where's the remote?"

"Take this water. Drink it. SLOW," he cautioned.

She grunted and accepted the plastic Taco Bell Batman collector's cup. Jared went back into the kitchen, got the dust pan and brush from under the sink. It was strange to him. His housekeeper Rosie was the only one who normally cleaned anything. Doing this made him feel more grown-up.

He knelt before the glass mess that used to be two seagulls in flight. His father had got it for him shortly after he lost track of Fatso. Later he collected other figures: dragons, griffins, castles, some farm animals. They were beautiful—in high school he would sit on his bed listening to Nine Inch Nails and Tool and sketch the figures in different poses.

Now his favorite was just shimmering shards and glitter dust.

"I'm shawrry. Sorry, I mean," Kaitlin whispered, watching him solemnly from the couch.

"It's just a thing, Kait."

"Your dad got that for you," she said, wiping a tear from her eye. "Shoulda stayed on the couch. I'm stupid. No wonder nobody will ever have me."

Rather than go to the trash, Jared set the dust pan full of glassy debris on his coffee table. He dropped down next to her. "Why would you say something like that?"

"I cannot—cain't—can't—" she chuckled, but it was empty. Her eyes centered on something far away. "I can't love. The people I want don't love me back."

"And the people who love you, you don't want," he added.

She narrowed her eyes at him. "Everybody wants to be happy, to find perfection. I would just settle for a female version of you."

He grinned. "I'm not too shabby then, for a guy?"

She pinched his cheek, a little too hard. "Ouch!" he cried.

"Don't get me started." She glanced around in silent confusion. "Why aren't we watching Gremlins?"

"Because we both work tomorrow and you'll be hung over as it is."

"No shitting way. You need to get up and search that out. Nowsies."

He smirked, pushed up to his feet with a sigh, and went over to his tower of DVDs. They used to be in ABC order when Kaitlin visited more often, but now the discs were all over the place. "Gimme a sec. You haven't helped organize for a long time. You left me high and dry."

"Oh bite me."

"Don't tease."

Kaitlin hissed in amusement. "What's up with you and lover girl? You haven't said much about Denise lately. Thought... ugh, I feel raw."

"You okay?"

She smacked her lips and closed her eyes for a second. "Yeah. Yep. So what's up?"

"With Denise?"

Kaitlin looked twenty hues of green and her tone indicated her patience had run out. "Yes you douche."

"The kids. I don't like kids. It just didn't work for me."

She reviewed her feet with great interest, nodding, obviously too drunk to ask for elaboration. "I like kids," she said, and stared off for a second and then back to him in alarm. "Jared—I *need* to vomit."

He hurried to her and took her under the arms. She sagged and he fought to pull her to her feet. "Come on, to the toilet."

"Why?" she announced. "I'm... I'm fine."

"But you just said...?"

"No, I'm good. Stop copping a feel."

He sighed and gradually let his hold of her go. Kaitlin belched into her fist and muttered something about Tikka Masala. He found Gremlins 2 but rather than put it on, he set it near the DVD player and returned to the couch. After a few minutes she shifted closer. "I miss your mom and dad."

"You and me both."

"They were good people. Taken too soon."

"Agreed. Though I guess everybody feels that way about loved ones."

"Weren't you supposed to put on Gremlins?"

"Weren't you supposed to upchuck?"

She glared daggers at him and he laughed. She folded her arms and looked away.

"So what happened, Kait? Janice seemed special. Why don't you ever tell me about your dates?"

She was about to say something and stopped short. Shrugged. "My head hurts."

"You're worried about me, right? That is what this is about. You never feel right leaving me alone. My parents didn't either."

With a roll of her eyes, Kaitlin sat back deeper into the couch. "Ugh. I don't feel as sorry for you as you think."

"Have your water."

She grudgingly took a sip. "Ya know, you've told me dick-all about Denise, too. I thought you and I were best friends."

"We are."

"So why the secrecy?"

"There isn't any."

"Yeah right. You had your head up her ass for months. You'd take forever to answer my texts. I had to always invite myself over. I was like unwanted leftovers stashed in the freezer."

"Not like that at all. I just didn't have as much free time." He sat there uncomfortably for a second. "So yeah, not like that at all."

"It... is."

"Well fine, I can say the same."

"I know you can, and just did. That's why we need to never be stupid again about love. Just... because... ugh. I think I feel sick again."

"You okay?"

"We should never let love dominate us."

Jared smiled. "Kinda what love does though, right?"

"No!" she said sternly. "To hell with that mess! Friends are more important. New love is... dumb."

"Maybe," said Jared.

"If I'd ever said something bad about Denise, would you have believed me?"

He caught a stock answer in his throat and consciously squashed it. "No, I guess I couldn't bear anything negative said about her."

"That's right. Love is built on a foundation of self-delusion and untruth. Is *untruth* a word?"

"Who knows, but I think you could say *lies* just as well."

"That's too harsh."

"I don't think love is built on that though, no matter what you call it."

"Keep telling yourself that," she said with a nod.

"I will."

She burped into her hand again and grimaced at the flavor. "I'm glad you're such a romantic."

"Hardly."

Kaitlin scooted closer to him and grabbed him by the wrists. "Jared."

"What?"

She stared him deep in the eyes. "There is no perfect person for us out there."

"You're entitled to that opinion."

"I know I am, you ass – I know."

She stood, swayed. Her hand pressed to her mouth. Jared knew it was really time now and guided her to the bathroom. He held her hair back and let her purge her stomach. He wiped her face, got her shoes off, and helped her into his bed, turned the fan on, left a pair of

Advil with a piece of bread and a cup of water on the nightstand, and left the bedroom window cracked for fresh air. He loved this. It was the first time he'd ever taken care of someone else when they really needed him the most. He couldn't even say that for his parents when they'd become older and ill. Doing this for his friend indeed made him happy. He desired to have a chance, someday, to help someone else, and he wondered who that future someone might be.

Chapter 26
The Banshee

Banch measured her every movement in the city. For her, a being who did not have full residence in this world as it was, colliding with something generated by the Disturbance Paradigm could make more problems. Not that a worst case scenario could even be conceivable at this point. So far, she'd escaped buildings from other dimensions appearing around her, streets changing shape, trees and other exotic plant life cropping up in her path, wild animals emerging from the shadows and then vanishing as soon as they came—this fading out of view was an excellent sign though; the Assembly was helping to hold off the collision of dimensions. It was their function anyway—even though this task was more severe than what they normally handled; akin to asking a surgeon to operate on a three-hundred-ton heart from an alien life form.

She had to admit, as much as she wanted them all to rot, the Assembly were doing a hell of a job. There had only been twenty—thirty—Banch thought a moment and nodded. No, it had been more now. Eighty or so lives had departed before the death schedule. The fault for those lives truly rested on Banch's shoulders. She should have left Jared alone. And yet, there was no other way it could have happened, and that time with him in the hotel, so selfish and used to death as she'd become, the collateral damage was almost worth it.

You have a cold heart, Utumm Resona.

Or perhaps it just burned with a fire of its own? She didn't want to feel regret for the dead anymore. They'd almost become, she hated to say, annoying. They were so willing to go from this wonderful existence, all for that empty, bright white nothing. That had to mean there was something more, right? But how did they know? Nobody knew.

Banch had a theory. The power of that light reminded her of an intense furnace. Not a hellish place to roast and suffer, just a gateway that refined your soul into fuel. All burdens were gone. All pain immediately resolved. There would be no need to think about death anymore because you became everything. This wasn't resting in peace, this wasn't eternal torment, this was becoming the lightning that laps at the heels of Gods, this was purpose beyond purpose. The soul had much power in it, and that power needed to be reclaimed somehow; the universe had countless instances of doing just that, so it had to apply here as well.

She stopped near a department store and patted the tube of lipstick she'd rolled into the hem of her undergarments. It might be the last reminder of Jared and she didn't want to lose it; she wanted to keep it until the very end. Too many thoughts filled her mind and she leaned against the building, with hopes it retained its structure while she rested.

The previous week had brought many deaths. She alone made the call for over one hundred thousand and seventy-three. Some she'd followed since their birth and some were assignments other banshees had no energy for. Banch had suppressed her feelings for so long she didn't think anything could break her, but learning about Jared becoming the Gift and experiencing that long last week of calling deaths had made a permanent mark on her. Oh, that week. How beaten down she'd felt—it lasted forever. She could remember some of the faces easily.

Alice Henning, a seven year old who was physically, emotionally, and sexually abused by her mother's boyfriend since the age of four. He beat her to death when she tried to escape the makeshift prison he'd created. Dumped her body in a storm drain culvert. Pissed on her.

Joseph Delphy, a twenty-eight-year-old mechanic, had acquired stage four stomach cancer. His friends at the auto shop rallied around him, pitching in everything they could and being an unexpected support group. For three years he battled the chemo and radiation and at last went into remission. He went back to work for about a week. Things were going well until the hydraulics on a lift failed and F-350 truck crushed him. That was the day before his coworkers would hold a giant

Welcome Back Party. He had no family, just his clan of devoted grease monkeys. They were with him while he bled out in the shop's trench drains.

Jessica Bunsing, twenty-eight and just married. She thought no other man would have her after she'd been raped by a high school student and embroiled in a legal battle where the defense tried to turn it around on her. Many had sided with the teen. Many had called her a cradle-robbing whore. Winning the case cost her. Close to bankruptcy from legal fees and nearing severe depression, she turned to crystal meth for several years. When she finally got help she met a wonderful therapist, a brilliant, wonderfully nice man who had just opened his own practice. He asked her to be his wife after a year of dating. After they married she planned to go back to school, mostly because he convinced her she was smart enough. They had a gorgeous wedding ceremony on the beach with his family. During their first dance, a large blood clot traveled into her lungs. Several hours later, she met Banch at the hospital and walked into the light.

Those were just a few lives among many, but then Banch's work week rounded off with a drone strike in northwest Pakistan that ended twenty-five people, all under forty years of age and, save for one individual, all non-terrorist affiliated.

These people lived and loved and died. The common thing to all of these circumstances: there wasn't meaning to any of it. Her sisters would warn her not to look for meaning in a chaotic universe, but Banch couldn't help herself. She loved her duty like any other banshee, but what about that light? Did it love? Did it hate? If that's where everything ended up, why not stop living now, right?

She sighed through her teeth. *Yes, what is the point? Love dies as easily as flesh, except it disintegrates faster than decay.*

No matter what, Jared would leave. He would die. Everybody would. They would become the light and Banch would always be left on the outside looking in. Perhaps she was flawed to worry over this. None of her sisters had expressed a need to end their life, even the most psychologically disturbed. They always had that greater need to serve the Deeper Unseen. Banch remembered what that was like, but now it held so little value for her. Maybe if two of her favorite assignments hadn't been made Gifts, she might have remained honored and bound by duty, but in some way she was grateful for having her eyes opened. She wasn't depressed. She didn't hate life. She loved it. But she had a resolve to close the book. It couldn't last forever. The pain was getting to be too much for her; she couldn't be numb anymore. It had to stop. That's what would make her finally content.

Even if Jared thought otherwise. This was the only way it could be.

Relief washed over her. After the hotel she'd really speculated if she could go through with the Paled Ocean, but now it was clearer than before. She couldn't go on. It was too much and she'd rather be the sheep than the shepherd for a change. The beautiful thing she had with Jared wouldn't endure for a millennia. It wouldn't even endure for a few months. Love planted a seed that sprouted, grew tall and unique, shared its pollen with the world, and then returned to the ground, as though it never had existed.

So fatalistic you've become...

Fear latched its frozen fingers around her mind. What if Jared died out there? What if another banshee led him to the light?

Jealousy grew inside her, but she tried to tramp it down. *Stop being silly. Remember you had a renewed resolve. You need to end this at the beach. It would actually be good right now if Jared died before schedule; the Assembly is too busy to capture him and he could walk into the light.*

But with someone else.

She imagined any number of her sisters making the call and Jared looking at them longingly, in bliss, hand-in-hand, led deep into that burning white.

She shook her head, stomach queasy.

Your job is to keep him from getting caught by the Assembly. And you've done that. Don't freak now. You will get to the ocean and break this endless cycle that has been your life.

She moved away from the wall and hurried along the sagging sidewalk. At the precipice, she didn't want another banshee with him. She *really didn't* like the thought of that. It had to be her there with him.

So you aren't ending this, foolish Utumm Resona? You've changed your mind yet again? Out of jealousy? Out of fear? What will convince you about what must be done?

Banch really didn't know what she needed anymore. What she did know was that she had to get to Jared. And soon.

Chapter 27
Jared

Jared's first slide down the windows took him halfway to the edge of the building. One more like that and he'd go right over the side. He'd managed to stop his body and plant the soles of his shoes against the glass. The expanse of pure, cold blue sky faced him. He still couldn't see the world beneath and he really didn't want to. The instinct to survive still fired on every cylinder. He didn't want to believe death really waited for him at that office desk, but it might be much less terrifying than dropping off a Mount Everest sized skyscraper. Either way. He wanted to live.

Banch, on the other hand, wished to die. He understood this; she came by that wish honestly, and it wasn't that she wanted to commit suicide out of despair, but rather to stop the weariness in her soul. She saw so much, knew so much, experienced life through countless people. It was debilitating. Disheartening, disillusionment and exhaustion didn't even cover it. And yet it was still a mistake. It was a mistake to give up.

Jared's forearms burned. He dared not readjust his position. It was so lonely up here. There had been so many lonely moments in his life, and he hadn't needed to feel that way at all. His banshee had been with him much of that time. For all he knew, she might be watching him again. Maybe his note, followed by the Disturbance Paradigm, had been enough to change her mind.

"Banch," he whispered. "If you're watching, like you once did, that means you took a corridor to the Free Zone. Hopefully, if you got through all this stuff. I don't know, I mean, I hope that happened. Maybe things are as messed up there as they are here. I want to believe you got away, that you're safe. I want to believe one good thing came of my screw-up. I know now why you wanted to help me. The need to care for someone was our connection. You'd never felt such a powerful need before. I could have been another number amongst the sad stories. You wanted to cradle someone and tell them the universe does sometimes care. Every banshee hopes for the same thing, but you wanted to collect."

Jared grinned at the strong wind blowing in and daydreamed it might be her presence. "You wanted the universe to put its money where its mouth was. I love you for that... and I wish I could have been more worthy to take a chance on, and to show you how great your job really is."

He closed his eyes as they burned. He tried again not to move. The wind dried tears to his cheeks almost immediately.

"You show us a way through our fear. You make it possible to finally care, no matter what happens, because there is beauty, such beauty in the end."

Silence. The blue void before him smiled back as though to say, *Care for some of this?*

Jared, feeling crazed, answered the void: "No, I want to have as much time as I can, but I'm not afraid of you anymore. Not of you. Not of a damn thing. I will go on."

With a loud squeak under his soles, he slid down the windows. His hands went out but there was nothing to grasp. The edge rushed toward him. He'd thought of this moment for a solid hour now but couldn't ponder it anymore, not like he'd imagined. It happened so quickly—he twisted his body, threw out his hands, and slapped at the slick surface like an animal begging to be let inside its home, and that's how he felt, so wanting and desperate. He wasn't afraid anymore, but he still had wants.

Oh god, how he *wanted*.

To just.

Get hold.

Then his body fell off the side of the building. The sky vaulted overhead. He sensed the space around him, dangling over the open mouth of a ravenous divinity. His hands locked on the edge. His fingers pinched it so fiercely it sent pain into his elbows.

The word PLEASE ran through his mind. But it wasn't a prayer; he wasn't a believer in a higher power. With all he understood about the Deeper Unseen it appeared *other* dimensions didn't know for sure either. There were powerful entities like the Silent Kings, but that didn't mean they were Gods. In the end, there might still be nothing inside that beautiful white light. Living might ultimately be better.

Of course it was. It was all he knew, all he could—

His fingers dragged closer to the edge.

—hold onto and cherish. Life made his love for Banch exist and even if it meant three more months, it was three damn months *more*.

He growled and pulled himself up.

His right hand released.

His focus intensified. He needed to swing his arm over but didn't want to overdo the motion. His left arm pulsed. A drop-beat thumped in his chest, different than it had in the past, but though it didn't feel as strange, it alarmed him his heart might give before his left shoulder did.

Avoiding it until now, his eyes traveled down. The street, so far beneath, looked two inches wide. He couldn't even distinguish the cars as more than smudges of color. The building had some narrow outcroppings. The closest had to be about fifteen or twenty feet down. It would be impossible to swing his body to drop the right way without two arms for leverage.

Impulsively, to his shock and dismay, he risked everything and swung his right arm to catch the ledge. His adrenaline warmed him top to bottom. The stress his left arm had taken became clear right away and it almost turned numb and useless. He needed to get closer to the building, and quickly. Or he'd be down to one arm again. Then no arms.

Jared pumped his legs. He planned on getting into a good swaying motion, but that didn't happen. Both of his hands came off the edge.

And he fell.

His feet struck the outcropping, knees buckled with the impact, and body sank back. For a split second he sensed the wind behind him and he flung his arms forward to get hold of something. His fingers brushed against a crack in the concrete and got caught inside. He pulled himself flush to the wall, so close his cheek pressed against the burning stone surface. Delirious and dizzy, he sucked air into his lungs and tried sidling even closer, though it was impossible.

His heels hung off the ledge, but other than that he'd secured a safer position. He almost wanted to cry for joy, but he wasn't exactly back on the ground either, so celebrating was definitely premature.

He promised himself he wouldn't look down again and took a second step. Seeing the distance below would only freak him out, if it didn't make this dizziness worse, so he soon went back to waiting. Time proved to be excruciating right away. Birds flapped around and he hoped they didn't investigate the out-of-place human. The shallow cracks in the concrete seemed to give less area to grip with every passing minute.

Then, piercing through the wailing wind, his cell phone rang. It startled him and his heart leapt into his throat. He closed his eyes and tried to calm down. A laugh, so dry it might have been a cackle, came from the depths of his chest. "Lettin' that one go to voicemail." He tittered for a minute more, feeling desperation shroud his mind. What if the call had been Kaitlin again?

Don't risk it. You'll do her more good unsplattered.

The building hummed beneath his hands, tickling his flesh. It was almost as if it *wanted* him to fall, but then the humming turned to quivering and trembling and shaking. Large blocks of concrete and rebar pushed out, surrounding him. He thought to grab one of these wide platforms but he feared the structures might be too tentative—here he was on this little ledge and the building around him rearranged itself like a backwards game of Tetris—a disassembling Transformer—a live action version of an oscillating sound graph.

From above, the sky warped in and out. Jared clenched his eyes. He didn't want to look at it—he didn't want to think that the atmosphere might pop and something unimaginable would rain down on him, washing him off the side of this Rubik's Cube Mount Everest he'd found himself trapped on.

The crack in the concrete slowly started to seal. He pulled his fingers out with a curse. Large portions of the building glided back inside. A falling sensation bloomed in his stomach. The building lowered itself, steadily. This brought little relief, however, because the tiny ledge under his feet began to retreat inside the building as well. He searched around for something else to climb on, but everything had tucked inside the face of the building.

"No," he breathed.

He stood on his tiptoes and hugged the flat surface with all his strength. Wind rushed around him. The ledge vanished from under his feet and he dropped at once—

Four feet into the planter of island bush poppies below.

He screamed and sat there, wild-eyed for a moment. He thought for sure he still had hundreds of feet to fall. Through the office window he could see a balding dentist, drill in hand, staring at him, along with his patient in the chair, open-mouthed and confused.

Jared scooted out onto the planter's brick border. He surveyed the surrounding area. The building was no longer in the dead center of the street. All the cars sat in the parking lot rather than parked in a circle. Nothing moved. Nothing reshaped. Nothing appeared and then vanished.

The Disturbance Paradigm had ended.

He swung his legs off the planter and hopped down. There wasn't any time to lose. If he could get a cab to the beach he'd maybe get there in time.

Before *they* showed up.

He took out his phone. MISSED CALL.

There was a voicemail. He didn't recognize the number but the area code was local.

"Banch?" he whispered. She knew everything about him, so it would stand to reason she memorized his cell number. She must have found a phone somewhere.

He went to the voicemail and selected the message. It started loading. The streets were still quiet—people probably trying to get their heads sorted out.

Why was this phone taking so long to load the message? What if Banch was in trouble?

You're the one in trouble, dummy. She's immortal. She's fine.

The cruel possibilities dominoed through his head. There could be all kinds of things happening to her—things he'd caused—and he had no way to know.

"Stupid shitty service!" He smacked the phone's screen. "Load, damn you!"

He aimed his phone to the sky, to the ground, left and right—he got another reception bar. He followed it, moving with his phone extended like some divining rod.

The bandwidth wasn't improving. He walked faster, phone wagging back and forth, trying to catch that sweet nectar of signal. He passed a parked gray Audi with a man sitting there, staring ahead, stunned. An upset disc jockey on the radio stammered, "For all these events which are being called... spatial... is that... hold on folks. Yes, a *spatial interruption,* says NASA, anyway. There haven't been many reported deaths. Plenty of injuries, but few deaths reported so far. This thing seems to have only ended fifteen minutes ago, so it's way too early to say for sure. Let's pray its over for good. No other reports have come in yet. But as stated, if you're just joining us, these spatial events have—"

Jared lowered himself and looked at the man in the car. "You okay?"

The man, sandy-haired and sunburned, dragged his beaten eyes over to Jared. "I was inside a pyramid made of tinfoil. The sun was in there with me."

"Whoa," said Jared, unsure how else to respond.

"The sun!" The man smacked his steering wheel. "The frigging sun!"

The man twisted the key and stabbed at the window button, sealing Jared off from him.

After the car peeled away, Jared checked his phone again. Only two bars but he decided to check the voice message once more.

It came on.

"Jared this i—"

He waited, but nothing else was said. The recording indicated a message almost a minute long. The voice sounded familiar but he couldn't place it. An older man though, not Banch.

He shook his head in disgust, watching the message struggling to load. "You've got to be kidding me. Really?"

He attempted to call Kaitlin back. It rang five times before going to her message.

He took off walking again. It was really bizarre, but with his new outlook, he'd given up on fearing the Assembly. If they came, they came. He probably deserved it, but another part of him, a wiser part cultivated by Banch's knowledge, knew they would use their last grant for direct passage to the beach; they wouldn't risk trying to take him here and having him slip away somehow again. They'd avoided the beach as long as they could but now there was no getting around it. They would be cautious.

They'd also be extra-pissed at him for trying to kill their offspring.

He suddenly felt sick. "Got that to look forward to."

The sun sunk in the sky. It would be dark in a few hours. He thought back to scheduling his doctor appointment last month, how he'd almost decided to go in late afternoon, rather than early morning. What a different day that would have been.

His thoughts swam languidly in his mind. Maybe in one of those other dimensions he got to be with Banch all day long in the hotel room, enjoying the food, the warmth and gift of their bodies together, and the appreciation of what they'd been given. Maybe the Divine Scream hadn't slipped out. After he washed away his taint, maybe he saw her die on that beach.

Was that a better ending than what would happen today?

He grumbled and hurried on, stabbing his phone left and right, up and down. If service didn't get better in the next minute, he was done with this. He noticed three bars and tried the voicemail message again. This time, success.

"*Jared this is Peter Revel, your dad's primary care physician. Remember me? I used to come over and play poker at your house? You and Bob put me in the loop on all your medical stuff a while back. I'm sorry I didn't get back to you earlier, but I slipped and hit my head in the kitchen. If that's not enough,*" he paused and chuckled, "*I ended up on a neighbor's lawn just now. Embarrassing. Anyway, I'm heading into the county hospital to get checked out, but if you haven't already spoken with your doctor, I needed to discuss your test results, buddy. This is critical. I'll probably be in the waiting room for a bit, so do call me back when you can. Really, Jared. This is VERY important. Please call to discuss this.*"

He gave his number and said his name again, then hung up.

There was a time when Jared would have ignored this message. He might have summoned the courage to have Kaitlin call back for him, but in reality he would have pretended there was no direness here. Would have pushed it completely out of his mind. Or written himself a note he'd never read: *Schedule with Doc.*

Now, after everything that happened, he had to know. He had to know what took him that day three months from now at his office desk. That was the day he was supposed to meet Banch for the first time.

And the Assembly.

If those facts had changed, he didn't see why knowing his cause of death would make a difference. The Assembly was likely to get him now anyway. So the whole thing was moot.

If anything, knowing would bring him closure.

Finally.

He put his thumb over the CALL BACK button and pressed it.

Chapter 28
The Banshee

Banch's feet buzzed from all the running. She had to slow down and shuffle them a bit; breaking connection from the ground even slightly had her legs shaking and her toes numb from the constant electric discharges. She considered whether she could risk taking some corridor shadows to the beach, but she had a feeling she might run into some people along the way who would best be avoided.

Ten-some people to be exact.

And "people" was a kindness not completely true to heart.

"Certainly, and we aren't known for our kindness either, Utumm Resona."

Banch flinched. "Who tastes my thoughts?"

She searched the alley and found no one.

"Your thoughts are mine. Your entire life is a play for me to watch. Over here, near the stairs."

Banch glanced over to a door with four steps joining it. A corridor shadow stretched to the left, spreading out like an auburn starburst of darkness. A figure stood just outside of it. Long, flowing vermillion hair reached to her hips. Her eyes held such benevolence, but belied the eagle features of the face. Despite such fierceness, Banch was drawn to her—she really would follow this person anywhere, because this was her banshee, the one she'd expected to take her to the light at long last.

Her voice cracked. "What are you doing here, sister?"

A thin smile. "Not leading you forward. Well, not yet."

"I must go. I haven't the time to talk."

The banshee folded her slender bronze arms and pressed them to her flat stomach. "I will be brief."

"Please do."

"Reconsider your plans. Now that the human knows your life through the Divine Scream, the death schedule has changed dramatically several times. It isn't stable for you or for him."

"How did it change?"

Another smile, this one coyer. "You know I cannot reveal that."

"Of course."

"I just took a chance to meet with you, to ask you to reconsider your plan."

"I already have. I will not disassociate in the Paled Ocean. It means more to me to continue seeing my assignments to the light. My weariness is over, sister. I'm ready for my duty again."

The banshee's expression didn't change, and why would it? Banch knew how they were raised: protect the schedule at all costs.

"That may be," her banshee replied, "but I want to reiterate my suggestion to rethink your plans."

"Which plans?"

"I cannot elaborate."

"To END myself?" Banch snapped. "I told you. I only want to protect my assignment from the Assembly. You can appreciate that."

"Indeed."

"So what is this visit about?"

The banshee took a step back. Fluttering red shades touched her one exposed shoulder—her uniform was a different style and material from common banshees. She'd been around for a *very* long time.

"I cannot say more—"

"I know." Banch groaned. "But you haven't shown any reason to be here. If I didn't know better, I'd say you're obliging the Assembly."

The other banshee's eyes burned. "You *know* that is untrue."

"Then why?"

"I don't often lead other banshees to the light. It happens so seldom. Eons."

"Even if my assignment is taken, I've decided against the idea. I'm not being deceptive."

A short nod answered this. "The schedule shifts sometimes."

"Yes, I suppose, but I've resolved to stay alive. I swear this to the Deeper Unseen."

"Good, but be wary. I don't have a firm schedule for you, Utumm Resona. It is in flux for you and for the gift."

"Why?"

"Just... rethink your plans."

"That again? What does that even mean?"

The banshee took a step back and was gone.

Banch looked at the wall where the corridor shadow used to be. She turned away and increased her pace, ignoring the blinding pain in her ankles and legs. She'd make her way to the beach, where this would be finished, once and for all.

Chapter 29
Jared

When they finally got in touch, Doctor Peter Revel had to call Jared back. He'd made it to the hospital but the place was a zoo. This was double confirmed when Jared tried to call the hospital directly about Kaitlin and got a busy signal. He didn't even think such a thing was possible anymore at a reception desk.

The good news was that a cab stopped when Jared flagged it down. The driver was an attractive black man with cornrows and a blue tattoo on his right bicep of Africa wrapped in barbed wire.

"Hospital?" he asked.

"No, the beach."

He twisted around in the seat and lifted a thinly scarred eyebrow. "Which?"

"Seal beach."

"Okay." He started typing into the GPS.

"You take credit?"

"Sure do," he replied.

Jared settled back in the seat, relieved but still anxious. "Did anything... weird happen to you today?"

Africa lifted with the man's shrug. "Slept through most of whatever it was. Crazy stuff happened though. I get it." The man seemed completely disconnected with the event, which Jared took as good news.

"Anywhere in particular at the beach you got in mind?" he asked.

"Just get me as close to the water as possible."

"Can do."

The cab took off with a promptness Jared appreciated. He decided to keep his further questions to himself; he didn't want to press his luck. He tried Kaitlin's cell phone again but got her message once more. He dialed the hospital. A frantic voice came on the line, "Can you please hold?"

Click.

Like he had a choice whether to hold or not.

He set the phone down on his knee for a moment and studied his blue shirt, sweatpants, and shoes. Going through the laundry at the Kangjun's seemed from the distant past now. And the adventure on the building had caused him to sweat so profusely the soil from the Deeper Unseen had purged itself from his skin. He had a notion of these things now, having so much awareness into Banch's mind and history. Since the soil had purged itself from his skin, the color of his clothing made little difference now—the Assembly would smell him coming, miles away.

His phone beeped. The call to the hospital was lost. He sighed and shut off his screen.

Two minutes later, a call from Doctor Revel came in.

"I'm so sorry for making you wait, Jared. What a mess it is here. I had to take a number. No strings to be pulled for this guy, I guess."

"No, that's fine. Did you hurt yourself bad? Are you doing okay?"

"My head feels fine," he admitted. "But ending up next door with my face in some fresh cut grass got me thinking I might have juggled some brain cells."

Jared gave a commiserating laugh and said, "Yeah."

"So... all right. I, uh, I just want you to know that I really liked your dad and you. Your whole family really."

"Thank you."

"Oh, of course. Of course. I just, I know this is a strange day and weird stuff is happening. It's not the greatest time to be laying more heavy shit on you. But because I care, this just couldn't wait. I still thought we should talk about what those test results showed. What did your primary care tell you?"

"The appointment was canceled, so please go on."

"So you don't know anything?" asked Peter.

"No, I don't."

He grunted and cleared his throat. "Well, all the deficiencies in your blood lead me to believe you have APS. Your own doctor, Saxon, probably would make the same conclusion. Some of his notes were already in the file they faxed me. You case is way worse than your father's, unfortunately."

"I'm sorry. AP...?"

"S."

"I don't know what that is."

Peter went silent for a beat. "Holy shit. I mean, your dad died from it. Nobody told you? He didn't say anything? You never asked?"

"I didn't... know what to ask. I guess."

"Sorry?"

"Tell me please. What is APS?"

"Antiphospholipid Antibody Syndrome. I tentatively diagnosed him after his three heart attacks."

"Dad had three heart attacks? I don't even remember him having one!"

"They were minor, but significant. He really didn't tell you? He had to come home from work twice and I think the other happened on the weekend."

Jared scrubbed his face and wanted to strangle himself. Why hadn't his father said anything? Why hadn't he noticed? "I must have been too busy thinking of myself. He was probably too scared it would freak me out, especially after losing mom."

"He told me he said something to you about it."

"Well, Doctor, he *lied*."

Jared's tone got the cabbie's attention, and he glanced through the rear view.

"Come on, Jared," said Peter.

"What is APS then?"

"Abnormal blood clotting. You may not even have traditional APS, but it's the closest diagnosis to make at this point. You'll need further screening, possibly require a heart bypass and need to take an antireplase injection daily to keep your clotting under control."

"I need an injection every day?"

"*Yes.*" Peter's surprise sounded like this was common knowledge.

"So I need to go to the hospital every day?"

"No, no, you can give the injection to yourself."

Jared was silent.

"Is that a problem for you?"

"Oh... oh, um, no."

"Jared, this is serious, serious stuff. You need to get all this done. You need to take care of yourself or—"

"I'll die," he finished.

Peter cleared his throat again. "It's serious. Like I said. A big fight waits ahead of you. But there's no reason you can't win."

"Will I need to take pills?"

"An assortment, why?"

"Nothing. I can do that. Every day though?"

"Yes, Jared. Have you worked on applying for that county health insurance?"

Shit, totally forgot about that, for like the hundredth time. "Not yet. I will though."

"Well, don't let those run-around fuckers kill you—I mean, sorry for the language."

"It's fine."

"Nip this in the bud. Take care of yourself."

"I know."

"Keep me in the loop. I'll send some articles your way from approved sources. Nothing too technical. Ask anything you want and if I don't know the answer, I will find it for you. I want to help in whatever way I can. Bob was one of my favorite people. One of the best hearts on this big blue earth."

"I agree."

"So you'll schedule a follow-up with a specialist?"

"Of course," said Jared. "Thank you so much for calling."

"You're welcome buddy, any time. We'll talk soon. Take care of that heart."

"Sure thing. Bye."

Jared realized that this was the conversation he was supposed to have this morning with his doctor. In different words perhaps, but the substance should have been the same. And he hadn't listened. Peter would have then called him later today probably, and he probably wouldn't have listened to that either. *So afraid. So very afraid. So unsure of how to proceed, how to take that next step.* Without Kaitlin to coddle him and make calls and schedule appointments and go with him to the pharmacy to get his meds, it would cost him his life. How would that have made her feel? She finally gets a part in something she auditions for and leaves Jared when he needs her the most. Of course it wasn't her fault but she'd undoubtedly feel guilty about it. It made him ashamed of the person he once was and at the same time made him dread becoming that person again if he managed to escape the Assembly and this day from Hell.

Images of the hotel drifted into his mind.

And a day from Heaven.

He sat back into the musty seat and rolled his head to his shoulder and watched the buildings whip past. Warehouses. Industrial complexes. A Stater Bros grocery store. A Chase bank. A Carl's Jr—

Jared sat up. He recognized this area. Him and Kaitlin got cash out at that Chase bank and ate at that Carl's Jr on their way to a Future of Mankind concert. He'd seen and remembered this place earlier while walking, before he got the cab.

The driver was driving him away from the beach.

Jared tensed, gripping the legs of his pants. His back straightened.

The door locks clicked in place, the driver checking them. He must have read Jared's body language.

"Not quite time yet," said the driver with a new rasp to his voice. "They haven't recovered fully—we'll drive a bit, and when the Assembly arrives to the outskirts of the Paled Ocean, this will be over. They will have their gift."

Jared tried to pull the lock up but couldn't grip the nub.

"You might want to just accept it and relax, Mr. Kare."

"Who are you?" Jared asked.

The man's jade eyes regarded him in the rearview. "I'm a cabbie." He smiled tenderly.

"Why are you doing this?"

"One of my colleagues decided to speak, *to interfere*—some of us would rather the Assembly lose their gift this time around. However, that desire is not shared by all of us, especially those who don't have the luxury of living outside the boundaries of the fortress."

"You are another Silent King then?"

The green in his eyes went fierce. "Just stay quiet."

"You can't do this! You aren't supposed to interfere with mortal affairs. That's mandate!" Jared was surprised how loud his voice had suddenly become.

"This interference is justified to keep the Assembly performing their function. I'll not spend the next century managing their depression and angst. I remember the days before gifts were appropriated to the Assembly, and despite what some of my other colleagues believe, it's a necessary practice. The gifts give them hope and focus. I will *not* be made to bail out the Assembly when they are too tormented to endure. I will not suffer again under the stresses of the dimensions. That's their job. *Theirs.*"

Jared struck the back of the seat with his foot. "Let me out! You've got no right to me. I don't belong to you."

"Calm it down, Kare."

"You all can go to hell."

"No such thing, but the Fortress is a hell of place." A dark smirk. The eyes glinted in amusement, seeing Jared's fear. "They'll eventually invest their energy in other gifts. They might take a little longer with you though."

The Silent King laughed.

Jared dipped into his pocket and pulled his phone free.

Another laugh. "Calling mama? Dada? Oh right, I forgot, they both croaked and left you alone."

"Get screwed."

"I like this new you, Kare. Troublesome, but fiery."

Jared started the text message: 911. *Anyone nearby, help me. This is Jared. Heading northbound on Bolsa Chica Rd. Yellow taxi. Driver locked me in.*

"You've been a pain in the ass, sir," said the King, scratching delicately behind his ear. "You and the Utumm Resona."

"You've no idea yet," Jared replied. He added recipients to the text and sent the message.

It was almost five minutes later and the Silent King's head canted to the side. He nodded for a while. Flickers of a smile touched his mouth, as though he received fragments of a radio signal directly into his brain. He must have received the entire message because his smile grew fuller suddenly.

"Oh, this just in—okay. We've got it. The Assembly have collected themselves from the disaster you caused." The King stopped at a red light and slapped the turn signal, making a gleeful *bam* sound. "Looks like we can head to the beach now. I'm sure they'll be relieved to know they don't need to find you—that beach makes them a bit skittish, poor souls."

The light changed and they u-turned.

Jared sent another text. *Southbound. Headed for Seal Beach.*

He hadn't received any reply texts to his call for help. Everything was probably still crazy in the aftermath of the Disturbance Paradigm. He was going to be driven right to the Assembly. Hand-delivered.

"You're thinking this is unfair, aren't you?" The jade eyes regarded him in the mirror.

Jared folded his hands in his lap and stared at them. *Bye Banch. Bye Kaitlin and the Kangjuns. Bye world.*

The King clucked his tongue. "You know, in one dimension I'm actually helping you escape right now. In another, I was destroyed long ago by the Assembly. And in yet another, I told a doctor your story and he helped to save your life. You see Jared, I'm not always the monster, nor am I always the hero—*I am many*—and when you are many, you cannot control or feel regret for one instance. Multiple ripples in the pond. Some cross. Some don't. But it all fades. You should try to understand that. Despite your inadequate appreciation of the multiverses, it's the only concept that should make peace in a person."

"I'm a toy. What difference does peace make?"

He snorted. "I'm overjoyed you realize that actually. I'm sort of speechless—that's a joke."

"Funny."

"Maybe that death-fairy taught you much more than I realized."

"She did."

"Seems so."

"She taught me," said Jared, "to go after what you want."

A group of cars turned at the intersection ahead and paired up side by side.

"And I don't want to be a gift," Jared added.

The Silent King's eyes widened in the mirror as the cars accelerated toward them. "What the hell is that?" He glared back at his passenger. "What is this, Kare?"

Tires screeched as a Jeep and Ford Explorer turned in opposing directions, almost impacting. They effectively blocked the street ahead. Jared could see the surprised faces behind the windshields. He recognized the look because he recognized the feeling they were experiencing—doing something you never dreamed yourself capable of.

With a wild growl the Silent King punched the brakes. More engines roared around them. Brakes whirred from behind. Jared searched out the back windshield. Screaming up the street were three other vehicles: a Toyota pick-up truck, Cadillac, and the Mustang Shelby from earlier. They formed up around the taxi cab.

Doors opened, almost in sync, and the Gilded piled out, hunting rifles wedged under their arms.

"Shit yeah," Jared said with a grin.

A younger man with shoulder-length brown hair trained his rifle on the car. "Out, out, out!"

Jared couldn't contain a little jab here. "Looks like things have chang—"

But the Silent King was gone. The driver seat, empty.

A knock on the window startled Jared.

"Are you okay?" asked a woman in a waitress uniform from the Bayou Cat restaurant. She held a rifle across her chest.

"Yeah," he replied unconsciously. It was really insane how fast they'd mobilized. It had only been twenty minutes since he sent the text.

The woman went around to the driver's side, opened the door, and unlocked the car. Jared got out and a group of the Gilded surrounded him. The air hung with the scent of burning fuel. All these vehicles had been pushed to their limits. A chorus of different questions rose at once, but when Jared held his hand up, the Gilded silenced.

"I need to get to the beach, as fast as possible," he told them.

No further questions asked, they guided him to the Mustang.

"I need a great driver," he admitted. "Every second counts."

"I took stock car racing lessons for six summers," said the waitress. "Did ride-alongs with several NASCAR drivers for my last two birthdays."

"What's your name?"

"Carol Drayers."

"You'll do, Carol." Jared rounded the car to the passenger side. He got inside, noting the familiar interior.

"Buckle up." She stashed her rifle in the back seat.

"Right, of course. We're going fast."

She sat in the seat and yanked down her seat belt. "Do you freak out easy?"

"Uh—"

"So, yes?"

"Why?"

"Just hold on. I'm going to drift around street corners. We might fishtail a bit."

Jared checked his seat belt and pulled it tighter. "Let's go. I'm ready."

Chapter 30
The Assembly

We never lost perspective on our existence. Not every life form in the Deeper Unseen was immortal. Some creatures lived out their respective lives for two minutes to two million years, from the lowliest of bacteria to the high vaulted grandeur and power of Silent Kings. But the Assembly was indeed immortal. That was to say the consciousness remained undying, not the individual members. There were ways we could disconnect from all realities and therefore "die," move on to the light and so forth, but if we were left on our own without such circumstances, nothing could kill us as a whole. Chop off our heads and new ones would grow back. Tear out our guts and they would slither back into our chests like homesick snakes.

We shared this form of longevity with genies, with lichs, with... banshees. Living forever made one obsessed with the concept of death—and we had to imagine that a banshee, working around death as often as they did, became powerfully fascinated with it. We did not wish for death, but it interested us as well. The fear of death even more so, because it was so foreign.

When we gazed upon the Paled Ocean for the first time in this world, it was a new concept for us. It was so large. So terrifying. In our world. In this world. In countless dimensions. This. Here. Deadly. Forever. It was the origin of life. On different planets this ocean might be comprised of other chemicals and minerals, but regardless, life always pulled itself out of the sludge, slime, and slurry, out of the fluid. Strange how something could be the dawn of evolution and the ending of it with such simplicity.

Our twenty eyes raced across the rippling dark blue surface. The familiarity of it disturbed us most of all. This ocean, in the Deeper Unseen, was harmless to us, and yet it looked *exactly* the same here. Nothing in this world looked the same so far—that was unnatural, an abomination, as though this body of water lured us into a false sense of security by disguising itself like an old friend.

We loathed this ocean.

In fact, we vowed then and there to never look upon it again, even in the safety of our own dimension.

Swallowing fear, we took a few steps forward and several of our number collapsed. Perhaps we'd overestimated our recovery. The Disturbance Paradigm had been more than we'd ever prepared for. In fact, it wasn't accurate to label it like any other. We would call this a Grand Disturbance Paradigm. We really prayed to never see another again. Hopefully the universes would collapse on themselves before that could reoccur. If we had to do it again, we wouldn't last. We lost close to a hundred thousand people from countless dimensions—in this world, only around eighty or so. But without our intervention, it was possible that hundreds of trillions of lives might have been lost without our effort. The death schedule had changed, but in a manageable fashion. The Silent Kings were pleased with the outcome.

This served to remind us of something important. We were the heroes; we saved more lives keeping the dimensions in alignment than any force great or small. And this last effort was cosmically significant. We saved the multiverses. In our collective, we'd never known anyone or any group who could say the same, since the very inception of time.

And who had threatened all existence? In this universe and all others?

Jared Kare.

Our gift.

If ever there had been a soul more worthy of being denied the light, it was him. People like him were a drop of acid that ate through everything and never stopped. Continue and continue. On and on.

Forever eating through all structures with the potency of their weakness. And he WAS weak. That was a misconception that many should keep in mind and never did. The weak were always more dangerous than the strong. Destruction and chaos loved the weak because it unfolded so sweetly, in a poetic fashion, whereas the strong initiated it through free will. With the weak, destruction and chaos were in control, and those entities, still alive and well in this day and age, happened to enjoy the hell out of that.

So this was all to say that our gift, our Jared Kare, was the greatest Satan of all time. Unintentional maybe, but the scourge of dimensions, no doubt about it.

"The Lance?" we cried. Though the words had been shared on all of our lips, the idea had come from the Seventh, lustful for torture. All others, the nine of us, nodded, though we were slightly upset the Seventh would choose to have a thought outside our minds. If it happened again, we would need to break him away from our collective.

Perhaps it was the appeal of the lance that prevented us from being so harsh on the Seventh, however. The Lance was a GOOD idea for our gift. We had many instruments to choose from in our fortress, but selecting the correct pleasure was an art, and the lance might complement our needs like a fine entrée in a masterfully constructed meal.

And as fine meals went, thinking about that, as wrecked, weary, woeful, and worked to the bone we were, it would be blissful to grill Jared's body and ingest his every piece. In the Deeper Unseen our gifts could not make contact with the ground, so they had to wear thick boots and clothing, but if we took those protections away from Jared for a day or so, he would be nice and charred by supper time. Crisp down to the bones. That smoky flavor was nicer, twice as nice when it was caused by dimensional disruption.

A few of us, at this thought, brought up our heels for a few moments to feel the sweet pain of the electricity arc between our flesh and the ground. As though the past few hours hadn't been painful enough, but then again, we lived through pain; it was our job and our tired friend. We were saviors of the people, but misunderstood, like a wandering rock star who picks up a guitar at a music shop during an exhausting world tour. Despite the exhaustion, he picks up the guitar and starts riffing anyway, because it's what he knows, how he breathes and remembers he's still living. It was our essence, our color, our form, our purpose, we were Those Who Endured the Pain, and we loved to hate it.

Our thoughts returned to the lance. We would work Jared up to that device. Although the Silent Kings granted physical immortality to our gifts, pain and shock on the physical form functioned the same as with any life form, and having Jared black out before the lance widened through his core, would spoil the effort. He'd miss out on the most important aspects of the pain process—it didn't make for a satisfying build up and climax. And watching the lance destroy a body from the inside out was a masterful display—it deserved the quality of careful brush strokes with fine oil paints, not the careless impulsive crayon work of rushed afterthought, lacking wisdom or work ethic. No. He would need our training to sustain himself through the process, and that required self-taught meditation and numbness.

Oh, how we were excited for the prospects this would deliver! Perhaps we could simulate the grave pain our three children endured during the Grand Disturbance Paradigm. Crushing our gift for revenge wasn't beautiful with brilliance however—we would think of something more fitting for Jared. Perhaps we would leave him in a dungeon without food for three weeks and then bring in a corpse formed in the shape of his friend Kaitlin. He would not know the corpse wasn't authentic. Our flesh molding was quite convincing. After presenting the body, we'd give him a knife and tell him dinner was served. Perhaps we'd roll the corpse in salt and spices beforehand. Exit from the dungeon would depend on how bare Jared left Kaitlin's bones. *Waste nothing*. It couldn't end there though. We would use those bones in a cauldron of stew Jared would tend every day, and eat from throughout the year—*yes*. Unless he came to the point when it no longer disturbed him, and then we would need to rethink our approach. That was when our gifts started losing something. Their minds became vacant places where heartbreak could live easily and cause no damage whatsoever.

So we couldn't rush the torment, just as with the lance. Jared Kare needed to endure as much as necessary to make us smile, but we had to be disciplined. We couldn't be greedy. This mountain would need to be climbed steadily.

A thrill went through us as we stepped out onto the sand. It gave a surprising relief from the concrete. The connection was stronger here. We were almost fully resident in this world. How ironic that fifty feet away in that rolling, foaming water was the exact opposite. All other versions of us would be torn away from the pattern of every reality as well. The Silent Kings would create a new Assembly of course, but our shared consciousness would be gone forever. "WE" would no longer be. A newborn "WE" would take over and develop shared consciousness in a different manner. A completely different personality. Perhaps the Silent Kings would forego gifts, like they did to us in the beginning. We weren't strong enough to do our duties without some prize at the end—perhaps the new Assembly would not need any compensation. No gifts, no fortress, just the joy of suffering in space attending to the dimensional hinges.

It almost made us jealous to consider we could be replaced with others less needy and demanding. But we had no doubts, if we ended up in that ocean water, we would be gone from every page of time, and the Kings would certainly need others to keep the dimensions stable; they were too high and mighty and cowardly to do the job themselves.

We flexed our toes through the sand. It was delicious, so welcomed. Gritty, yet smooth. We enjoyed it for a moment. A very distraught woman yelled in the distance: "Jose, our house was upside down! I'm not taking the pills again! Believe me!" A second later, "Goddamn it, don't call me CRAZY again!"

We groaned.

Our gift had made such a mess of things. All would be well, however. It wasn't possible this world or other versions would catch on to the source of these issues; the knowledge on this planet was too limited. They would try to figure it out. Try to apply meaning. It wouldn't matter. It never did. Even those planets with higher understanding still would not be able to do more than just discuss the atrocities they'd faced.

A briny wind blew in, ruffling the hair of those of us possessing it. Along with the wind came a sharp scent. It was like blood and sweet cream and vulnerability.

Our gift. Delivered as promised by the Silent Kings.

But the scent was slightly different now. Not so vulnerable. Jared Kare had been much changed over the course of one day. As alarmingly different as he'd become, it wasn't a problem, for he still had enough reluctance and self-doubt to make him taste sweet to us. He'd been brave on that building. We'd monitored it closely. Although we did what we could to allow him to survive, if he hadn't kept his wits, it might have been impossible to help. We had no doubt about that. The Jared from this morning would have fallen, despite our help.

How could he change so quickly though? Despite being through the trial of today, nobody became a different person in twelve hours. Something else was at play. He was changed from mind to heart to guts.

And as though an answer, we caught another smell coming from the east. This smell converged on the beach as well.

The banshee drew near.

Fortuitous. We'd figured she had found a corridor shadow and slipped away to a safer place once the Disturbance Paradigm ended. This was welcome. It almost brought us equal joy taking our gift as it did with dealing with the likes of her. Yes, we would disintegrate the bitchwhore in the ocean, and laugh with mirth as we at last, deservedly, took our gift home.

Chapter 31
Jared

When the stretches of sand appeared, Jared got numb. Staring. Staring. Staring. His trembling hand still gripped the door handle.

"Where do you want me to go?" asked Carol, his driver.

He shook his head to regain his thoughts. Had to focus. The drive had been expertly performed but had twisted his already queasy stomach into several thousand new knots.

"I can get us closer," she added.

"No, Carol," he said. "Thank you, and I think you probably could race NASCAR."

She waved him off and leaned over the steering wheel, squinting at something in the distance. "Are those guys painted red?"

Jared swallowed and his eyes slowly scanned the beach. "What guys?"

"Over there by the lifeguard station. Is that paint or... blood all over them?"

"Pull to the curb."

"Sure, but—"

"Please!" he insisted.

Carol jerked the car quickly to the right and cranked up the parking brake. She was still looking intensely ahead. Jared couldn't locate who she saw, but he had a horrible hunch.

"Suspenders? They're wearing suspenders and no shirts? Where are you looking? Point, Carol!"

She pointed and Jared followed the direction of her finger. He saw them then, probably less than half a mile away. His eyes weren't as good as Carol's apparently, but he saw the ten men slowly treading through the dense brown sand. Jared took a quivering breath into his lungs, and looked out past the long pier to the water and back to the approaching monsters.

He would run. It didn't seem like they could catch him before the water, but he couldn't sit around debating that theory; it was time to move.

"Thank you so much, Carol." He unlocked the door and pushed it open.

"I'll drive right to the water if you want," she said, brown eyes sparkling with failing sunlight.

Jared judged the distance of the Assembly again. The sand looked wet enough. They'd had to go over the curb and take out a small blue picket fence. He considered it a moment more and shook his head. Too many factors. No way would he get this woman closer. Even if they weren't inclined to change the death schedule, it was too risky, and he couldn't be responsible for another life.

"Thank you, no."

He shut the car door and jogged to the bent blue picket fence half submerged in the sand. He hopped over it, his knees protesting when his feet struck down. He checked the lifeguard shack but no longer saw the Assembly. He started toward the ocean, but his eyes still desperately raked the beach.

He saw them again.

They were running.

Shouting.

Crying.

Screaming.

Like warriors of a savage planet.

Like wise men of a disturbed era.

As though running to a long lost brother.

As though moving to the last stage of a brutal gauntlet that had lasted since the invention of murder.

Jared put his head down and took longer strides. He'd run so much today it was pathetic how slow he went, but he had to make it to the water or everything Banch sacrificed would be for nothing—as well as those other lives lost and the pain caused to innocents.

He pushed harder. The beach rose and fell with his labored breaths. His heart still beat strong from the tense ride in the Mustang, but it had a good rhythm now and if he hadn't known better, would have thought it was trying to pump in sync with his steps. His mind wandered and he grew dizzy. He was such a klutz. What if he tripped? What if bloody hands grasped him around the neck just as he was pushing up from the ground?

His legs nearly failed him when his shoe caught something under the sand. He dropped on his side. He kicked up again, throwing sand behind him and a neon green beach toy with it.

"Damn it!"

Scrambling to his feet, he moved with renewed effort, throwing sand every which way.

"Kare!" the group of men snarled.

He powered on. The sand came off his soles in sheets. His foot went down wrong and sent him reeling again. His arms thrashed forward, comically reaching for something that would never be there. And then: Knees twisting. Jaw snapping shut. Air sucked through his teeth. Hands gripping the cool sand. Thundering ocean tableau. Keening sound in his mind.

Over his shoulder he saw them. They rushed forward with blinding speed, but judging from the distance they still couldn't reach him. He knew he'd be in the ocean water in less than a minute.

Thanks, Banch. I'm so much more real than I used to be.

The ocean was in ten feet when a hard impact to his hip buckled his knees. It caught him by surprise and he yelled out, "What?"

Jared lifted his head, spread out his hands to push up, but a blunt gray-red-rusted thing burst into his view and in seconds it was inches from his face, like an entire planet of metal had descended on the world at once. The impact made his front teeth jiggle in place and shards of pain leapt up deep into his gums. Stars shattered. Darkness lit. Sea air stuck in his collapsed sinus. The sky spun sideways. Reality became sand in his ear, under his eyelids, up his nostrils. He tasted blood on his tongue.

A treacherous plowing sound went through the damp sand. Jared's eye cracked open in a sheet of blood. The Assembly pulled back one of those grappling hooks of theirs. The sight of it joined with the pain in his skull made him gag. He turned to his side to vomit but the diamonds of pain in his hip all the way into his chest made him re-focus and gasp. He could hear the sounds of waves crashing. So powerful. So close. He couldn't see though. His vision was black-locked. Sand ran down the back of his throat with saliva, a mud that made him wretch and quiver for its intrusiveness in his body.

He forgot where he was.

Who he was...

What he...

Why?

Hard, bleeding hands, fingers like heavy fishing hooks, snatched him under his arms and ripped him up to a standing position. A bass collection of voices forced itself deep into his ear drums. "KARE."

A resounding sigh followed so raspy and full of need that Jared let loose a whimper.

They had him.

He hoped Banch had left as he'd asked. They'd certainly hurt her. Maybe throw her into the ocean out of revenge.

Don't show up, Banch.

Maybe she took his letter to heart and made it to the Free Zone. There were corridors all over this place. It would have been easy to just slip away. He scanned the beach as the Assembly pushed him forward. He almost pitched face-first but a thick hand seized him by the neck and another thumped his chest, almost knocking the air from him.

"Keep walking," they chorused.

"Why do you want me?" he coughed. "Haven't you tired of your sad games? Aren't you finished with being subjects to Kings who would have you suffer for one scrap of kindness every century?"

"We will never tire of you, Kare," they said.

Jared lunged to break away. Jumping in front of him, an Assembly member smiled and ran a sensuous hand down his tall afro into a face full of dried red, the aftermath of an endless bloodstorm. His eyes burned hot gray.

"You will not go," his mouth moved, and yet all ten said.

Jared turned his shoulder down and charged. He struck the other's body like meeting an ancient castle wall. Jared's teeth clicked and he flew back; his ass hit the sand, head snapped, and he went flat. Before he could even find his breath, a tiger-lion-bear-freakish hand clutched his throat and fired him into a standing position. "Stop resisting," the Assembly threatened.

He was shoved forward, not hard enough to fall to the ground again but just about. He could see the corridor shadow on a hill that sloped upward to the parking lot. It was one way to the Fortress.

"This won't make you feel better for your lot in life. It NEVER does," he told them.

They dragged their gift faster toward the hill.

A figure ran out in front of them. Her chest heaved. Her modern clothing, though normal, seemed foreign on her. The Assembly halted him.

"No," Banch cried through deep breaths. "I'll be your gift—just let him go."

"Funny," said the Assembly. "We will make you pay for this, Utumm Resona."

Banch lifted her hands. She looked so incredibly tired. "Come then," she whispered. "Make me pay."

The Assembly didn't take her cue—they turned away and surprisingly headed closer to the ocean.

"No!" Banch said. "No!" she yelled at them. "Please!"

Jared felt like he'd collapse on the sand every two steps but they kept going—not toward the ocean anymore though—they'd quickly headed away, intent on shoving him up the hill toward the parking lot. He could see the shadow where they would plunge.

The view of that shadow became blocked.

Banch put herself in their path.

Ten growls sent out at her.

"I'm warning you," said the banshee. "Let the human go. Can't you see? It was me you needed, all of this time. Take me and leave him. You won't be sorry."

Silence.

The two members who had Jared's wrists tightened their grips and he noticed the others balled their fists, veins snapping up in the blood stained skin.

"Give way, Utumm Resona," they said.

"You really won't take me instead?"

"Don't you dare act surprised, bitchwhore. You knew we wouldn't."

Banch took a deep breath and her eyes settled on Jared. There was love and sadness there. He knew those unique versions; he was married to them, and his heart sank at how this failure would affect her. He couldn't think of her in that ocean, but if they took him, what else was left?

That's what she'd wanted. Just not on the terms she'd hoped.

"I understand now, Banch," he said, raising his voice through the wind. "This is how it has to happen. Do what you have to."

The expression in her eyes didn't change. The sun was low, but there was enough light to paint a gleam in them. Jared felt his own eyes fill with that same emotion. He knew in the next moment, somehow, against all probable reasoning, he knew this would be the last time he saw the banshee he'd fallen in love with today—the soul who made him more than he deserved to be.

Banch's mouth opened. This sound he'd heard before, but after the Divine Scream it meant more. It was odd how a sound, a stretched out, brutal force of vocal magic could mean different things from second to second.

But it did.

And this scream was one Jared recalled, but it was so removed from everything, and felt brand new. Until his molecules started to race away and he then did remember this particular scream.

It was a Swell.

He couldn't believe Banch had the power to do another. This would rip her apart. She'd have to heal for a long time to recover from something so catastrophic to her body. Jared didn't have a chance to say a word. His mouth atomized and rushed out. Eyes turned to the Assembly—watched as their bodies broke into glittering fragments and surged to the ocean, along with him. Jared's head filled and he realized he was about to be scattered glitter as well.

It took only a few seconds. His body had been starlight and now it was whole again. Banch had not sent them far. The ocean crashed, high and loud around him. He felt the taint of the gift wash not from his skin, but from deep inside his bones. And just as he thought he might black out and fall face-first into the ocean, Jared heard the Assembly die.

Chapter 32
Jared

Jared slugged through the water. A pungent fiery odor hung in the air and meat cooked to ash. A few bones floated on the water and dissolved into white, ropy strands, which fizzled and lifted off the waves in claps of steam. The Silent Kings must have been scrambling right now—Jared was sure of it. They'd need to build another collective consciousness and teach it how to work the hinges between the dimensions. Hands-on training. It would not be pleasant.

A pleased smile touched his lips at the thought.

But the smile faded when he caught sight of the body. His heart drummed so heavy black starbursts exploded into his vision. He concentrated on breathing and steadied his pace. As he approached, a fountain of blood erupted from Banch's throat and she twisted slightly in the sand.

"Coming Banch! Coming! Hold on!" He limped through the soft wet mush of the beach.

Her body was still. He tried to calm himself with the facts. She was immortal—it was only a matter of time before she'd heal. She'd be fine. There was no question about that. This was a reality she'd lived with for thousands of years. It was only a matter of getting through the pain. He couldn't bear thinking she'd endure it all for saving him, but endure it, she'd have to.

When he reached her, he fell to his knees, heart stutter-stopping, popping, jerking in his chest. He kissed the side of her mouth. Unconsciously he licked his lips. The blood tasted different, sweeter, yet still rich in metal. He put his hand over the flowing wound in her throat brought on by the Swell. He leaned his mouth against her ear. It was hot and gritty with sand.

"I'm sorry I went against our plans," he whispered. "I thought there was another way. I thought I could help. But we did it, Banch! We did it! You'll heal and, and, I'm free of the taint."

He stroked her hair. It buzzed under his hand like dying electrical current. "I—I just didn't want to think of you going. I couldn't... selfish, I guess, but I know it's not what you really wanted, right? I saw my life through your eyes and I knew somehow you didn't want me to go forward without you. I bet on that, but..." He looked around a moment, searching for the right thing to say. "I also know why you want it over. I'm just one life. When I'm gone, you'll have to continue watching the senselessness of it. I get that, Banch."

The tide surged forward and for the first time Jared noticed its proximity. It would reach Banch soon. He'd have to drag her away, since he couldn't lift her off the ground. Her healing had already begun and strands of flesh had reconnected in her neck. A good sign, but it would be some time before she could scream again. Maybe days before she could even speak whole sentences.

"Banch, I'm gonna have to drag you above the tide." He put his forehead against hers. "I'm sorry to have to move you."

He slipped his hands under her arms and readied to draw her up. She was immobile and couldn't say anything. What would she say if she could? Tell him to get his hands off her? Let the waves come and end this thankless job once and for all? Let her walk into that light, since this was her only chance?

His hands eased under her cold back and a chill went through his body to settle in his stomach. He trembled so hard his teeth clattered and he had to steel himself. "Banch? Do you want me to let you go? Do you want to just stay here? Do you want to go into the light? Can you blink for yes?"

Her eyelids didn't move. Her eyes were distant. It was obvious. She wasn't even listening. She was in shock from the pain. Jared thought about it a minute more. He knew how she felt. He knew that ending her existence meant far more than her love for him. Why was he not giving her what she needed? He'd be walking into that light soon enough himself. If there was an afterlife, doubtful that it was, his only chance to ever see her again was to let this happen.

"Okay… okay, Banch," he said, a tear spilling from his right eye. "I'll stay with you until the end."

Her gaze moved to him but she still looked out of it.

"Did you hear me? I'm with you. I'm with you." He kissed her cheek a few times. "Come on, Banch—what do you want me to do? Hold you?" A dry laugh trailed off his lips.

He studied the tide and tried to make an estimation, though he could only recall back to his sandcastle-building days. It seemed like the water might be upon them in the next ten minutes, but he couldn't be positive. Banch's eyes started moving back and forth, probing around. She was becoming more coherent, but the glazed-over surfaces still indicated her miles from clarity.

Jared's mind crept into so many different locations, scenarios, and resolutions. He started vacillating. Maybe he should just wait until she healed? Then she could decide for herself. He could call the Gilded again. Get some painkillers. But what if she missed the chance? She'd resent him. She really did *want* this. He'd read it on her heart. He had to be strong and give her release. There had to be a moment where he stopped being so self-consumed. His mother and father had loved him, even though they enabled him to be broken, but he knew what it meant to love. *Deeply.* You had to give up everything. You had to eat your fears and use them to grow into something bigger.

He stretched his body out in the sand next to Banch and put his hand on her thigh. "You'll never know how much it meant to me, what you shared. So much sorrow, but it was you, the whole time. Having so much of your life inside my memories now… it's a gift like no other. I always wanted a moment with a perfect woman—you gave me countless moments, Banch."

A small sound bubbled in her throat.

Her eyes were tranquil.

The tide had inched forward a few more feet. It would be quicker than ten minutes—maybe even less than five. Banch's neck wound had fully closed by now—just a reddish discoloration in the skin. Her head twisted around. The hiss of the tide sounded much louder. Soon. Jared would need to deal with her being gone. But at least he knew it was what she wanted. At least he could finally get something correct for a change. For how he'd held so many other people back—people he cared about, family and friends alike—this was his chance to rise above that. In a way, he was excited at the prospect.

"No..." Banch mumbled.

He startled and tossed his head toward her. "What?"

A rapid gurgling rose from her throat and her face moved again. Jared couldn't decide whether to be hopeful or full of dread with how quickly her head swiveled and body shook violently. Jared took her arms, bringing them close near her body. She growled and kicked her feet in the sand. He struggled to keep hold of her.

"It's okay. It's okay. Hold on! The water's coming."

"No!" Banch said.

"*No?*"

She caught his wrist with surprising power and brought him close.

"Don't," she said. A horrible sound clicked in her throat.

"Shit!" Jared scrambled to his feet. He went behind her, took her under the arms.

The tide washed over Banch's feet.

"God no!" he shrieked.

Her feet folded into themselves and burst into a bright hot light. Shimmers of clove colored starlight snapped around them.

"I'm disassoc—" Banch retched. "—iating."

He helped her up and her groan was dreadful enough to taste. "I'm sorry! Hold on! I know where the corridor is."

Jared's heart thrummed and punched inside his chest. Dark stars dazzled before him. He could imagine passing out so easily, he began to think he *was* passing out, but he stumbled backward, dragging Banch through the sand. Her lower legs were gone. Her knee caps bubbled with cosmic illumination.

"It's not far," he told her. "I can get you there."

He pulled on her harder, his joints about to give, his heart about to stop. He checked her again. She'd vanished up to the hips, and yet he could still see where her heels made trails through the sand—her legs were invisible but still had physical residence.

"Have to crawl... out of corridor on the other... side... or I'll be stuck," she said.

Jared got a better hold on her and stumbled on.

"Almost," he said, and heaved.

Banch had lost her body up past the belly button and the disassociation continued to climb. He wheeled her around and aimed her at the wash of auburn shadow on the sand. The flesh vanished just at her collarbone.

He had no time for a final goodbye and pushed her into the shadow—but couldn't tell if she'd vanished completely before. The diminutive corridor led just outside the Free Zone. It would only be a matter of crawling a few feet, if his memory of the maps served accurately this time. He wasn't sure, though, she hadn't disassociated in the corridor. He prayed not.

Death was far better than eternal limbo.

Either way, Jared realized then he stood on the beach alone. The shadow sealed. He would not see another corridor again unless the way was opened from the other side. In the Free Zone, there were no direct paths back here large enough for a full sized person. Even if Banch made it, she could never come back to this dimension. And she would not risk returning to the Kings' territories. She'd be captured immediately.

Jared twisted down to the sand to sit.

For better or worse, it was over. And his banshee was gone.

For a time, he watched the waves crashing. He really hoped he'd saved her, but he could never know.

Unless she was waiting for him when he died, making the call.

His heart rumbled in its strange way, as though to answer that morbid thought.

"In three months, will you be there, Banch?" he asked. His eyes went deep into the waves as the sun set. "Will you?"

Epilogue

THREE YEARS LATER

Kaitlin pulled the car into the space. Robotically, she got out and went to put money in the meter. It was too much of a chore to fish out coins with her prosthetic fingers, so she slid out a debit card and paid for a few hours, though she wasn't sure she needed that much time. After she got the receipt her nerves got the better of her and she returned to the driver's seat. She didn't think she was ready to do this. It would make it real, make her finally face all the feelings about Jared she'd bottled up over the past few years. She brought up an old photo on her phone of them together at Disneyland and couldn't look at it for very long.

She turned on the radio. The first song that came on was Tom Petty's "Free Fallin" and she had to turn it off. Tears surfaced in her eyes. So many memories. He'd been such a big part of her life for so long, the loneliness of the last few years felt crushing right now.

Changing the channel she found NPR. *Tune in tonight for our new "Explorations in Science" special in tribute to the three year anniversary of THE EVENT. A panel of physicists and astrophysicists moderated by Neil Degrasse Tyson will discuss the remarkable space-time phenomenon that occurred on our planet and with a special focus on new string theory revisions based on the Event's epicenter in Southern California. It should—*

Kaitlin pushed off the radio. Losing a best friend was bad enough, but remembering that strange day where the bed curtains in her hospital room nearly crushed her wasn't a particularly great recollection either.

"Shit hell," she muttered. It made her feel somewhat better and she popped open the door. The salty air wrapped around her. She could do this. The Pacific Ocean filled her vision with its dark blue infinity. Even though she should have expected it, the honk of her car alarm when she armed it made her jump. Again, for the tenth time today, she wondered if she should have brought Shelly. It would have been good to use her woman as a shield, or crutch, or whatever, but Kaitlin supposed she owed it to her old friend to do this alone.

The way to the memorial wasn't far, even though Kaitlin wished she'd worn different shoes. Shelly had really girled her up, which Kaitlin guessed was an okay thing if it made her fiancée happy, but something had to give, and walking on a beach in Manolo Blahnik pumps had to be one. She slipped them off and walked barefoot through the moist gray sand.

This was the first time she'd been to the memorial and she hadn't had any expectations, but it was a beautiful space in the sand up past a levee only twenty yards from the ocean. A few people walked down the wooden stairs, softly conversing. Kaitlin gave them a smile and marched up. The garden was meticulously cared for. Every shrub was clipped to perfection and the lawn mowed to an inch high. The eighty-two bronze plaques glinted in the afternoon sun. Kaitlin didn't have to count them—she'd heard on the news that number enough now for it to be ingrained. She'd also been to another memorial site in Chino Valley, which had been commissioned by the state—that was the larger of the two and more widely visited. This place was a second stop for tourists wanting to pay their respects to those unfortunate people who perished in The Event.

Kaitlin dragged her eyes across the half circle. Each bronze plaque had a different breed of flower growing to represent the individual lives. Once again, these plants were cared for with expert hands. She walked around them and read the names. None of the names rang a bell as far as the biographies she'd seen on TV.

The caretaker's house opened then. A man came out with a curly haired toddler on his hip. He was telling her what a great job she did on her art project. Kaitlin couldn't help a small grin. She almost felt easier about being here.

Then the door opened again.

And it was him.

She'd never seen Jared with so much facial hair before, but the thin beard suited him. She tried to control herself but wanted to sob. Just hearing his voice on the phone had almost brought her to hysterics as it was. He'd kept away from her almost exclusively with no real explanation. At first she was angry, and then sad, and then grudgingly accepting. They'd only spoken one Christmas and a couple of her birthdays. When he was completely silent this past year, she'd thought he might be dead. In many ways she'd prepared herself to just consider him gone from her life forever.

He rounded the semi-circle memorial with grace she'd not remembered he possessed. He opened his arms and she ran into them. She wanted to shriek but bit her shaky lip still. They embraced for a few minutes, only listening to each other's hearts and soft breathing.

"It's okay, Kait," he finally said, stroking her hair. "I... I'm sorry it's been so long. I just had to have time."

She pulled away from him and looked deep into his eyes, searching.

"It was never about you. Understand?" he asked, putting his hands on top of her shoulders.

When she said nothing, he smiled. "Okay?"

She scratched a few tears away. "Of course, okay. Yes. Thanks for calling me, you jerk."

He snorted. "Forgive me?"

She leaned in and kissed his cheek. They held each other for a few moments more before breaking away and both quietly admiring the memorial. "I love this," she said. "It was such a big thing, doing this for them. And finding so much success as well. Congratulations."

"It's a small thing," he explained. "The least I can do. We're here and they are not. I've learned we can only control what we can though. Everything else we have to live with."

"That doesn't sound like my Jared."

"You have no idea," he laughed. "Come on, I need to see the rest of my kids out."

"Kids?"

"Students." He playfully tugged her toward the beach house.

"Since when did the West Coast Database Excellence pay enough for you to afford a place like this?"

"They didn't. I quit there a week after The Event."

"Then how—"

"I have private investors... let's just say they are a dedicated group who make sure my every need is taken care of. I don't take advantage, but some of them have very deep pockets."

"Must be nice!"

"Uh, yeah!" he said, and they both laughed.

Kaitlin didn't know how to react when he opened the door to his home. The living room walls had an array of pen and ink drawings, mostly landscapes and ocean scenes, which Jared had always enjoyed. It was a genuine art gallery, something far more sophisticated and complete than any of his previous sketch books might have held. A large rectangular window provided an astonishing vista of the beach. None of this was as shocking as the gathering of tables lined up in a classroom formation. Children and their parents worked on a project together.

"I thought you lived here?" she asked.

He nodded. "I do. Bedroom's in the back and the kitchen's on the other side of the studio through that hall there." He shrugged. "There's a small dining room, but I manage."

"So, what is this? I mean, are you an art teacher now?"

"Sort of—I've kinda set myself up as an instructor to teach shy kids how to communicate through art. Some of the parents like to join them. You just missed lunchtime in the kitchen. We all make the meals as a group. It's nice. I really enjoy it."

"Getting innocent children to cook for you now?"

He slipped his hands into his jean pockets and chuckled. "No, I cook and they help. Sometimes."

"You? Cooking? This is pretty odd for you, I must say. I'm feeling Twilight Zoney here."

"It's not so odd. I'm just playing catch up."

Kaitlin lowered her voice. "But you don't even like kids, right?"

He smiled. "I've made my peace with them."

She took another gander around at the quietly focused art workshop. "All day instruction sounds pricey—no wonder those investors signed on."

"It's free," he clarified. "Limited seats, of course. My investors provide me with food and supplies. We do encourage parents to spare something for the families devastated by The Event. There are several charities I vouch for."

She stared at him, her mouth agape.

He snickered. "You look fucking impressed."

"I *am* fucking impressed."

He put his hand on her arm. She put hers over it. "I missed you so much," Kaitlin told him. "I thought you'd finally given up on me."

He shook his head with a wry smile and strolled over to one of his drawings and ran a thumb down the side of the black lacquer frame. "I had health issues, Kait. Some serious ones."

"Jared? You... you what?" She held back a sudden flash of rage. "Why wouldn't you tell me?"

He continued to look at the drawing in a stoic, distant manner. The image was a depiction of a building, more like a surrealist skyscraper than the typical terrain and sea tableaux.

"I needed to handle it by myself. If I didn't, if I let someone hold my hand, I'd never be able to walk on my own. The hospital time was extensive and I was fortunate my investors insisted on helping with the costs. I had three heart bypasses and tried several different chemical therapies to regulate my condition, which is abnormal clotting of the blood. It's what took dad."

"That floors me—you wouldn't call or, or, or even let me know?"

He shrugged and looked down. "I'm sorry. Believe me, I had my hand on the phone a lot these past years."

"No calls to the Kangjuns either?"

"A couple of times. They're doing well. In fact..." He pointed across the room. "That's their niece, Mi-Cha. She's been coming here the last year with her daughter."

A beautiful woman glanced up at Jared and smiled. There was something more in her eyes than just politeness.

Kaitlin leaned in close to Jared. "She's a looker. How long have you been going out?"

He coughed abruptly and his face flushed. "I haven't—I've thought. But. No. It's. We're not. We haven't, I mean."

"You're ridiculous if you don't take her out. She's married?"

"Divorced for three years."

"What in the green hell, buddy?" said Kaitlin. "What *in the* hell?"

He shrugged again.

"Is it Banch? It can't be right? You hadn't heard from her since she left. That's what you told me last Christmas. Did she come back to the states?"

Jared pressed his lips together and shook his head. "I won't be hearing from her again, unfortunately."

"Hey, I'm sorry and I liked that one, but I think three years is enough of a pining period. Don't you?"

"It's nice to see you're jumping back into the position of my dating coach."

"Don't start with all that, nimcomshit."

"Oh, that's a new one."

"I'm taking it for a spin," Kaitlin laughed.

Jared sighed and put his thumbs through his belt loops. He looked more like a man, but still the boy who missed the bus all those years ago. "Thing is Kait, with Banch... some days you're right. Three years should be long enough." He glanced outside, past the workshop to the beach through the window. "Then some days, not entirely enough."

"But—"

"Nah nah nah," he cut her off and seemed to shift moods. "Enough on all that. How's your hand doing?"

Kaitlin pulled her glove off so he could see the prosthetic fingers.

"Can you believe it's given me an edge at auditions? It's great for Hollywood bleeding hearts trying to prove their fairness."

"You are a fingerly challenged American?"

"I prefer to call it the Luke Skywalker syndrome."

"Yeah, but he lost his whole hand."

Kaitlin struggled to bend down her fake digits so she could flip him off. Jared roared with laughter and brought her into another tight embrace. "So amazingly glad you're here. Hey, I'm closing class in about five minutes. Want to help me see everyone out?"

"I'd love to."

All the students and their respective guardians thanked Jared profusely. When it came time for Mi-Cha, she was very shy, but respectful to Kaitlin.

"It's nice to meet you, and hey." Kaitlin slipped an arm around the woman's slender shoulders. "I'm getting married in a few months. This guy needs some arm candy to take with him. I can't have my best man showing up alone. It's embarrassing."

The woman bowed her head and blushed deeply. Jared grabbed his face in dismay. "Kaitlin—you, what?"

Giggling, Mi-Cha reached out and patted Jared's arm. "If he wants me to go, then I'm there."

He pinched between his eyes, trying to let the redness in his face fade a little. "Oh, you're so in for it, Kait." Both women giggled. "Can I call you, Mi-Cha?"

"You know you can, Jared," she replied. "And please do."

He tried to compose his embarrassment and saw her and her daughter outside. When they were well into the garden, he fake-strangled Kaitlin. "Married? You never mentioned—"

"How could I? You were busy being some hermit art teacher with clandestine financial endowments."

"Do I get to meet her first?"

"Shelly? If you're nice."

He rolled his eyes. The last two people walked up to leave. An older black man with his granddaughter, from the looks of it. "Kesha wants to tell you something, Mr. Kare."

Jared took a knee before the seven year old, who twisted shyly. "Of course."

"Mister... Mister Kare."

"Yes?"

Her voice lowered. "You're my favorite teacher."

Jared cupped his hands over his heart and patted it. "And you're mine, sweetheart."

He stood, shook the man's hand, and confirmed another session for next Thursday. They said their goodbyes and Jared shut the door.

"I guess I was pretty assuming," said Kaitlin. "Thinking you'd be in the wedding after all this time."

His eyes misted, looking at her. "Like you could ever keep me away."

Hers misted as well. "Hey, your birthday is next week right?"

"Yep, the big 3-0."

"Wanna do lunch at the Bayou Cat with Shelly and me?"

"Love that place," he said with a wink. "I'll definitely be there."

* * *

When Jared was thirty years old...

He came home to a silent house. This wasn't a change. He'd forced himself to become used to it. No more TVs and radios on, just the sound of the ocean outside. Tonight was somewhat different, however. Kaitlin and Shelly had taken him to the Bayou Cat and they'd all had a great time, stayed well over two hours after dinner talking. He didn't know Shelly that well yet, but he got a great vibe from her. And with how Kaitlin gazed at her while she was talking... Jared recognized that look.

It was therapeutic being around friends, but now he was alone and had to give himself his injection and take his round of pills. His phone would alarm him to make an appointment with Doctor Saxon tomorrow; he was already way ahead of it and had several post-its placed strategically so he could call when they opened tomorrow.

Scarce was the night that passed when he didn't think about Banch. Had she made it out of the corridor before disassociating? Three months had stretched into three years and he'd not died yet. He'd changed the death schedule by taking control of his life. The doctor said he could live into old age if he kept regimented. Would he live long enough to forget Banch? If she was no longer his banshee, would he think about her as he went on?

No, he thought. *Not likely I'll ever forget her.*

He sat at the table letting the meds soak in before he retired to bed. He took a deep breath and enjoyed how great he felt. His heart no longer beat irregularly and he was in the greatest shape of his life—even better than high school. All those runs on the beach had helped him beyond measure.

He yawned and moved a salt shaker next to the pepper. He stared at the little glass jar for a mundane moment. Something bright passed over his vision. He blinked and glanced lazily around. A streak of auburn slid to the floor and puddled there, just hardly the size of a fist. At first he couldn't move, thought perhaps he'd nodded off at the table and was consumed by dream, but he pushed up from his chair and staggered into the table, feeling the reality of its solidness. It was there. A corridor shadow had opened in his house!

He got down on his hands and knees and examined the watery brown-red color. Something thin stuck out from the center of the shadow. He reached inside to pinch it between his fingers but his nails were too short. He brushed his thumb over it.

Paper.

If he reached into the shadow completely, he'd run the risk of losing the paper, but he hadn't come three years this far to let this chance go.

Jared plunged his hand inside.

And pushed the paper out of reach.

"No!" he cried, his brow suddenly dappled in sweat. "No!" he shouted again when he lost hold once more.

Not thinking, he rammed his arm inside, almost to the elbow. Electricity flowed into him, spiked micro-insects chewing on the nerves in his hand and sending messages of fiery pain into his shoulder and brain. He bit his lip and cold iron flooded his mouth. The feathery touch of paper between his fingers—he caught it and pulled his arm out.

The pain was too much to do anything but lay there clutching his arm for a while. His mind kept going to the paper in his hand and what it would say—what he *wanted* it to say. When his arm finally numbed and tingles ran out of his fingertips, Jared rolled over and looked at the thing he'd pulled from the corridor shadow.

The envelope had an impression of the first syllabary symbol from the Statemen's district in the Free Zone. From Banch's visits there as the Assembly's currier, Jared recognized the quality of the stationary. It was from Felderman's wood pulping facility. There was an invisible seal on the back, one of Felderman's most recognized inventions: transparent wax. Jared almost felt bad pulling the substance away, but this wasn't a letter he would think of leaving unopened. Whoever sent it had to go to great lengths to ensure opening a route here. It had to have been sent outside the Free Zone somehow, since no known routes led to this world. Dangerous. But he'd received the missive. It was in his hands and there was a single card inside.

After he read it, Jared felt dizzy. He started laughing and shouting and fought to stand up. He took the card and ran to the front door. He shoved his feet into his tennis shoes and bolted outside to the beach. In only minutes he was hip deep in the Paled Ocean, the one place they shared in common. It was the only thing he could think to do in response to this, the only way he could feel closer.

To her.

Still giddy, he sloshed back toward the shore. He held the card up to read it in the moonlight, but it slipped from his fingers and blew away. He yelled out in panic and tore toward the place the card had landed. Luckily the wind carried it no farther and he snatched it up in time.

He let himself drop down and sit there on the sand, looking at the card: the lipstick imprint of Banch's lips on the boiling white surface. He recognized the shade of lipstick immediately and the memory warmed him, made him feel like he'd found something ancient inside himself, lost even before Banch, something primeval in his thirty year old mind.

Then he read her note under the painted lips once more.

I'm with you, Jared.

He couldn't go to sleep that night. He'd promised the students his chicken tacos tomorrow and wondered how he'd get through the crosshatching lesson and still have time. He could grill the chicken now and warm it in the oven tomorrow. That would give him a buffer. He had to do something productive anyway since he couldn't very well sleep right now.

So he took the chicken out to the grill, along with a bottle of his dad's favorite Dark Heineken he'd had in his fridge for the entire time he'd lived on the beach. It was the first beer he'd ever try. He'd never understood what occasion he'd been waiting for, but there could be no other more important than this night and the soaring in his heart.

The flames on the grill were the same brand of red as the setting sun. As he flipped the chicken breasts, he'd occasionally pull out Banch's card from his shirt pocket. He pressed his lips into the impression—and somehow it felt just like kissing Banch's full moist lips. Another one of Felderman's creations, the sensory responsive parchment paper.

"Love you," Jared whispered, and tucked the note back into his pocket.

He opened his beer then and took a long swallow. It actually tasted a lot better than he'd expected. He continued then to cook and sip beer, a smile stretched on his lips. Everyone he'd ever loved seemed to be present at that moment. Kaitlin, his mother, his father, the Kangjuns. They were his energy, and Banch was the racing world beneath him.

He hoped every Jared in every dimension had a moment like this one.

A pair of seagulls squawked and took to the sky. Jared watched them, his heart filling with an exaltation he'd never expected to find in his lifetime. The gulls, soaked deep through their feathers, flapped away, crossing over and trading flight plans with each other, merrily calling, back-dropped against the copper dome sinking behind the remaining stupor of sapphire sky. Night had fallen, and after a long harsh day, with all of its trials behind them, it was clear the birds had found themselves ready for what would come next. Without a doubt, they were heading for an unseen brilliance beyond the dark, and they were finally content.

THE END

Benjamin Kane Ethridge is the Bram Stoker Award® winning author of the novel BLACK & ORANGE, NIGHTMARE BALLAD, BOTTLED ABYSS, as well as countless short stories and articles on writing and being human. Benjamin lives in Southern California but would very much love a corridor shadow to take him to Florida whenever he chose.

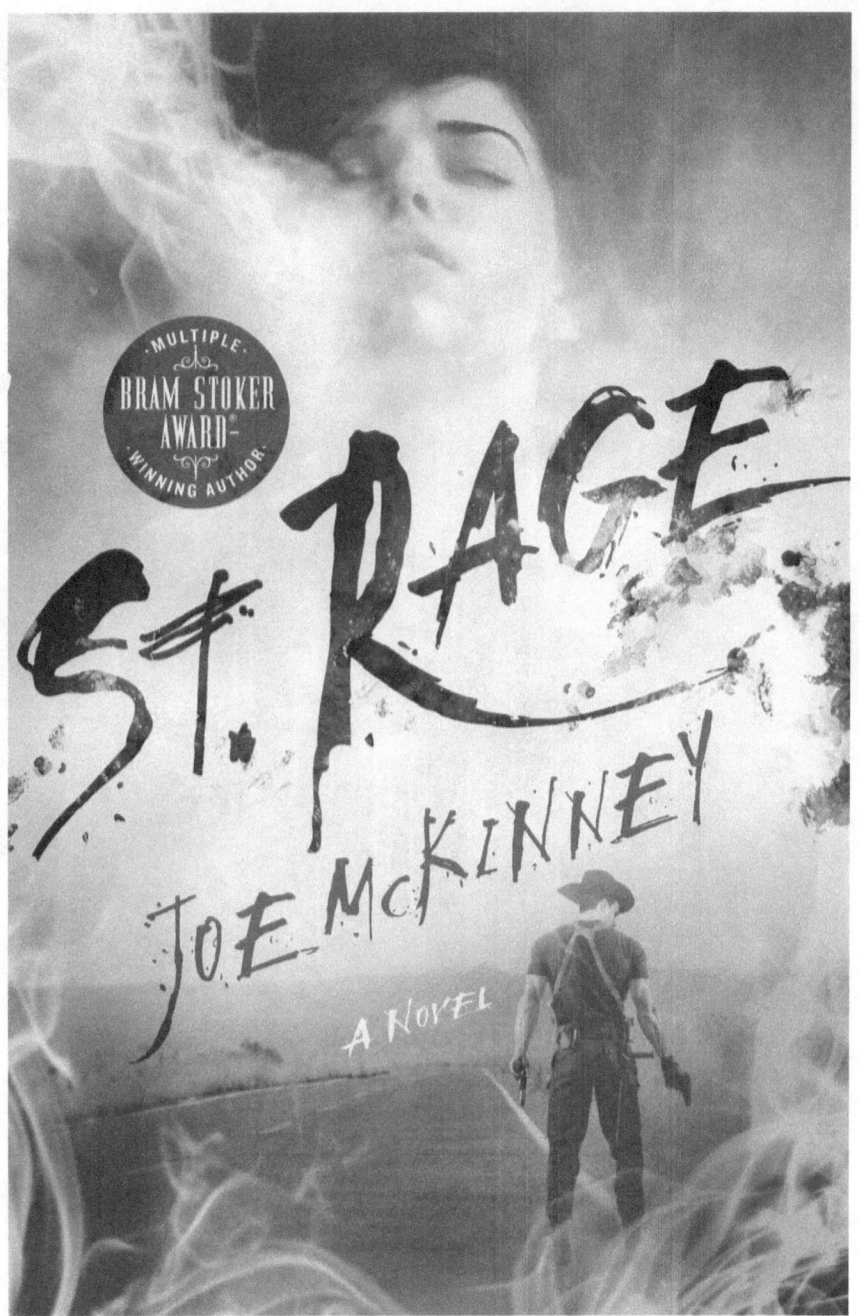

MULTIPLE BRAM STOKER AWARD-WINNING AUTHOR

ST. RAGE

JOE McKINNEY

A NOVEL

BLACK
TIDE

PATRICK FREIVALD

• A MATT ROWLEY NOVEL •